BANGKOK BURN

SIMON ROYLE

Also by Simon Royle

Tag

About the author

Simon Royle was born in Manchester, England in 1963. He has been variously a yachtsman, advertising executive, and a senior management executive in software companies. He lives in Bangkok, with his wife and two children.

BANGKOK
BURN

SIMON ROYLE

PRESS

First published in Thailand by I & I Press 2012

This I&I Press trade paperback edition 2012

Copyright © 2012 Simon Royle
Afterword copyright © 2012 Simon Royle
Cover copyright © 2012 Simon Royle

This is a work of fiction. Any similarities to people
or places, living or dead, is purely coincidental.

ISBN 978 616 305 502 6

A CIP catalogue record for this title is available from the
National Library of Thailand.

Typeset in Adobe Garamond Pro and
Franchise for Chapter Headings.

I&I Press
249/17 Lat Phrao 122,
Lat Phrao Road,
Wang Thonglang,
Bangkok 10310

WWW.SIMON-ROYLE.COM

For Nicholas and Naomi

The Sauna in Heaven

12 May 2010, Bangkok, 2 pm

"I'd like you to help me with something…" He paused and waited until I had lowered myself into the still-steaming, hot water.

I wondered if he was clairvoyant. Was I just an open book to him? I had come to tell him I wanted out of the family business. By the look in his eyes, I could tell he knew why I had come, and was preempting the discussion.

"Yes, Khun Por." He insists I call him Father, Khun Por, even though he is not my natural father. Everyone else calls him Jor Por Pak Nam, literally Godfather of the River's Mouth. Unless you're Thai, that won't mean much to you. And that's how it is meant to be; it's better you don't know. I eased myself onto the narrow shelf in the pool, the heat vicious. A tingling sensation covered the sunken part of my body as veins expanded and blood rushed.

I waited. This wasn't a request. We both knew that. Whatever he asked me to do, whatever, I would do. It's a way of life. People in the west – you – you don't understand this. Perhaps in Sicily. But blind obedience and loyalty, it's mainly an Asian thing. The Thai word for it, Griengjai, has no equivalent in the English language. You don't even have a word to describe this cultural trait. But it is what holds us together: our cultural glue. Quitting the family business would have to wait.

"I need you to go see Big Tiger. I owe him a favor, and he needs…" He smiled, and I knew what was coming next: Dek Farang, Foreigner Kid in English. I'm hardly a kid, but I've been called Dek Farang by the family for as long as I can remember. Except Mother, she's called me Chance since the day she gave me that name, on my fifteenth birthday.

Dek Farang, coming from Por, is a term of endearment, a bookmark in time to when he first laid that name on me forty-one years ago. On the street, everyone else calls me Khun "Oh", a Thai nickname, shortened from Ohgaat, which translates as Mr. Chance. In business, I use an entirely different name. Complicated? Sure.

We were in a suite in "Heaven" – a high-priced sauna and massage joint on Ratchada – a safe place for us to meet in private. My image as a respectable businessman is something we both want to protect. The suite looked like Ikea meets Bali in the French Revolution. Minimalist sofas, Louis XIV chairs in white and gold, mixed with slate gray post-modernist wall art, the baths of hot and cold water, narrow and long. Not my taste, but it was private, and we weren't there for the decor.

Bank and Red waited outside the door. His "boys". You will never stop at this floor, and if you called them boys, you'd either end up dead or in hospital for a very long time. Bank is at least sixty-five; Red, maybe a bit younger, but these are two guys whose wrong side you never want to be on. There's a story about a Farang, who insulted Por in Patpong one night. This was back in the early sixties. Bank and Red, then in their mid-teens, waited a week to let things settle down. Then they beat the guy a breath short of death in the middle of Patpong Road. He was in hospital for four months before he could eat anything larger than what fits down a straw. The day he came out, they beat him again on the steps of the hospital. I heard it went on for a year. Somehow, the police never found out who was doing the beating.

I waited to see if he'd give me any more instructions about seeing Big Tiger. It would be impolite of me to speak first.

Por let his legs float up and waved his arms slowly outward to rest them on the side of the pool. His legs, skinny and white, contrasted with the teak color of his arms and face. I watched as the ripple in the flat pool spread towards me, bracing myself for the pain. He turned and looked at me. The brow on his square Chinese Thai face furrowed with thought, and a little smirk, come frown, on his mouth. His lips hardly moved when he spoke.

"I spoke to your uncle last week. He mentioned you. He hasn't seen you for a while."

No more talk about Big Tiger then, just an admonishment that I hadn't been to see Uncle Mike.

"I've been busy, Por."

"Too busy to go and see your uncle?" An eyebrow raised, a question mark in his large doleful weepy eyes.

"No, Por. I'll go see Uncle Mike." The white eyebrow raised a fraction higher.

"This week, I promise."

He smiled. I smiled back. It'd cost me a day to fly to Phuket to see Uncle Mike. With having to see Big Tiger, what I had on at the office, and Bangkok's streets heating up, this was going to be a busy week.

"Ai yah, this water is too hot," Por said, his Chinese roots showing. He started to slowly lever himself upright. I got up quickly before him and took him by the upper arm, just in case he slipped getting out. He shuffled slightly, a bit wobbly, till he got his bearings. Turning to me, his eyes became deadly serious, hard. He grasped my forearm with a thin bony hand.

"You be careful with Big Tiger. He's up to something." He smiled and squeezed my arm. Chat over. I gave him a deep wai. He waied me back, ruffled my hair, and turned towards the master bedroom. I headed for the shower in the guest room.

Freshly showered and wearing one of my best Armani knock-offs, I pressed the button for the elevator and had a quiet word with Bank and Red to look out for the old man. His parting words had me worried and had been in my mind while I was getting dressed. Red's eyes slid to the woman sitting on the fake Louis XIV chair opposite the elevator.

Por's newest girlfriend. She was waiting for me to pay her some attention. I didn't. Half my age, she pouted as she stood with a flounce and a shake of her million-Baht, made-in-Seoul tits. The Koreans do good tits. I looked at her. She paused a second in defiance, which melted as she dropped her eyes and gave me a wai. Respect has to be earned from the inside out. It's just the way we are.

She brushed past me, the hall wide enough to drive a bus down. Bank opened the door to the suite for her, and with a last glance, she gave me her back like it was a victory. Bank chuckled softly at the look I had received and sat down on the chair she had warmed in her wait. He opened up his Thai Rath newspaper and licked a thumb. Por would be busy for at least a couple of hours.

The elevator pinged, and Red held the door open as I walked into its red velvet-lined interior. So elegant, the designer should be garroted with the gold brocade tassels. I turned and smiled at Red as the doors began to close. I looked at my watch. 3:30 pm.

The blast knocked me off my feet, and life went into slow motion. I was punched into the rear of the elevator and dropped like a sack of lead to the floor.

I came round to the sound of the elevator door pinging each time it bumped against Red's body. I sat up, legs straight out in front of me, a high-pitched ringing in my ears. Over Red's dead body, I could see to the far wall of the suite. The whole wall had been blown out. Three meters away, her eyes wide open and staring at me, Por's girlfriend.

It took me a moment to realize I couldn't see her body because it wasn't attached to her head. I wiggled my toes and fingers. Everything still there, or at least it felt like that. One hand on the wall of the elevator, I struggled to my feet, lurching into what remained of the hallway. My legs, no, all of me shaky, I was shaking all over.

Further up the hall, Bank lay face down, a scarlet blood pool around him. On the white marble floor, it was turning to a faint rose color. Water from the sprinklers rained down, mingling with the blood. Dizzy, disoriented, high-pitched ringing in my ears, I walked over the debris of the hallway into the suite. The wall and door of the master bedroom were missing. I stumbled on the slippery rubble beneath my feet.

The lounge and pool area were ripped apart; small fires dotted the room. The water from the pool sloshed around my feet. I saw rubble move in the far right corner of the room. I tore at the brick, shredded furniture, and mattress on the floor in the corner. Por was underneath. Blood poured from his nose, ears, and the smashed remains of his right leg. He tried to sit up. I knelt beside him. Taking my belt off, I got it around his right thigh, pulling it as tight as I could, till he screamed. Getting my arms underneath his armpits, I lifted him until I could put him over my shoulder.

Staggering, my knees still wobbly, I turned. Chai, my driver and bodyguard, stood in the doorway. He was saying something, but I couldn't make out what. He came over to me, pointing at his left eye, and took Por onto his shoulder. I reached up, feeling my eye, and my hand came away covered in blood. I could feel bits of something stuck in my forehead and cheeks. I pointed to the hall.

We went back into the hall, and bending down, I grabbed Red's legs and pulled him out of the doorway of the elevator. As I straightened up, everything went sideways.

Lucky Number Nine

"It's a nine, a nine for sure," Aunt Malee was saying, looking down at me. She saw my eyes open and smiled, a heavily jeweled finger pointing somewhere on my chest. I raised my eyes to see Dr. Tom, our family doctor. He raised his eyebrows, and then a mirror angled so I could see my chest. The mirror wobbled, I shook my head. The angle changed, and there, halfway between my right nipple and my collarbone, was a perfect, dark purple circle, almost black, and embossed in red-tinged white, the number 9.

"The elevator button," said Dr. Tom, shrugging his shoulders. Constructing magical formulas of lottery numbers is a national pastime, a habit as addictive as smack that kicks in twice a month in The Kingdom. Cambridge-educated doctors aren't immune.

"He's awake," Aunt Malee announced to the rest of

Por's wives sitting on the sofa behind her. I could barely see out of my right eye and nothing out of my left. But I knew they were all there. I am the son that none of them have produced. Por has four minor wives, Mia Noi, and twelve daughters. Four, the Mia Noi limit set by Mother: Joom, his Mia Luang, Major Wife. Joom wasn't in the room.

"Khun Por and Mother?"

"Mother is with Por. She said she'll come and see you later. Por is in the room next to yours. He's in a coma, and he's lost his leg, but he is still alive," Aunt Malee, Jasmine, said. "Now you must rest. You have been badly wounded. Are you hungry?"

I shook my head slightly.

She turned, unblocking my view of the other aunties sitting on the sofa, cards on the table in front of them. Ever since Casino Royale, the movie, came out, their game was Texas Hold 'Em, and they drank vodka Martinis. Aunt Malee reached over and fished a black elevator button from the white plastic kidney-shaped bowl on the side table next to the bed. Doctors and car mechanics have a lot of the same habits. They both start by asking you what your problem is. They both rip you off. And they both leave parts replaced in the boot of a car or a kidney-shaped dish as assurance of work done.

The muted sound of a girl sobbing in a Thai soap opera laid a pattern for the general hubbub of activity in the room. Everything is a social occasion in Thailand: birth, death, and everything in between. I was in a big room, and it was filled with people. Hospital rules don't apply when money, the butt of a gun, and four angry aunties are thrown into the equation.

"I see your five and raise you ten," Auntie Ning said to Aunt Su. Looking at me from the sofa, she smiled and said casually, as if asking what I'd watched on TV the night before, "Nong Oh, did you see anything when you were, um, you know, on the other side?"

The volume dropped. I could practically hear the sobbing girl's TV tears hit the ground in the hushed expectation.

"No, I can't remember anything, and no one gave me any lottery ticket numbers."

The suspended breathing exhaled with a whoosh.

"But this morning I dreamed about an elephant."

A sharp intake of collective breath, then the volume went back up. I just couldn't resist it. The girl sobbing on the TV forgotten, cards by mutual unspoken agreement folded, the aunts turned to compiling.

Counting off in reverse order the number of sutures I had, 120; the number on the door, 24; and how many pieces of glass, metal, and brick Dr. Tom had taken out of me, 14; then, of course, the piece de resistance, the 9, embossed on my chest ... and an elephant in a dream.

These numbers, turned upside down, added together, subtracted and manipulated with seemingly logical extensions that would have floored Einstein, were then compiled as lottery numbers and jotted down on napkins with jeweled Mont Blancs. The cell phones came out, lottery number consultants, Monks and Mor Doo's, Fortune Tellers on speed dial.

Auntie Dao, Star, wife number two, her fifties bouffant hair-do shimmering with glitter, got up from the sofa with a heave and rocked her way over to the bed. She reached across and took the elevator button from Aunt Malee, then looked at it as if inspecting a flawed diamond.

"You know it might not be 9; it might be 6," she rasped from her smoker's throat. A collective gasp at the perception. Six is "hok" in Thai, but in a slightly different tone also means fall, as in fall down, with connotations of death or bad luck.

"No. I had a chat with the police forensics team. It was definitely a nine." Doctors and teachers are infallible in Thailand. Everything they say is the truth. In Dr. Tom's case, I had no doubt that he had called the forensics team. After all, it wasn't every day that someone standing five meters from a bomb survived and, more importantly, had a 9 embossed on their chest. I had just become an urban legend. What amulets I wore on my neck, such information to be gained by bribing hospital staff had increased tenfold in value.

Dr. Tom put a hand up to the beeping IV machine and fiddled with a knob. "Sleep now. We'll talk later."

The aunts' chatter faded to the beat of the girl still sobbing on the TV. At least sixty percent of Thai soap opera is spent sobbing. Not the watchers, the actresses. There was a reason for that, but I fell asleep before I could remember what it was.

I was born in Goa, the son of two heroin-smuggling hippies from Boston, John and Barbara's inconvenient accident of free love. They came to Bangkok on the trail of the Double UO with me in tow. The Vietnam War was going full blast, and smack was the drug of choice of the hip set. A lot of people made a fortune smuggling smack. John and Barb got dead, shotgunned on the stern of a yacht. Por had bought the yacht for them in Singapore, their Valhalla craft off a beach at Boracay Island an early template for drug deals gone bad. I have the news clipping. It's on the Internet, an old, forgotten article in an Asian boating magazine, a couple of druggie's five minutes of fame, all used up.

Their last name was Collins. Mine is Harper. Samuel C. Harper. It was a name Por got off a clothing store in New York. He took me there to get some suits made. I get a good discount. I'm glad he changed my name. It saved me the job. There was no fucking way I was going to go through life as Sunrise Krishna Collins. But Por had bigger reasons than my problems with my love-child name. The Germans who'd put the hit on my parents and ripped off Por for a couple of million were looking for me.

I became Samuel C. Harper, Por became my father, and when the time was right, the Germans became dead.

I woke up thirsty, weird dreams taking me back to my childhood, my mouth feeling like the bottom of a bird's cage. The IV machine cast a green electronic light over the now darkened, vacated, and quiet room. I took a drink from the glass of water waiting on the side-table, and noticed the 9 button was missing. The aunts would have had it cut up by now: five ways. Mother would get the largest piece, and they'd split the rest.

A huddled shape on the sofa snored, the glint of the distinctive curve of an AK-47 magazine cuddled in his arms. His back to me, I couldn't make out who it was – one of the "boys". In the nurse light of the hallway, Chai was sitting in front of the door, his back to me, his head held high.

"Chai," I said softly. I didn't want to startle the sleeping shape with the AK. Chai turned his left ear toward me.

"Help me up."

Chai got up from his sentry position and walked over to me without making a sound. His eyes held a question, and he hesitated. Dr. Tom or Mother had left orders.

"I'm going to see Khun Por." It wasn't a request.

He dropped the steel bar on the bed. I got my legs over the side. Everything hurt. Chai wrapped an arm around me and helped me onto my feet. Taking the wheeled IV drip stand with me, we shuffled to the door. Chai paused, holding me steady, he then let go of me. I wobbled, but I had the drip stand for support. He took out his Uzi, and opening the door, gave the hallway a quick scan. He turned and nodded to me, holding the door open. I had a flashback to Red. It wasn't pleasant.

Shuffling forward, the bright light of the corridor bit into my eyes. I had a serious headache. I stood, wobbling. Chai took my arm in his left hand, his right held the Uzi pointing down the corridor. Chai's a "shoot first, ask questions when everyone's dead" kind of guy: my kind of bodyguard. He parked me by the door, tapped the cell phone on his belt, and whispered into a mouthpiece.

"Chance has come to see Por."

The door opened. Beckham stood in the doorway. Not David, Opart. But David was his favorite football player, so he'd changed his name to Beckham. Five foot tall and about the same wide, no neck, he filled the doorway, a sawn-off pump action shot-gun swallowed in his hand. Beckham opened the door and stepped aside. I shuffled in, walking carefully, keeping an eye on my tether to the IV drip. When I finally reached the bed, I sat down in the chair next to it.

Khun Por had a tube stuffed down his throat and little white pads with wires leading off them stuck on his chest. A machine, with a large black accordion trapped inside a glass case, thumped down and sucked up with a hiss. He looked so small, this huge man. His energy was his size. The energy inert, he'd shrunk. Mother lay asleep on the sofa next to him, her long barrel .357 Ruger Blackhawk on the coffee table within reach.

His usually neat hair was tussled from sleep. I reached out and smoothed it into place. Normally, I could never touch my father's head. Us Buddhists are particular about such things. I stroked his head, smoothing his hair into place, quiet tears rolling down my face.

"Boss."

I turned at Beckham's whisper. He was pointing at a flat screen monitor on the sideboard near the sink: CCTV split in two, the right and left views of the corridor. I wiped the tears off my face and, getting up from the chair, shuffled over to the sideboard. Three men in the picture in the corridor to the right, standing at the end of the corridor. All were dressed in black.

Men in black, there'd been a lot of speculation and talk about MIB over the past few weeks, but these guys didn't have anything to do with politics. Chai reached into the inside pocket of his jacket and pulled out the fat tube of a silencer. Moving with a speed and efficiency born of practice, he screwed it onto the end of the Uzi, doubling its barrel length. Beckham put the shotgun on the sideboard, nodding at it and looking at me in the same motion. I picked it up in my right hand, the left still occupied with the IV drip. Beckham took out a gun from behind his back and screwed a silencer onto it.

I heard a noise behind me and turned to see Mother coming around the coffee table, the Blackhawk in a two-handed grip. It looked ridiculously large in her dainty hands, but she knew how to use it. The phrase "nuts off a gnat" springs to mind. Chai spoke rapidly into his hands-free mike, telling Tum, identifying the guy sleeping with the AK in my room, what was happening.

Beckham and Chai moved quietly to the door.

KILL THEM ALL

13 May 2010, Bangkok, 2 am

The three men in black were still at the end of the corridor. Judging by the amount of hand-waving going on, they were arguing. There's a tip for you: get the details sorted before you go to assassinate someone; it's a lot simpler that way. One of them turned away, his back to the camera. He got hit on the arm by one of the others. He turned, tall, with a thin face and a moustache. I didn't recognize him. The fat one doing the waving, his black T-shirt exposing his belly, a dessert-plate-sized amulet hanging from his neck, grabbed Skinny and pushed him down the corridor towards us. Skinny walked a few steps then, looking back, flicked the bird at the other two.

"Only one is coming. The other two are staying down the hall," I said. Chai nodded at my whisper, and told Tum next door. Skinny was getting closer. Chai made hand signals. Wait – one – go in – open door. Good at charades. I watched the monitor. One of the waiting two men lit a cigarette – smoking in a hospital. Skinny reached the door to my room and stopped. That really pissed me off and set my mind off in a hundred different directions.

Skinny reached behind his back, his gun snagging on his belt as he tried to tug it free. Standing next to me, Joom said into my ear, "Amateur." Skinny's tongue curled over his upper lip as he turned the handle and pushed in. Beckham, his hand on the door handle of our room, was waiting on me.

Skinny disappeared from sight. I nodded. Beckham quickly pulled the door open. Chai went into the corridor and dropped onto one knee, Uzi pointed down the hall. The monitor showed Beckham disappearing into my room. The Uzi made clacking sounds, an echo of the spent cartridges rattling on the door. Five bursts and amateur minute was over. The two bodies hadn't even pulled their weapons.

I watched as Chai walked down the corridor. He looked into my room, but didn't stop. Reaching the fallen bodies, he knelt down. I couldn't really tell what he was doing, and I felt dizzy. I went and sat on the sofa. Mother got on her iPhone, beginning the cleanup.

Chai and Beckham stashed the bodies in my room and brought bedding over to make up the sofa proper. I needed to get some sleep. Just as I was nodding off to the muted conversations Mother was having on her phone, Dr. Tom showed up, jeans and T-shirt replacing his usual hospital garb.

His very round blinking eyes were evidence that Chai

had taken him next door. He looked paler than usual, which made him seem ghostlike. He gave Mother a wai, his hands settling on his well-fed paunch with a nervous wringing. He pulled the chair over and, pretending to listen to my heart, whispered.

"Chance, please, this is a hospital. What am I going to say?"

Joom put her hand over the mouthpiece on the phone.

"Thomas, this is a hospital, it's filled with dead people. You don't have room for three more?" The arched eyebrows above the fierce glare nearly made me crap myself.

"I'm sorry, Mere Joom, but…"

"Thomas. Nothing will happen. Nothing has happened. I've spoken with the police district commander. One new Range Rover, okay? The police are not interested. Stop worrying. They were Khmer. No one will miss them." Mere Joom did not have the same sense of awe for doctors and teachers as most Thais.

"Mother, we should use them. Someone wants us dead. Let them think they succeeded. Start the funeral day after tomorrow. Give it the full works. Cremate two of them. Feed the other one to the crocs." The famous Pak Nam Crocodile Farm, largest in the world with 60,000 hungry crocs every night. It's a service we provide to other families. Tourists often comment on how lazy our crocs are. Equivalent to your mobs' funeral homes. Ours is a more environmentally friendly concept.

"That's not bad thinking, Chance. I've been asking Khun Por to retire for a while now. Maybe now he'll agree. Yes," she nodded briskly, "that's what we'll do. Thomas, you'll sign the death certificates for Chance and Khun Por, and get those bodies next door sealed in body bags. And I mean sealed, padlock them. I don't want anyone peeking inside. Say it's because of disfiguration from the bomb if anyone asks why."

Thomas remained sitting by the sofa.

"Go. Go." Mother, with the iPhone in one hand and the Blackhawk in the other, shooed him towards the door. Thomas jumped up and backed out.

There's a villager's joke, which goes something like this. The Poo Yai, mayor, of a small town heard that the men of his town were all afraid of their wives. The Poo Yai's wife ordered him to solve the problem. So he called the men of the town together for a secret male-only meeting. And he asked them, "Who among you that is afraid of your wife raise your hand." Everyone in the meeting raised their hand, except one little old guy, sitting in the far right corner at the back of the meeting hall, his hands clasped firmly together in his lap, his shoulders shrunken inwards trying to make himself as small as possible.

The Poo Yai noticed the little old man and asked him to come out to the front and explain to everyone how it is that he alone is not afraid of his wife. The little old man shuffled to the front, his eyes darting left, right, and back to the door. The mayor lowered the microphone a little and said, "So come on, tell us the secret."

The little old man took the microphone and in a quavery voice said, "Well, this morning when I got up, my wife said, there's a secret male-only meeting being held at the town hall today, and every male in the town will be asked by that fool of a mayor…" At saying this he shrugged apologetically towards the mayor, who in return shrugged his shoulders, nodding his understanding and waving at him to continue speaking. The old man continued, "So my wife told me that when that fool of a mayor asks you to raise your hand if you're afraid of your wife, I do not want you to raise your hand. So that was why I didn't raise my hand."

Thai women have carefully cultivated and crafted a legend around their being innocent demure females. They get together for card games and laugh about it.

An ice-cold fear went through me. Uncle Mike. He wasn't involved, well, not directly, in the family busi-ness, but he was known, in certain circles, to be "family". Chai looked at me; we had that kind of understanding. Por had put us together when I was six. We've been on the street together since then. I raised a fist with my thumb to my ear and my little finger to my mouth. Chai handed me a cell phone. I dialed Uncle Mike's number. I checked the time on the cell. Four am. It rang, and rang, and rang some more, until a polite recording of a female voice said to leave a message. He slept with his phone on. Always. I'd never not been able to reach him.

All thought of sleep vanished. I felt a deep shame for not thinking of Uncle Mike. I remembered Por's simple words, "Too busy to go and see your uncle," and here I was too busy to even think of him. Shame and anger: "Griengjai".

It was mid-morning before all the preparations were

made. These were tough times in Thailand. Yesterday another M-79 was fired. These seemingly random attacks had been going on for weeks. All part of the red shirt versus every other color that Thai politics had divided itself into. These attacks had put a strong military and police presence on the roads. Clearance to drive Por and myself, armed, out of Bangkok, to the East and the South was needed. Clearance cost money or favor, sometimes both.

Mother finished another call to Aunt Malee, distributing orders like a general in a live fire zone, which in a way she was. She hung up without saying goodbye and hit the green phone button again, this time calling an army colonel. It was trade favor time. I recognized his name as Mother sweetly said hello. She'd introduced him to his wife, the daughter of her third cousin. I wasn't paying attention and only caught the last fragment. Something about Pornsak's college fund. If I remembered right, Pornsak was his son. I was too busy trying to work out who was moving on us. So far no one had showed their hand.

"All right, yes, he'll meet you downstairs. Yes, now." She pressed the off button on the phone with a flourish and put it on the table in front of me. Legs straddled, hands on hips, she looked down at me.

"It's arranged. You're to leave now. You'll have a police escort as far as Chumphon. There's a black VW van waiting downstairs." Her phone beeped. She snatched it off the table, attacking the screen with her thumbs. "Okay, Beckham has checked them out. It's all okay. Call me when you get there. Do you need money?"

I nodded, and she went to the sofa. Picking up a Nike shoulder bag from the floor, she tossed it on the seat and spread it open. Then she lifted a pilot's suitcase onto the sofa, flipping open the twin back lids. 1,000 baht notes wrapped in bundles of a hundred thousand. I counted about fifty bundles before she zipped the bag and handed it to Chai. He slung it over his shoulder. I got up and gave her a deep, respectful wai. I felt worried for her and was scared for her. She smiled, stepping forward, and mindful of my wounds, gave me a soft hug. Stepping back, she looked deep in my eyes.

"Don't worry. I will be fine. And Por, if Buddha wills it, will survive this. You don't worry about us. You get well." Then her eyes turned tough, taking me back years. "You take care of things, Chance."

"Yes, Mother."

She leaned in close. I could feel her breath on my ear. "Promise me. Kill them all." Each whispered word said distinctly.

"Yes, Mother."

Behind every powerful man, there's a powerful woman. In Por's case, five of them.

Tricks For Free

We cleared Bangkok's traffic and were well on our way south. The VW was comfortable, with in-seat DVDs and individual mp3 listening. I plugged in my earphones and sat back. It would take at least eight hours, depending on traffic, to reach Uncle Mike's place in Phuket. It's about 840 km or 530 miles from Bangkok. We're cruising at a steady 160 kph, about a hundred miles an hour. No one's going to stop us. Everyone is profiting from our speed and uninterrupted passage. Chai's in the seat opposite me, cleaning his Uzi.

The question of who was trying to kill us was gnawing at me. I shut my eyes, listening to Edgar Cruz playing Bohemian Rhapsody, singing along in my mind about it being too late, time's up and my body aching. Yeah, that'd be about right.

The most obvious choice was Big Tiger. Big Tiger was the younger of Por's generation and hung out near the Ancient City. He'd grown in wealth and power under Por's umbrella of peace between the gangs of Samut Prakarn, Pak Nam. Was he making his move before I came on the scene? Ironic, since I didn't want it. According to the radio broadcast we'd heard as we passed Hua Hin, I was dead. There's something quite liberating about that.

Khun Por's funeral rites and mine were announced on the news. I checked the time on my cell phone. Two hours since we'd left Bangkok. Por should be in the army hospital in Cambodia by now. It was announced the governor would send his deputy to the funeral as he had to be away on a foreign trip; code for I can't be there, but I need to show respect. All he could do in the circumstances. I received an SMS from Beckham: A-okay. The news of Por's death was big news. Even with the red shirt stand-off and politics dominating everything, all the local Thai stations reported on the funeral.

Using my wireless Air from True Move, I plugged into the social networks: HiSO and Dara Facebook pages awash with the same article. Comments about tears ran freely. Many no doubt hoping that their debts had died along with Por. I turned the radio off. We understand crocodile tears. We have a farm of them. An SMS from Mother confirmed she was okay. We'd bought ten new phones on the way out of town, and Chai had stocked up on SIM cards, spending the first part of the trip out of Bangkok sending the numbers to Beckham, Mother and the aunts. It wasn't likely anyone could trace the calls.

I called Uncle Mike again with no more success than

the earlier times. Frustrated.

Uncle Mike and Por had run together in the early days. A New Zealander by birth, Uncle Mike had met Por a couple of years before John and Barbara. Uncle Mike only smuggled weed. Lots of it. That's how he met Por, who supplied the weed – those days, Thai Stick; these days, Cambodian. Sailing the ocean blue from Thailand to Perth, dropping the loads off on islands before coming in to drink gin and tonics in the Royal Perth Yacht Club. He'd made a fortune, and the cops never knew he existed. Until one sad day he was pulled over for speeding with fifty kilos of weed tightly packed in the boot of his car. Arrested and jailed with his trial date near, he bribed a federal judge and got bail. Por waited just over the horizon in a Thai fishing boat, the decks covered in drums of diesel. Enough to get them home.

A lot of guys who smuggle drugs never make money from it. They always reinvest, and eventually they all get busted or killed. Part peer pressure, part nature of the business, they don't know when to quit. Uncle Mike did. He put his hard-earned money into land in Phuket in the late sixties – huge swathes of beachfront property. He used Joom's name to do it. We don't let Farang buy land in Thailand. Yeah, right. Apart from the land, he'd bought technology stocks. Everything that Warren Buffet did, he followed. It made him a very wealthy man. But you'd never know or think that the guy in shorts, flip flops and a T-shirt full of holes, riding the little Honda Dream motorbike was worth about 450 million dollars: a conservative estimate of a moving number. Some reckon, my aunts in particular, that he's worth over a billion.

Thinking of my aunts and Uncle Mike made me smile.

For years, Por had tried to give one of them to Uncle Mike. When he'd send me to Phuket, he'd take the newest wife or girlfriend, sometimes both, with him, me riding in the back. He'd stay at Uncle Mike's place, back then, a simple villa with a pool overlooking the Andaman Sea. Por would stay for a few nights and then head back, always suggesting to the aunt that she stay on with Mike. It wasn't that Por didn't want them. He just wanted his best friend to have a good wife, and he'd done some pre-qualifying. The aunts weren't opposed to the idea either. They would look at Mike with that "I promise you everything" look – another tool in the Thai women's toolkit of Man Management. He'd smile and say nothing. Por would leave, pressing a few thousand baht in my hand, leaving me with Uncle Mike for the summer.

Bangkok time was surviving the streets, learning the rituals of structured society, and the responsibilities and intricacies of a modern mafia business. Time with Uncle Mike was learning how to be free. To abandon preconceived ideas and live simply: eat, drink, think, play, and sleep. Rock climbing in the Hindu Kush so we could watch a sunrise; rock music at Madison Square Garden and my first joint; sailing across the Malacca Strait to Langkawi; reading Frost under a full moon, to the sound of water slopping against the hull.

> When a friend calls to me from the road
> And slows his horse to a meaning walk,
> I don't stand still and look around
> On all the hills I haven't hoed,
> And shout from where I am, What is it?

No, not as there is a time to talk.
I thrust my hoe in the mellow ground,
Blade-end up and five feet tall,
And plod: I go up to the stone wall
For a friendly visit.

With a groan that didn't get past my lips but wracked my body, I thought again of Por's admonishment. Frost reaching me from the grave.

He took me back to Goa, had me showered by a Yogi for a karmic body wash. The images flashed, warmed, and scared me. Por was left brain, and Uncle Mike was right brain. Is this all I will have from them, melancholy thoughts?

Suppose it wasn't Por. Suppose it was me. The reluctant hit man had gone straight to my room, not Por's. Was that simply because it was first in the corridor or was it the only target? I couldn't know, but it presented at least a fifty percent chance of being a problem. I stared out of the black-tinted windows as the isthmus narrowed and we got closer to our goal; the road through the mountains twisted, slow, frustrating.

Dr. Tom's final instructions about rest and staying on the drip for at least two more days came to me as I took the IV tube out of the needle. I taped the female needle to my arm – might need it later. The evening air was warm and carried the smell of jasmine and burnt cooking oil. Patong's lights glittered in the distance. The dirt road was quiet, dusty. Uncle Mike's house was about half a kilometer further up the road. The driver on loan from the army colonel was taking a piss on the side of the road – the splashing noisy. Chai, standing next to me, poked out his elbows sideways horizontally and swung sharply side to side. I heard the crack. He rolled his shoulders and, shouldering the Uzi, nodded at me. We never talked much. We didn't need to. Given our track record of visiting people over the past 24 hours, I had decided to approach with caution. We set off.

We stuck to the dark shadow of the bushes lining the dirt road until we were a hundred meters from the house. Chai, moving faster and with an impatient flick of his head at me, slipped away into the bush. Uncle Mike owned all the land around his villa and left it as it was. Free grazing for buffalo earning a fortune as a land bank. Uncle Mike hated guns almost as much as any form of authority. The Glock 17 is light, compact, and reliable. I had two of them. One in a shoulder holster supplied by the colonel, and the one in my hand. Slide racked back ready to fire. Some things I agreed with Khun Por, and some things with Uncle Mike. Guns I went with Khun Por. Uncle Mike lived in paradise. We lived in Pak Nam.

Uncle Mike's villa was surrounded by a twelve-foot-high wall made of red brick. The sliding gate was metal alloy, colored to look like teak, with a door set into it. I tried the handle on the door. It opened. The front of the villa was dark. Uncle Mike had to be missing or worse. I kept to the side of the sandstone-paved driveway, staying on the grass. I edged around the deck and to the steps leading to the front door. The smell of death came heavy, crushing the jasmine-scented air. I walked up the steps, Glock ready, but knowing there was nothing there.

The door started to open. My heart tripped. I raised then lowered the Glock as Chai appeared in the doorway.

He shook his head once and went back inside. I followed, putting the gun on the side counter next to a ceramic bowl with rotten black bananas. The smell of rot got stronger in the hallway, and it wasn't bananas. Chai hooked his head towards the back of the house. I walked that way.

Lilly, Uncle Mike's maid, was dead on the floor of the kitchen. The white tiles around her head black with her blood. Chai turned the lights on in the kitchen, revealing a modern, efficient island in the middle of brushed chrome. And Lilly on the floor with a cell phone stuck in her mouth. I went over to the sink. A drying cloth neatly laid by it. Lilly, always cheerful Lilly. An empty sink. He was taken in the morning. Probably yesterday, might have been the day before. I'd need someone to examine Lilly to find out. I puked up in the sink. Turning the tap on, I rinsed my mouth out and splashed water on my face. I went back to Lilly, cloth in hand, reaching for the phone. It rang. Dire Straits, "Money for Nothing", the ring tone. They had a sick sense of humor and a camera in here. I stood up and walked through to the living room. The phone still ringing.

A black box on the rattan side table. I reached behind the box and pressed the little black button on Uncle Mike's router, shutting off the Internet connection.

"Chai, call Mother and get her to put a trace on any phone calls out of towers within reach of this house."

Chai nodded, his hand dropping to the cell phone clipped to his belt. I walked back into the kitchen and took the phone out of Lilly's mouth. Holding it well clear of my ear, I hit the answer button.

"Don't bother getting your mother to trace the call.

I'm using Skype from another country, and go and turn the Internet back on." Bugged as well, then.

"Fuck you. How much? When and where?" The caller had an accent, but I couldn't place it. Scandinavian, German or Dutch, dunno. Keep him talking.

"If you don't do as I say, your uncle is going to be killed. Slowly. Do you understand?"

"I understand that you want something. My guess is that you want money. So you listen to me. If you hurt him, I won't do what you want. You'll have to just kill him because I won't play your game. Do you understand?"

"Khun Chance or should I call you Mr. Harper, hey Sam? What do you think?"

Shit! Not good, is what I think.

"What I think is that you should get to the point of this call. Are you going to do that anytime soon?" I was looking at Lilly on the floor and getting angrier by the second. Cool heart, jai yen, but I couldn't let this guy think I was going to dance to his tune. That would just make everything more expensive.

"All right, Mr. Chance." He pronounced it "Chunce". "I'll get to the point. We want your Uncle Mike's money. All of it. By the end of the day tomorrow, or we kill him".

I knew this was where we'd been headed ever since Uncle Mike didn't answer the phone. Felt it in my gut. Now it was here for real. Front and center.

"Look, maybe you're not aware, but there's a bit of a problem in Bangkok right now, and moving a million doll…"

"You fuck! You shut up with a million. You fuck. You think we're stupid, mister. We know all about you, your dead Godfather, and your uncle Mike, the farm, everything, so don't fuck with us. One hundred million United States dollars by tomorrow."

"Can't do it. It's not possible. First of all, Mike's not worth that much, and second, it is physically impossible."

His accent got thicker the angrier he got. Scandinavian. "Do it, or he's fucking dead." And he had a slight lisp – he'sth.

"He's fucking dead, then, isn't he," I said, just trying to keep him engaged. "Are you really going to blow this because you're too fucking stupid to understand the word impossible? Look, I can get you five million by tomorrow night."

"One hundred million in a week. I will call and tell you how and where to deliver it. One week, that's all you have. One hundred million. Keep this phone charged. You fuck up, and he dies."

The phone went quiet. Holding it carefully, I walked over to the sink, opening one of the cupboards above it and taking out a Ziploc bag packet. I got a bag out and dropped the phone in it. I put the cloth over Lilly's face.

We closed up the house and headed back to the van. I got on the phone to Mother. She answered on the first ring.

"Chance, are you okay? We're getting the numbers that called into the towers around Mike's place. We should have them in an hour."

"Mother, I'm fine. We've just left Uncle Mike's. Lilly is dead, murdered by whoever took Mike. They've called me. There was a camera and bugs in the house. This seems to be a sophisticated gang, and they know about us."

"What do you mean?"

"I mean they know about the family, the business, and Uncle Mike's money."

"How much do they want?"

"A hundred million."

"Baht?"

"Dollars."

"I see." She paused, and I heard a sigh. "When?"

"A week from today, the…" I looked at the date on the phone, "the 19th."

"All right. You get out of there. I'll make arrangements for Lilly, poor woman. So sad, it breaks my heart, all this violence."

"I know, Mother. I have some things to do down here, but I'll try and get back to Bangkok tomorrow."

"Be careful. Call me before you come so I can arrange an escort. The situation in Bangkok is getting worse. I'm hearing rumors of all sorts, everything from another coup to armed insurrection by the army regiments from Isarn."

"I'll call. Bye, Mother."

We went through the rest of the rooms. Apart from the art scattered around, Uncle Mike didn't keep any valuables at the house. Nothing was out of place. Even in his bedroom, everything was neat. It meant they'd taken him in the morning. During a day, Uncle Mike created havoc with neatness.

THE BEST ENEMIES...
ARE DEAD ONES

13 May 2010, Phuket, 11 am

One of Por's favorite sayings is "A good enemy is intelligent and sane. A bad enemy is intelligent and crazy. The worst enemy is dumb and crazy, but the best enemies are dead ones." He'd always chuckle when he delivered the punch line, and so would I. Uncle Mike would frown and then smile, shaking his head slowly from side to side. My happiest memories, days when the three of us were together.

My Twitter account was filled with new tweets. Bangkok Crazy. I had a list of journalists, people "in the know", cops, army, and then friends. Some the cops' tweets were hilarious, but I couldn't laugh. Lilly getting killed had really upset me. Her life had been miserable and tough as hell until she met Uncle Mike. She'd deserved to know happiness for longer. No more chance to tilt the balance in her favor. I felt, sad, sick, and really pissed off all at the same time.

From the rest of the tweets, it seemed like Bangkok was going into meltdown. The red shirt leaders were playing games in the negotiations with the government, and it looked as if the government didn't want to play anymore. The center of Bangkok, occupied by the red shirt camp since April, was now a medieval fortress. In April, the street protests had turned into street battles with over 14 dead. It was possible that Big Tiger was using the protests as cover for getting rid of us. The bomb attack at Heaven had been reported as being either political or business related. Astute reporting that covered 80 percent of all possibilities and didn't actually say anything.

I couldn't see a Farang getting a bomb into Heaven. It just didn't stack up, unless the Farang had help. I went with the idea that the bombing and the kidnapping were two separate incidents. I sent an SMS to Mother. Check with cops about any Scandinavian criminal gangs operating in Phuket or Thailand. I knew the Bandidos had put together gangs in Pattaya, Phuket and Samui, and they usually preyed on foreigners. But they had been quiet since '06, when a bunch of their leaders got busted. I was tired, forgetting things.

"Chai go back inside and get Uncle's backup drive. It's in his bedroom."

The army driver was outside having a smoke. I was inside the van with the air-conditioning. I got out and bummed a smoke off him: a Marlboro red. On the packet, "Smoking Kills". I was already dead. The nicotine fired up long dormant endorphins. It made it easier to think and wait. I needed to get some sleep and have Uncle Mike's place fingerprinted. We could get prints run through local and Interpol cops. It'd take a day or two, but it was worth a shot. I was thinking about who to get to question the neighbors in the area when Chai returned, a square black box in one hand and a blue cloth bag in the other.

I needed a place to stay which had access to the Internet, was quiet with good security, and out of town. My face was too well known by other "families". A quick search, Absolute Chandara seemed like a good choice. I gave Chai the phone number and asked him to book us rooms.

I set up in the main living room. Chai had booked me into a two-bedroom suite with a private pool and put himself and the driver in the villas either side of me. The infinity pool in front of me dropped 80 feet down a cliff to the sea below. It was a good choice.

I'd hooked up the back-up to a USB port and was trying passwords. Uncle Mike always used Rolling Stones songs. It was the only way his acid-scarred mind could remember them, the passwords, not the Stones, he remembered all of their songs. Written as one word with prime numbers in between the words, it wasn't foolproof, but I hadn't got in yet. I knew a guy in Bangkok that could do it. An Israeli whose business it is to recover lost data, but Bangkok, and waiting was out of the question. I kept going, using the song list I'd pulled up from the iTunes store. I was halfway down the list.

Honky2Tonk3Woman5
Lets2Spend3The5night7Together11
You2Can't3Always5Get7What11You13Want17
Please select Drive and location:

While Uncle Mike's hard drive copied over to mine, I went and had a shower. It's hard taking a shower when you're covered in bandages. Drying myself, I took a look in the mirror. I was covered in bruises from midriff to my neck. The patch over my eye hid a two-inch cut that had taken most of the eyelid off, and missed my eyeball by less than a millimeter. The number nine on my chest was as clear as ever. I wondered if it was permanent. The four-poster bed with its white linen sheets and fluffy soft pillows looked very tempting, but I still had work to do.

I hooked myself back up to Dr. Tom's IV drip. He'd sent me an SMS while I was in the shower. "Por settled army hosp. nr Sihanoukville. Still in coma but stable. Take your medicine. T."

I had the TV on while I was working, watching the stuff that was happening in Bangkok. It was getting worse. Deputy PM Suthep had turned himself in for arrest as the red shirt leaders had requested, but he'd turned himself into DSI. Since he was effectively the head of DSI, the red shirts rejected the move. PM Abhisit, Mark to you, wasn't going to be resigning any time soon, and Dr. Thaksin had been making phone calls in the background. U.S. Assistant Secretary of State Kurt Campbell had flown in seagull style. Done breakfast with red shirt leaders, crapped everywhere and flown off. The arrogance of ignorance is not bliss. It was getting too hot to cool down now. If the lid blew on the protests, there'd be fighting in the streets. I had to be back in Bangkok.

I got an email from Mother. A list of phone numbers calling into and from the base stations around Uncle Mike's house. Money is information. Information is power. I left the numbers for later and made a call myself.

Cheep was an old friend of Uncle Mike's. He'd been a loader on a few of the runs to Australia, helping to catch the 10-kilo bundles of weed as they were tossed from the deck of a fishing boat, usually during a bad storm. The Thai navy didn't like bad storms, and tended to stay in port while they were happening. He owned a couple of the bars in Patong and had a small crew. Mostly retired but still connected, I could trust him to keep his mouth shut and get things done.

"Khun Cheep Sawadee Krup…" There was a scream, and the sound of the phone hitting something hard. Disconnected. I hit redial.

"Khun Cheep. Hello. Khun Cheep. Are you there?"

"Who is this?" His voice sounded weird. Oh shit, of course.

"Hey, Khun Cheep, don't worry, man. I'm not a ghost."

"That's exactly what a smart ghost would say."

"Khun Cheep, it's me – the this-life me. I'm alive. We faked the death for reasons I don't have time to explain, but I've got some problems, and I need your help."

"You scared the hell out of me. I nearly pissed myself." He was half angry now, his voice petulant with indignation.

"Would sending an SMS have been better?"

"No. Okay, what's the problem?"

I outlined the situation to Cheep. He was as furious as I was about Lilly and promised to work with Mother to arrange a good funeral. Meanwhile he'd put his boys on canvassing the area to see if we could come up with anything.

"Keep the news that I'm alive to yourself, okay. And tomorrow, go get a few phones and some SIM cards. Chai will update you with numbers to call."

"Don't worry, Chance. Your uncle is my best friend in the world. Whatever you want, you call. When we find these people, we kill them all. Yes?"

"Yes, Cheep. We kill them all."

Uncle's internet history came up with a bunch of investment forums, stock trading sites, news, music, Amazon and eBay. Nothing unusual. I went through his cache. Nothing. It was nearly 1 am. I debated having a drink, but with the painkillers Dr. Tom had given me, I persuaded myself not to. The pain was good for keeping me awake. I went back to the hard drive. More out of hope than conviction, I kept looking.

An hour later, I still had nothing. And I had nothing left. Something was nagging at me, something that I knew I should be getting, but I wasn't. The thought spun out to the sound of a fishing boat heading out to sea.

Natasha from Odessa

Skype. The first word in my mind when I woke up. The Lisp had said don't bother trying to trace him because he was using Skype. Was that how they found Uncle Mike? Did Uncle Mike use Skype? I jumped out of bed, excited, heading for the living room. This was what had been nagging at me. A sharp pain in my arm, I turned. The IV drip machine hit me in the face, I'd forgotten to disconnect. I sat back down on the bed and got the plug out of the needle. I taped the needle back up. Not the best start to a day. It was 7:15 am. I was late getting up. I usually get up at 5, gives me more day.

Chai was in the open kitchen of the living room making coffee. It smelled good. The TV was on with the volume muted, Government Spokesman Colonel

Sanserm all dimples. Sitting down on the sofa, I grabbed the remote and turned the volume up while I booted up my notebook. I hoped that during the night a solution had been found to the political mess we were in. My hope was short-lived as Colonel Sanserm laid out the terms by which protestors had to leave the Ratchprasong rally site or face forceful eviction. To give you Farang a better idea of what was happening here in the Land of Smiles: imagine if a group of armed civilians took over Times Square and then fortified the area they had with a twelve-foot-high wall of sharpened bamboo stakes and rubber tires. And every now and then, someone fired an M-79 grenade launcher at groups of people protesting against those behind the bamboo stakes.

The notebook was up, and I switched to Uncle Mike's back-up drive. Yes. Skype was there. I disconnected from wireless before I started the app; didn't want anyone knowing that I was in Uncle Mike's Skype. I turned his status to invisible and went straight to the conversations tab. I was working on a single piece of logic. Whoever kidnapped Uncle Mike must have been known to him. His house was hard to approach unnoticed; even the roof had sound sensors on it. Free-spirited he may be, but he wasn't blind to the idea that houses get robbed, especially Farang houses. So his security system was tight, and he had a panic room. But nothing was damaged at the house, which meant he had let them in or at least one of them. That meant he knew them.

All the conversations between happy_hippy45 and the people he was having them with made sense. Except one. Natasha. Natasha's profile gave me little to go on: female;

user_name: Natasha_Odessa; Country: Russia. But there was a photo. Of a very beautiful woman. Whether it was a real photo, who knew? I went to the hard drive and searched for strings containing Natasha. Three files came up, with an extension I didn't recognize,.sgf. I left Skype on and then Googled "file extension .sgf". At the top of the list, screen grabber file, a proprietary format of the Screen Grabber application used to capture video from Skype or MSN. I hit the url and landed on their site. A free download, valid for a 30-day trial. Two minutes later, it was installed in my hard drive. I clicked on natasha_1st.sgf.

She was real. She was beautiful. And the only thing she was wearing was the microphone she was using to talk to Uncle Mike. She looked like she was in her late twenties maybe early thirties, everything firm and perky. Now call me cynical, but True Love is not the first thing that springs to mind when I see a twenty-something hanging off the arm of a sixty-something.

To her credit, though, she was giving one heck of a performance. It was hard not to get a hard on. I mean, it didn't look like she was acting. I focused on the room she was in, but it didn't give anything away. She was sitting in a straight-backed, wicker-bottomed chair, the walls of the room white. A single painting, I guessed a print of Van Gogh's "Sunflowers", hung on the wall behind her above the wooden headrest of a single bed.

So, maybe, Lisp wasn't Scandinavian. Maybe he was Russian. I'm thinking this has "Honey-pot" written all over it. The other two files were more of the same, except in the last she was dressed at first and then disrobed. I couldn't hear what she was saying. Apparently Screen

Grabber only grabbed video, no sound. That was okay. I had a photo, a direction, and an erection.

I closed the notebook and walked out to the pool. Easing my butt over the edge, I slipped in, the water deliciously cool. Conscious of the need to keep the dressing on my eye dry, I floated on my back, feeling calmer. So here's what happened: Natasha is searching for a mark. She finds one, Uncle Mike. She eases in. No video at first, just a sexy Russian voice. She didn't dive straight into amateur porn, she waited till the fourth chat. Good online girls don't do porn on the first date. She probably hit him with the, "Honey, good news. Guess what? I'm coming to Thailand," line right after show #4 where she showed him she could be a "good-girl" all dressed up – expensive executive chic.

Could Uncle Mike fall for that? Sure, why not? With her body and looks, any guy with a pulse could.

There was only one problem with the scenario above, and that was how did they get to know about me and the family? Rolled in with that, while I could see Uncle Mike falling for some cute Russian pussy and inviting her for a holiday, I couldn't see him telling her his net worth. Just not his style. I mean some guys like to talk about how much money they've got. Uncle Mike is, sort of, gleefully ashamed of his wealth.

I climbed out of the pool and went in for a shower. Washed the chlorine off. Got dressed. Down to my last T-shirt. I'm thinking to head back to Bangkok. Not likely to find out anything new here. They wouldn't stick around once they'd got their man.

I called out to the living room.

"Chai."

"Yes."

"We're heading back to Bangkok. Can you give me a hand with this eye-dressing? We should change it?"

"Yes."

A lot of people think that Chai can't speak English. His language skills are superb. He just doesn't like talking. He likes listening, especially to monks. Donates a fair part of what he earns to restoring temples. Maybe it's insurance.

Chai peeled the eye-dressing away. I was watching his face for any change of expression. Impassive, the dressing off, I waved Chai to one side so I could get a look at the damage. It wasn't pretty. I had a backward L-shaped set of stitches running from my forehead near the bridge of my nose, right across my eyelid, just under the eyebrow and finishing at my temple. But it didn't look too puffy and pink, so not infected, just fucking ugly.

A trip to Korea, I thought, and segued into the staring dead eyes of Por's girlfriend.

Chai finished with the dressing.

"Settle up with the front desk."

He nodded.

While Chai was checking us out of the hotel, I sent a screen capture of Natasha to Mother. She'd get it run through the Immigration Police database. Everyone coming in or out gets their photo snapped. If she was here, then she was there.

I scanned the online versions of the Nation, Bangkok Post, and the Thai dailies. Everyone's prognosis was the same. Bangkok was headed for a showdown. The big question on everybody's minds was whether the whole country would follow. Already, a train full of troops, allegedly headed for the three southern provinces where we have our own little jihad problem, had been stopped and held hostage. Only when the mayor of the town, and the army general in command of the train, guaranteed that the troops were really headed for the south, was the train allowed to continue. There's a fine line between protest and insurrection. It looked to me as if some of the reds had crossed it already. But again, nothing is simple in this land. On a simplistic CNN level it was reds versus military. The reality is far more complex: The military may wear green on the outside, but this is Thailand, so what they wear is their business, until the time comes when you have to take a side. Talk of watermelons, green outside red inside, and pineapples, green outside yellow inside, abounded on Twitter.

The problem with trying to figure out what is happening in Thailand politically is that you have to under-stand that Thais are masters of deception. The "third hand" or "invisible hand" is there all the time. Oftentimes, more than one, and what looks like an open and shut case is actually a black box packed full of twists and turns, bubbling away in an atmosphere of rumor and vapor. CNN had the colors down to poor underdog red, versus rich elite yellow. Not getting that there are more colors here than a Dulux paint catalog, with a flip-side of shades of gray.

I checked my Twitter stream, email, and SMS. Nothing from Cheep or Dr. Tom. Chai came back. Stood in the doorway and nodded at me. I held up two fingers, starting to pack up the stuff. He walked over to the sofa I

43

was on and sat down in the easy chair opposite me – the short-barreled Uzi across his knees, the muzzle pointed at the door.

"Chance."

I stopped packing and looked him straight in the eye. It's an occasion when Chai talks.

"Yes."

"We're going to kill them, right?"

I thought of Natasha. Heels of her feet on the edge of the straight-backed wooden chair with the wicker bottom, head thrown back, neck long and taut, quivering. I imagined Chai behind her, slicing through the white skin with his carbon black K-Bar knife. It wasn't a pretty image.

"Yes, Chai, we're going to kill them all." He had a hint of a smile on his lips. Aunt Nings' Doberman had a look like that. Before it was fed.

MUSTANG SALLY

14 May 2010, Bangkok, 5 pm

Uncle Mike had a saying. "Behind every pair of eyes, there's a life lived." I was looking at Natasha's. It was research. The notebook on my lap. The red cell phone on the seat beside me rang. A last look, what's your story, Natasha? I closed the notebook. It was five in the evening. We were heading past Pinklao into Bangkok. Traffic was light going into the City, and heavy coming out. Rumors of an imminent military crackdown on the red shirts were all over the net. I answered the phone.

"Chance?"

"Yes, Cheep."

"People saw a black van yesterday and a white van the day before. The doctor said Lilly died sometime in the morning the day before yesterday."

"Anyone get a number on the van."

"On the black van, yes. On the white, no."

"The black van was us. Anything else?"

"That's what I figured. No, nothing else."

"Check around. See if anyone has heard anything about a Scandinavian or Russian gang doing kidnappings or extortion. I'll send a photo in a minute, but keep it low profile, okay."

"Sure."

I hung up. So the morning of the day that I was blown up, Uncle Mike was kidnapped. That was a big coincidence.

The army driver was snoring in the front seat while Chai drove, trying to set a new land speed record between Phuket and Bangkok. I ran algorithms on the base stations numbers, listening to the Rolling Stones.

I had already singled out the data for the morning of the eleventh. Calls in and calls out. For Patong area base stations, this is a lot of data. A SQL query sorted out those numbers that had made calls from that area in the week before. I focused on those that only made calls on that day. People passing through. For those calls, I took them down to the picocell level. A picocell (pico) is base station repeater within, say, carparks or a mall. A microcell would cover an area of a few malls, and of course, macrocells are the base station receivers and transceivers which can cover an area of up to, in the case of GSM, 40 km. Patong area has ten main base stations. Each base station has a collection of microcells and picocells within it. This is a lot of phone calls; however, a cell phone is simply a two-way radio. Triangulation is built into the network. All the data is there for analysis, it just takes a bit of luck and a lot of time. Normally, I'd farm this out. But I didn't know who or where all of our enemies were.

I eliminated any numbers that were present at tourist-spot picos. Kidnappers usually hang out in bars, restaurants, hotels and motels. I overlaid the numbers left on a satellite map of Phuket. Color-coded lines show the movement of numbers flowing from pico to pico. I color coded these according to average time spent at a picocell. If the average time spent in a picocell range was low and consistent, then they were moving. If erratic, then they were stopping places. I adjusted the algorithm to split a color for those which had a 10-20 minute stop at the microcell repeater for Uncle Mike's hill property area.

A thin neon-pink line emerged. It came in from the mainland, ran to the airport, and stopped there for 15 minutes. It then changed to 4 pink lines, went straight to the microcell area, and then all 4 pink lines went to a microcell east of the bridge. The four lines tracked southeast until they disappeared out of the data range. I needed more data. I picked up the green phone. Hit 1 on the speed dial. It didn't even complete the first ring before she answered.

"Hello, Mother. How's my funeral going?" I could hear the live pipes and cymbals in the background.

"Wait a second … there, that's better. I can hear you now. The funeral is going good, but four streets got hit for protection money last night: four different groups. No one we can recognize. The heads of the five districts are meeting tonight. It was Big Tiger's idea."

"Okay, maybe he's making his move. What do you think? Are you going to go?"

"No. I want to see what happens. We'll know more without showing our hand."

"Yes, you're right…"

"Of course I am."

I smiled. "Mother, I need some more data. Four numbers. I've sent you the numbers."

"All right. It'll take time. The staff at the telcos are pretty busy tracking numbers right now."

"Yes, of course. How's it going with the money?"

"It's going. Just like the trace data, it'll take time, another couple of days at least. You'll have to go to Singapore, though. We can't move it here. Too much is happening right now. The military is trying to shut down red shirt financing. All transactions in and out are being very heavily monitored. This whole mess, I just can't believe it. Did you hear the BMA plan to shut down the electricity in the red shirt camp? That's no good. The red shirts have generators. Anyway, is there anything else? I've got to get back to your funeral."

"Yes, couple of things. Can you ask Aunt Ning to visit her Mor Doo, this evening after the monks leave, and to ask him for an update on how I'm doing in the hereafter. She should describe in detail how she saw me dead in the hospital, and Khun Por, too."

"Hmm, yes. Are you trying to spread a rumor?"

"Yes. A couple of them. Is Sally there?"

"Yes, she's playing Hi-Lo outside in the Sala."

"Can you tell her to meet me at her salon at about five?"

"Yes. I see your game. That's good. Maybe draw someone out?"

"Yes, Mother."

"How is your eye?"

"It's okay. Throbs a bit when I think too much, which means its throbbing all the time. But it seems to be healing all right."

"Remember what I told you. All of them."

"Yes, Mother. I remember. I have to go now. Bye, Mother."

"Take care of yourself." Her voice nearly cracked. I hung up to save us both the embarrassment.

"Chai, Bangkok Noi."

He nodded.

I called Cheep again. "Cheep, have your guys ask around Yacht Haven up north. See if any of the boat boys know anything about a boat leaving day before yesterday. Should have been 4 or 5 people on the boat. Show the photo of the woman if you need to."

"Okay. I'll send some guys up there now."

Chai stopped outside Mustang Sally's Salon & Spa, blocking the view from the houses opposite. I took the blue and yellow phones, a few bundles of cash, and left everything else in the van. Chai went into the salon before me to check the place out, rolling his eyes at me as he came back, closely followed by a six-foot-tall, beautiful woman. I climbed out slowly, aching everywhere.

"Oh my God, look at you! I'm so sorry about Por. He was such a darling. Come in. Come in." At one time, Sally was Bangkok's highest paid call "girl", a katoey, specializing in femdom. Her reputation for blow jobs was legendary. Able to suck a golf ball through a straw, the most common metaphor. Still dressed in black, she offered me a hollowed, powdered cheek. I gave her a quick peck on the cheek and followed her inside the salon. Hooker to salon is a standard career path, but Sally's success was anything but standard. Known by the nickname "Dara CNN", celebrity gossip is Sally's way of keeping the salon full. Sally also does make-up. It allows her to get up close and whisper the latest hot secret in your ear. Sally locked the doors behind us. I needed a disguise and a rumor spread.

"Have you got a weapon. A gun or…" I put some urgency in my voice.

"Yes." She had a frown on her face.

"Can you go get it? Now." Her eyes went wider.

"Sure. Yes." She started to go back up the stairs off to our right, but turned, her foot on the first step, and looked back at me.

"Are we in any danger?" She had a sort of semi-accusing look on her face, as if to say thanks for dropping this shit on my doorstep. I figured the more she felt that way, the faster the news would go out.

"No. Maybe. Probably not. Could you hurry. I left mine with Chai in the van." You can always play the Griengchai card, as long as the other party feels it. She nodded her head. Mind made up.

"Okay, I'll just go get it." She pointed up the stairs. "It's upstairs." She started up the stairs, got about halfway up and stopped, leaning over the banister. "By the way, Chai, is he your driver or a friend? He's quite a…"

"Sally. Please."

"Okay. Okay, I'm going. Make yourself comfortable, I'll, er, okay, yeah…"

My nose was inches away from the valley of Sally's cleavage; she was putting extensions into my hair. At least that's what she said she was doing. I hadn't said a word since sitting down, and Sally was bursting to ask me a thousand questions. Time to start a rumor.

"Did you get these done in Korea?"

"No, Bangkok. Why? Do you like them?"

"Just curious. Sure. They look good."

Sally stepped back, long gray hair extensions in her right hand. She tucked her chin in, looking down, and pushed her tits together.

"Do you think they should be bigger? I was thinking about having them upgraded. Go up a couple of sizes. What do you think?"

"I think they're fine as they are."

"Would you like to see them?"

"No, it's okay. I can tell from here. They're fine. Can you hurry this up a bit? I've got to get to Cambodia tomorrow."

Sally pouted, flounced, grinned, all in one move, and went back to putting extensions into my hair. She leaned forward, giving me a close-up of her cleavage.

"So do you know who, um, you know, tried to kill you?"

"Yes, that's why I'm going to Cambodia tomorrow. It's better if we don't talk about this, Sally, and whatever you do, you must keep my visit here a secret. Okay. Promise me. Whatever you do, don't tell anyone."

"Of course, darling. I won't tell a soul."

Sally's salon is in the back streets behind Arun Amarin Road. The Chao Phraya River runs by her back door. I stood on her dock, waiting for a long-tail boat. Smelly, noisy, uncomfortable, but faster than rush-hour traffic. The long-tail that responded to the green light on the dock was driven by a little skinny guy. He gave me a leery smirk when he asked me where to go. He'd obviously picked up Farangs from Sally's before. The eye-patch had been the problem. Whatever the disguise, the eye-patch would draw attention. Thinking about the Bandidos had given me the idea. Now I looked like a skinny Hulk Hogan in denims. A long, droopy moustache tickled my nose. The black bandana headband, mirrored Ray-Bans, and skull-and-cross-bones eye-patch were Sally's work. I looked ridiculous, but I didn't look like me.

The river was only about 200 meters wide at this point, but the landing at the Shangri La Hotel was about 5 kilometers downstream. As the long-tail driver swung into mid-stream, I spent the time trying to figure out how many people Sally would have called by now, and how many of those would call someone else. She'd start with the senior rumor mongers, the ones with the highest celebrity value, and work her way down. Working on a 1+1 principle, with an allowance for degradation, it would take about another fifteen minutes to reach the landing and it had been ten since I left Sally's. I came up with a conservative estimate of ten million. It probably wouldn't be that high within 25 minutes, but by morning, everyone I wanted to know would have got the rumor that I was still alive.

The long-tail taxi pulled alongside the landing at the Shangri La. I handed over forty baht to the smirking driver and headed for the street. The Shangri La is in a back street off Charoen Krung Road, which connects to Silom. Center of the financial district, also Patpong and Thaniya Plaza are here. Thaniya is a little piece of Ginza and, at a tenth of the price, is the hang-out for Japanese "Sararee" men after a hard day's work on the golf course. Foreigners, especially ones wearing biker leathers and looking like Hulk Hogan, aren't welcome. It was where Musashi Shirotomi, head of the international division of the Yamaguchi-gumi, had his headquarters. No taxis were around, so I shouted to a kid sitting on a motorbike squeezing his zits in its mirror.

"Hey, man, take me to Patpong." Not that many of our motorbike taxi guys speak English, but this phrase is easily understood.

"Hundred baht." A rip off, but keeping in character, I nodded and climbed on, wondering what your average Hell's Angel might think of a biker on the back of 125cc Yamaha. Traffic was light, taxis scarce. It didn't feel like Bangkok. Way too quiet for rush hour on a Thursday. But then someone was firing a grenade launcher at the other end of Silom. Not normal times.

As we approached the other end of Silom, where Thaniya was, I could see fireworks rising from the red shirt encampment. On the opposite site of the street were army and police. Barricades had been set up in case the reds tried to invade Silom. A few days earlier, about a hundred meters from where the taxi dropped me, a young student had been killed and 70 others wounded by M-79 grenades. The government said the grenades were fired from the red shirt camp. The red shirts said the grenades came from the government hospital. The truth? Who knew? The guy who fired the launcher. Shades of gray.

About twenty meters into Thaniya on the right-hand side, opposite the new and second-hand golf shop, is a small alley running between two buildings. The first thing you notice about this alley is that it is spotlessly clean. The second is a door at the end of the alley that doesn't have a handle. I pressed the button on the speaker next to the door and took the Ray-Bans off. I stood back and looked at the camera on the wall above to my right.

"Please tell Ken San that Chance has come to see him," I said at the little box. It was hot under all this hair.

The door clicked open, and I went in to the hallway behind it. A Japanese guy was waiting in the hall. He patted me down, two fingers on his left hand missing. He nodded at me, bowed and, with a gesture of his hand, pointed at the door behind him. I went into a small room with a tiled floor and two wooden benches lining each wall. I sat down and removed the boots Sally had provided. The room was quiet, the slight humming of the air pump for the fish tank next to the door the only noise. The outside world kept out. I put on the slippers provided and opened the door.

Dogs Don't Have Money

Mushashi Shirotomi, Ken, to his friends, stood by the door. A stocky guy, shorter than my six foot, but broader in the shoulder, wearing a dark suit and white shirt. Ken's a new generation, no tats, Yak. While his crew controlled the hookers, drugs, and snakeheads, Ken spent most of his time on the golf course. Just like any other Japanese exec. I gave him a wai. He bowed back.

"I heard you were alive, just five minutes ago." My rumor had beaten me to Silom.

"Well, keep it to yourself, could you, Ken? Another rumor's coming out tomorrow that I am really dead. And that one will be supported by a grainy YouTube video of me being put in a body bag."

A low laugh from a throat made raspy by the Mild Seven cigarettes he chain-smoked, then his face turned serious, and he gestured towards the long white sofa at the far end of the room.

He sat on the sofa opposite me, a low Thai teak table between us.

"What's going on, Smart? Is Khun Por really dead?"

"No, but he's still in a coma, and he's lost a leg."

"I'm very sorry to hear that. Please pass my wish for him to have a full and speedy recovery to Khun Joom."

"I will, and thank you."

A guy came in with a tray and set it down near Ken. He moved the tray between us and poured me a glass of hot sake. Assorted sashimi and sushi lay on little plates on the tray. He waved his hand at the food, and taking his glass, raised it to me.

"Cheers."

"Cheers."

I took a sip of the sake and then put it down on the table.

"Ken, I will come straight to the point. I have a favor to ask. Two favors." I held up two fingers. Elbows on his knees, palms together, a steeple to a point resting on the tip of his nose, he nodded his buzz-cut head at me.

"One. I need some information on a Russian girl from Odessa. Her photos are on this." I handed him a USB memory stick. He nodded. "The second favor is I need one hundred million dollars by Wednesday next week."

Ken didn't blink. He sipped his sake and then put the cup down on the table.

"Australian, Singapore or US?"

"US."

"Collateral?"

"Stocks, bonds, gold futures contracts, a couple of coal mines in Indo and 45% of a tech company in K.L. that I'm in the process of taking over. Total book value for the whole lot of about 150 mill. If liquidated in a fire-sale, not less than 110. If you hang onto it for a few years, 500 mill, easy."

"How long will you need the money?"

"Not more than fifteen days."

"1% a day compound."

"Can you do 1% a day flat rate?"

Ken lit a Mild Seven. I reached across and filched one from the packet.

"I thought you didn't smoke?"

"It's a newly acquired habit, along with dying."

"I hope dying doesn't become a habit. It'll be hard to go for a drink with you. Have you figured out who's trying to kill you?"

"No, not yet. Night before last, in the hospital, whoever it was tried again. Funny thing, the shooter, stopped at my door first."

"You couldn't keep him alive?"

"No, Chai and Beckham were handling things. I was still banged up from the morning. And to be fair to them, the other two were hanging out down the corridor whilst this one guy went into my room."

"Which room came first, your room or Por's?"

"Mine."

"Maybe just a coincidence."

"Yeah, maybe."

The guy who brought the tray of food and drinks came back in and walked around to the back of the sofa. Ken leant back, and the guy whispered, in Japanese, something in Ken's ear. He could have shouted from the door, but I guess he was just being polite. Ken nodded and looked at me. His eyes thin slats in his tanned face, thick black eyebrows came together in a frown as he sucked hard on his Mild Seven and then stubbed it. Blowing the smoke out in one long exhale, he looked at me.

"Seh Daeng has just been shot in the head. Seriously wounded according to our guy on the ground."

"Shit. That's heavy. Things will get bad quickly now." Seh Daeng was a rogue Thai army general who'd allied with the red shirts, organizing their defenses and, some said, the M-79 attacks.

"Who'd you think? Army?"

"Could be. Most probably. Seh Daeng is widely thought to be behind the blowing up of the army colonel last month and also behind the M-79 attacks going on. But he has enemies on the other side, too. Some of the red shirt leaders are more scared of him than they are of the army. Nothing is what it seems."

I shrugged.

Ken nodded and took out another Mild Seven. He saw me looking and pushed the pack my way. I shook my head, lifting up the one I was still smoking.

"I can get the money. I'll have it ready by tomorrow. And forget about the interest. Get it back to me in 15 days, okay. Give me a call when you need it. Allow ten hours for delivery."

Between our business interests in Japan and his in Thailand, it was a safe deal. I stood and offered him my hand. He smiled, looking up at me from the sofa, rose and took it. Ken understands Griengjai, and he'd just earned himself a boatload.

Outside of the cloistered world of Ken's office, automatic gunfire crackled, interspersed with the loud "crump" of explosions. Negotiations were a thing of the past. No one was talking now, only shooting. The yellow phone rang.

"Chance?"

"Cheep – what have you got?"

"You were right. The woman and a man that sounds like Uncle Mike got on a big motor yacht from Yacht Haven. They left about midafternoon. Four guys, all Farang, with them. I got copies of their passports, I'm scan..." a series of loud explosions went off. They sounded close.

"What was that?" he shouted. "Are you okay?"

"Yeah, I'm okay. A shooting war's just started in Bangkok. Someone shot Seh Daeng about ten minutes ago. Hang on, I'm moving up the street a bit." I turned right and walked quickly up Thaniya and found a doorway which shielded some of the noise. "Yeah, okay. What were you going to say before the explosions?"

"Mother of God, that's going to set things off."

"You started to say something before the grenades went off."

"Oh yeah. I'm scanning copies of the passport and the yacht's papers. I'll send them up to you."

"Okay. Thanks, Cheep. I got to go."

I kept walking up Thaniya, typing out a quick message on the Blackberry to Chai. The bursts of automatic fire faded the further I got up the street. I needed to get off the streets and out of here.

- where r you?
- Chinatown
- pick me up Lob. Montien 15 min.
- k

Fifteen minutes from Chinatown was pushing it, but traffic was light, and Chai only knows one speed when he's driving. I stuck my head out to look up the street and to the right. Any shooting would come from there. It seemed calm enough, so I turned left, keeping to the edge of the buildings. There was a lull in the shooting behind me and then another series of loud bangs, and the automatics started up again. The Montien Hotel was about another hundred meters up the road. I thought running might be better than walking.

The lobby was nice and cool – a guy playing on a piano. You couldn't hear the shooting. The bar was empty except for the waitress and the bartender. The little war was hitting tourism hard. Numbers at our crocodile shows were seriously down.

The waitress, dressed in a dark green Cheongsam, showing lots of leg, came over and knelt by my seat.

"Can I get you something to drink, sir?"

"Yes. Hennessy Cognac XO." I spoke in English.

She gave me a strange look. I guess biker's don't usually drink Cognac, but to hell with it. The Blackberry buzzed in my pocket. I checked it. Mail from Cheep, with attachments. I left it. It was too hard opening attachments, especially large files, on the BB. The waitress went to the bar, and I overheard her say in Thai to the bartender, "The smelly dog wants a Hennessy XO, give him the cheap shit, and if he pays in cash, I'll split the difference with you."

The bartender looked across, smiled at me, and nodded. The waitress turned and smiled at me too. Land of Smiles. She came back with the cheap shit and, kneeling, put it down on the table in front of me, sliding the bill in a leather holder next to it. I smiled at her and said in Thai.

"Now go get me a Hennessy XO, and don't fuck around. I'm not in the mood."

She went pale and, grabbing the drink, went back to the bar. The barman quickly poured a very generous shot into a new glass. He didn't look at me the whole time he did this. She came back and put the Cognac down. I picked it up and swallowed the lot in one go. It burnt deliciously all the way down. She looked at me nervously. I spotted Chai out of the corner of my eye, waiting just outside the doors. Standing up, I bent and picked up the leather holder the bill was in and gave it back to her.

"Here. You can pay this. Smelly dogs don't have money."

She took it. Her eyes dropped. A 1,500 baht lesson. Got to do what you can for the country's tourism standards.

Chai saw me coming out of the bar and got in the driver's seat of a black Benz 500 SEL parked in front of the entrance. I slid in the back. My notebook was on the seat beside me, and I knew the Glocks would be under the seat in front of me.

Chai was sitting at the wheel, engine running, looking straight forward and waiting for instructions.

"Lat Prao 93."

We eased out of the forecourt of the Montien, Chai

driving at a reasonable pace, not wanting to draw fire from a panicked soldier or red shirt. I plugged in the BB and downloaded the message that Cheep had sent me. I wanted to get a look at this fucker.

Lucjan Kaminski, age 35. I figured the passport was bullshit. I had a Polish passport. I had four of them. They were the easiest to get, and they gave you access to EU countries. He had a pinched face and a hooked, long nose, with deep-set eyes. It was a black and white scan of a passport photo so the resolution was poor, and the contrast made the cheekbones high and dark. With the pinched face, it made him look evil, or maybe that was just the way I was looking at it. The yacht's papers were more revealing. I was sure the name was also faked, but the make would be real. The papers showed she had entered Thailand the day before the kidnapping and then gone straight to Yacht Haven. I started to forward the message to Mother with a note to get the photo of Lucjan around our contacts, and then I stopped. Little point, and it was a risk. I was pretty sure they'd left Thailand two days ago. The hundred million dollar question was where were they now? I canceled the format and instead hit reply, typing out:

- Find out how much diesel they put in the yacht.

Most big yachts sail with a full tank. Knowing how much diesel was put in would give us a range, assuming an average cruising speed of eleven knots, standard for a Hatteras. Also assuming that they were headed back to where they came from. Both big assumptions, but something was better than nothing. Got to have a start point for searching. If they came in straight from where they had last been, it would give us a radial within which we could search. A Hatteras 53 is not a small motor yacht, and the yacht clubs and marinas around SE Asia are not that many.

I looked up from the screen and over to my right, through the dark-tinted car window. There was an orange glow reflected in the clouds above Lumpini Park. Bangkok was on fire.

How You Doing, Baby

14 May 2010, Bangkok, 9 pm

Pim stood in the doorway, looking very pissed off, her eyes puffy and swollen. I smiled. No response, but she stepped aside to let me in. I slipped off my shoes and walked past her into the living room. I didn't sit down, and I didn't look back. That would be inviting trouble, and I already had enough. She walked past me, picked up a magazine from the coffee table, and sat on the sofa, her long, smooth, tanned legs pulled up underneath her. She was wearing one of my shirts, the top four buttons undone, and lacy black underwear. I didn't dwell there, afraid she might glance up and catch me staring at her crotch. She didn't look at me, focused on the upside-down magazine in her hands.

I retreated upstairs to the bedroom. It was easier than facing the barrage of silence, and I stank. I stripped off.

The 9 hadn't faded. I put on her shower cap and pulled it down low over the stitches around my eye and stepped into the shower. I like to use hot water first and finish with cold.

Pim and I had met at a function for a democratic MP trying to get re-elected. I'd been asked by Mother to go, and Pim was there as the dutiful daughter of the MP. The first thing I noticed, she wore no make-up. She was tall, had long, glossy, black hair and honey tanned skin. In a room full of starlets, models, and rich daughters, she was easily the most beautiful woman. It was lust at first sight. It still is. I leaned forward, allowing the cold water to pound my neck into submission. When the adrenalin stops, and just before the pain starts to kick in, on the cusp between the two, we have a chance to look at ourselves for what we really are. I was a fucking idiot.

Pim was the first person in my life who chose me. Everyone else had me thrust upon their lives one way or the other. To Por, Joom, Uncle Mike, and even Chai, I was a responsibility. To their creed of honor, an unavoidable duty. Pim chose me. Against the will of her parents and friends, those who knew who I was, she chose to be with me. I dried off, put on a pair of Levis and a T-shirt. I went back down into the living room and sat on the sofa next to her.

She didn't move and didn't stop looking at the magazine, now the right way up. Holding the magazine in her right hand, her elbow on her hip, her fingers twirled a strand of hair with her left. I swung my legs up on the sofa and slid my head onto her thigh. Not looking at her, I felt her muscles tense when I laid my head down. She turned a page in the magazine, being careful not to touch me, the snap of the page speaking volumes. I stayed still, she hadn't pushed me off.

Three more snaps of the page later, I was thinking of the best thing to say. Everything I thought of was lame:

- I should have called. (Give me a fucking break.)

- I'm sorry. (Every time I hear those words it reminds me of the song: Is all that you can say.)

- I've been busy. (Oh please or fuck off – take your pick.)

- How are you, baby? Wait a minute. That might actually work. Anything's better than this deafening silence.

I said softly, almost a whisper, "Pim, how you doing, baby?"

My head hit the sofa as she jerked her thigh out from underneath me. The magazine slammed down on the coffee table so hard the bang echoed off the walls. Jumping up, she spun around, one hand in a clenched fist behind her, the other holding a finger a millimeter from my nose. Her knuckles bone white.

"Fuck you, Chance. You were dead two whole days, and you didn't think to call me? No. Don't get up. Don't say a fucking thing before I'm done and I throw you out of here. I had to go to your funeral. Your fucking funeral, Chance. You aren't even dead. You're off doing fuck knows what, with fuck knows who, and when you're done you think you can just come here and it's all okay? Well, fuck you. Are you really that fucking arrogant, or are you just fucking stupid. For God's sake, Chance, I thought for two days, two fucking days, that you were dead. You can't do that to someone. You leave here, gonna go to talk with Por and get out of the family business, blah, blah, blah. The next thing I hear you've been blown up in a fucking massage parlor on Ratchada. Did you tell Por before or after you fucked the whores? And while you're fucking whores, I'm at your funeral surrounded by all the other stupid whores you've fucked. Snidey fucking looks: at least my boyfriend wasn't killed in fucking massage parlor. Shit. You are shit. You didn't even have the decency to get blown up somewhere respectable. No. You had to get blown up in a fucking massage parlor."

Pim grew up in London. Where she learned her English.

As I sat up, she slapped me. Luckily, on the right side of my face. I sat dead still, looking at her. She slapped me again. I looked at her. She punched me. A guy's punch, shoulder behind it, twisting the fist as she connected with my chest. She pulled her arm back for another go, and I grabbed her fist. Pulling her onto me, holding her close, she fought like a cat in a net. She'd never been as beautiful. I twisted us around until I got her back on the sofa, and ripped her lacy black panties down. She let loose a feral snarl and punched me on the jaw so hard I saw stars. Then she was on me.

She was kneeling between my splayed legs, a frown of concentration on her face as she daubed iodine onto the cut under my eyebrow. One of her wilder punches had torn a stitch. A satisfied smile played around her lips.

She poked her tongue out a little as she concentrated and then done, sat back, her hands palm up on her thighs. The satin gown she'd thrown on, open to the edge of her nipples. The right nipple kept winking in and out. I was getting horny again. She closed the gown with a look.

"Forget it."

"Okay, I was just thinking."

"I know what you were thinking, and forget it." She waved the cotton bud at my eye like a conductor wielding a baton. "You deserved it."

"I know I did. I'm an idiot."

"Yes." She nodded twice deliberately. "You are." Her eyes steady, going with it. "There won't be a next time, you understand me. Next time I won't open the door, because I'll be gone".

"I know."

"I mean it, Chance, and I still want you to leave the business."

"I have to clear up the mess we're in and then after…"

"After, there'll be another mess and another. There always is. You don't tell me what you do with the family, and I understand that. I'm not sure I want to know, but I read the papers. I read who's been killed for this or that. I read who's disappeared…"

"Uncle Mike has disappeared. He's been kidnapped, and the ransom is a 100 million."

"Oh." The cotton bud baton came to a rest on her thigh. "I like Uncle Mike."

"We all do. Por isn't dead, but he's in a coma, and he's lost a leg. Someone has been making a move on our territory, a new gang. Now you know what I know. Now do you understand why I can't quit right now?"

"A hundred million baht?"

"No, US."

"Wow. Do you have that much?"

"Wow, yes, and yes, we have that much. It'll wipe us out, but if we can't find him first, we'll pay."

"Let me help."

"I will. Tomorrow you need to go back to the funeral. Take a seat near the reporters and leave your phone on the seat when you go to burn incense for me."

"Okay, but why?"

"Because your phone is going to have photos of a dead me on it, and I need the papers to think that it's real."

"You think the reporters will steal my phone? Sorry. Dumb question."

"It's about the only thing I am sure about. And be careful moving around Bangkok in the next couple of days. Someone shot Seh Daeng in the head earlier tonight, and he's not likely to survive. It's going to get bloody out there."

"I don't get why you want people to think you're dead after you spread the rumor that you're alive."

"We still don't know who is attacking us. I want them unsure of whether I am dead or alive. If they're sure I'm dead, they may make a move that forces me to have to come back from the dead, but if they're not sure, they'll wait. Them waiting gives us time. Honestly, I don't know if it is helping or not. Just something I can do."

"Zombie."

"That's me."

"What are you going to do?"

"Keep tracking the phones. Find the boat, and tomorrow, I've got to go to Singapore."

"Singapore? Why?"

"I've got Samuel Harper stuff to get done, and I need to clear some of our funds over there. I'll only be gone a day. Fly out in the morning and back in the evening."

"So I'll see you tomorrow night?" She fixed me with a heavy-lidded stare.

"Not sure. Okay? The situation is pretty fluid. I'm following leads where they take me, so I can't promise because I don't know. If I'm not getting anywhere, I'll come back here. Is that good enough?"

"Yes."

I held my arms out, and she came in for a hug. I whispered in her ear. "Can you make me some coffee? I've got to get to work tracing those phone numbers." I felt her head move downwards in a nod. We stayed like that for a while.

The house in Lat Phrao is one of six I have around the city. Spare clothes, toiletries, instant noodles, cash, and passports in each of them. Pim had moved into this one three months ago. She'd made it her own, turning my bare walls minimalist approach into something warm and comfortable. She had converted one of the bedrooms on the second floor into the study I was sitting in, watching TV, Bangkok burning, thinking about the data I'd just mapped.

The phone data that Mother had sent me showed the

boat tracking down the coast of Thailand until entering Malaysian waters and out of the cell's range. My guess was that they were somewhere between Singapore and the border with Thailand. Now that's a big area, and if they were just in a quiet little bay, it would be tough to find them. But I didn't think they would because they could have done that in Phuket, and they didn't. There were a relatively small number of marinas between Singapore and Thailand that could take a fifty-three-foot boat. I was guessing that Lisp would be at one of them.

The red cell phone rang. It was after midnight. Mother.

"Chance."

"Yes, Mother. You need to rest. If you keep going like this, you'll collapse, and then where will we be?"

"Don't worry about me. I got some sleep today. Did you check your mail?"

"Yes. I got the numbers. I've traced them heading down the coast. They entered Malaysian waters. My guess is Langkawi. Do we have anyone near?"

"I'll check."

"Okay, let me know. I'm going to Singapore tomorrow. How are you going with the money?"

"Slowly, like I said, but I'll be able to transfer about fifteen in the morning."

"Okay, I'll clear the rest through Singapore. I spoke to Ken. He'll lend us the cash, here in Bangkok, for 15 days, no interest. That's if we need it. I'd prefer not to take it, but we owe him anyway just for offering."

"Yes, sure. When you see him, please tell him anything he needs to give me a call."

"Will do."

"And how are you. How's your eye?"

"It's okay. Itching."

"That's a good sign. Means it's healing. Have you bought a lottery ticket yet?"

I laughed. "No. You know I never gamble."

"You should, after surviving that bomb and the assassination attempt. What if you hadn't woken up?"

"If I hadn't woken up, Chai and Beckham would have taken them out anyway."

"Maybe. Anyway, you should think about it. Your luck is running high. If we have to pay out that hundred million, then we're going to be broke for a while. I've got to go. There're rumors the red shirts are going to move up here, and I've got to go talk with some of the residents. They're scared it will hit business and just be bad. It won't take long. You take care, Chance."

"You too. Bye, Mother."

It was one in the morning. The TV showed the street in front of the Dusit Hotel ablaze. The rattle of au-tomatic weapons could be heard as the Thai news guy hid behind a phone booth. CNN and BBC were reporting the same old tripe. Rich against poor. They didn't have a clue. Media fiction for ratings. You can't sum up Thailand's political complexity in a thirty-second sound bite, and these morons weren't even trying.

I switched the TV off, killed the main light in the room, and turned on the desk lamp. My eyes were sore from all the time spent in front of the notebook. I needed to sleep, but my eyes stung. I rummaged around in the desk and found the eye drops. Visine. I tilted my head back and lined up the nozzle. The liquid ran down my cheek, but it felt good. I had to be a bit more careful with the left eye. Just as I was about to squeeze the drop in, I heard a noise in the garden outside.

VULTURES IN THE NIGHT

15 May 2010, Bangkok, 1 am

I froze, listening: a scratching sound below the window of the study. Someone was trying to break in. Below the study is the kitchen. They were trying to get through the kitchen door. Shit! I'd left the guns in the car with Chai. I went quietly into the bedroom. Pim was sleeping. I knelt softly on the bed and covered her mouth with my hand, putting a finger to my lips. She woke, eyes panicked staring at me. I leant in close to her ear.

"Don't say anything, and quietly, very quietly, go and hide in the closet. Someone's trying to break in."

She nodded, eyes wide, scared, and got out of bed. I turned and went back out to the landing, listening. They hadn't got in yet. I had double bolt locks on all the doors. When they figured that out, they'd come in another way. Maybe through the window. I needed a weapon, fast. My golf clubs were downstairs in the cupboard under the stairs. Can't get at the kitchen knives if they're coming in that way. I edged toward the top step of the landing and heard the creak of the kitchen door. Shit. Shit. They were in already. I knelt down in front of the study door on the landing, the bedroom with Pim in opposite me. The stairs are made of wood and the fifth and sixth stairs creak. They've never been right since I bought the house.

I forced my breathing to slow, my heart hammering away. If there was more than one, I was fucked. I waited. Sweat rolled into my eye. I tried to keep my breathing quiet. Quiet and slow. I heard the stair creak and then silence. I waited. Had he skipped the next step? Another creak. I felt a desperate urge to take a leak. Fuck it. I went around the corner of the stairs and dived down. Shit! There were two of them. Slow motion time or fast brain time kicked in, seeing, as I dived, the first guy lift his gun and fire. I felt the bullet crease my skull as I crashed into his chest. The second guy was very quick. He ducked as we went over him, and we crashed to the bottom of the stairs. The guy under me not moving, his gun clattering away towards the front door. I dived for it, looking over my shoulder, sliding on the floor, reaching for the spinning gun. The guy on the stairs rose, turning, his gun coming up. I wasn't going to make it.

I saw the bedroom door open. Pim came out with something white and rectangular held above her head. The guy seeing my look, turned, his gun swinging towards her. I got my fingers on the spinning gun, bringing it up, and fired three times quickly. He went down, but I kept firing, getting up, walking towards him. Seven shots, good grouping.

The guy I'd tackled on the stairs was dead, broken neck. I went through his pockets. Nothing except a few thousand baht, a spare magazine, and a packet of cigarettes. If you couldn't do it with one mag, you wouldn't get a chance for two.

I wiped down the gun and put in in his hand. Holding his hand steady I fired two more bullets aiming at the other guy's chest. The last one missed and hit him in the face. Powder traces on the hand would now confirm this guy fell down the stairs, broke his neck, and then fired multiple shots hitting the first guy. Yup. I could see the words in the very expensive police report to come.

Blood dripped on his face, mine. I reached a hand up to my head. Above my ear, I felt raw flesh where the first bullet carved a groove. It stung and was wet with blood. Another fraction of an inch and I'd have been killed. Maybe I should buy a lottery ticket. My feet scrunched on broken pieces of ceramic toilet. Good choice. I went up the stairs to her. She was crouched on the landing, at the same spot from where she had hurled the toilet lid at the guy. She'd saved my life.

"Get dressed. We're out of here," I said, softly. She stayed where she was. I put my hand on her shoulder, giving her a squeeze. She was shaking. "Pim. Move it. Go get dressed."

She looked at me and nodded, still in shock.

Then the doorbell rang.

I glanced down the stairs at the door. Shit, someone must have reported the shots. I shook Pim by both shoulders and pointed at the bedroom. She nodded and moved. I went downstairs and peeked through the eyehole. One of the estate's security guards stood outside, talking into his radio. Bullshit or bribe? I opened the door. The guard was skinny, tall, long bony throat lost in a shirt collar four sizes too large.

"Um, excuse me, sir. Sorry to disturb you, sir, but we've had calls about gunshots being fired, sir. Is everything all right?"

"Come in," I said, opening the door.

He had a worried expression on his face as he sidestepped past me into the hallway, his eyes wary, body language screaming, "I don't want to be dealing with this." His mouth opened when he saw the guy with the broken neck behind me, and then he saw the guy on the stairs. The guard's Adam's apple bounced in his throat.

"What's your name?" I asked him, voice even.

"Somchai, sir."

"Okay, Khun Somchai, here's the thing. I just came home and found these two guys like this, but I don't want to be involved, so here's what I suggest as the best way for us to handle this. One, we could report this to the police and spend the next twenty-four hours explaining how these two guys got past you guards and into my house. Or two, we can keep this to ourselves and I'll tidy everything up. You remove the CCTV tape for tonight. I was never here, and this never happened. You go home twenty thousand baht richer."

Somchai looked at me and looked at the bodies. His Adam's apple bounced some more.

"Fifty", he said, his eyes almost apologetic. Almost.

I bought a packet of Marlboro red and coffee at the 7-Eleven opposite Big C on Lat Phrao, Pim's Audi 6, engine running, curbside. I put the coffee on the roof of the Audi and tapped on the window. I handed a coffee through to Pim. She took it, and the window shut again. Even at night, the temperature was hot, about 27 Celsius, and the fumes from the traffic on the road were heavy. It was 2 am, and normally a lot of traffic on the road now as closing time for the bars, clubs, and karaoke lounges hits, but tonight it was quiet, empty. Wars do that to a city. And not a good time to be driving around with an unlicensed weapon. The army had set up road blocks all over town. My mind was spinning with the latest attack.

A black Benz ran the red light on the other side of the road, used the U-turn, crossed three lanes of fast-moving traffic, cutting in front of an eighteen-wheeler, and pulled up behind the Audi. The truck slowed, the driver's boy yelling out of the window at the Benz. Chai stepped out of the car and took three fast steps towards the truck, his hand reaching into his jacket. It pulled away with a belch of black smoke. I thought I saw a grin on his face as he turned, but it was late, and I was tired.

I handed him the keys to the house and the entrance card to get into the compound.

"Two of them. One had Cambodian cigarettes on him."

Chai nodded, looked at the cigarette burning in my hand.

"Mother's sending a couple of guys to clean up. I need you to take Pim to stay with Mother."

He nodded again and handed me a sports bag. I raised

my eyebrows in question.

"Phones, I've programmed them all, cash, Glocks, and I put in a couple of hand grenades." He looked disgusted with me, his expression dark, eyes flat, angry, hot. "You shouldn't have been unarmed and alone. Next time, I'll stay."

"Okay. We'll talk about that later. Take Pim to Joom's place, and stay with her until I get back. I should be back about eight in the evening. It's the Thai flight. I'll leave Pim's car at the airport. If they knew where we lived, they might know the car. Pick me up tomorrow outside exit four, eight twenty. Bring Pim with you tomorrow. Okay?"

Chai nodded.

I went back to the Audi and got in, tossing the bag in the back seat. I reached over and stroked Pim's cheek. "You've got to go with Chai. Okay. You'll be safe with him. I'll be back tomorrow. Chai will pick me up tomorrow, and he'll bring you with him."

Pim reached across the space between us and put her hands on either side of my face, pulled me to her. Lips open, she pressed hard, her tongue hot in my mouth. She broke off and sat back, hair wild, still holding the sides of my face.

"I'll see you tomorrow. I promise."

She nodded, dropped her hands, and got out of the car. She walked over to the passenger side front door of the Benz, shoulders and back straight.

I pulled out into the sparse traffic. We don't even take curfews literally. Thinking. The thing about information is that it accumulates. You start off with one event or data, and then another occurs, and you start to gather information. The latest attempt worried me a lot.

Only five people, family, knew where that house was. Pim, Joom, Por and Chai. It was possible that they had followed Pim, but I doubted that. They had come late, and they had come for me. I hadn't seen the Benz that Chai was driving so there was no way they could have known by watching that I was there. The other piece of information was that they obviously didn't believe I was dead. And that was interesting. It meant my rumor was working. The cockroaches were coming out into the light. Dead cockroaches. I needed one of these guys alive.

I turned onto the expressway and up the ramp. An army Humvee was parked at the top of the ramp, with a few soldiers standing looking at me as I drove by. A sign of the times. I lit another cigarette and opened the window. Keeping the speed low, I wasn't in a hurry now, on autopilot. I was heading back to Ratchada area, on the Ramindra Expressway heading into the city. Alone on the expressway, a surreal experience.

I couldn't make sense of any of what was going on. None of it fit. Not the bomb in Heaven. The only people who knew we were going to meet in Heaven were Por and I. He set it up and called me. I didn't even tell Chai until we were about to drive there. So how did someone manage to plant a bomb in the room, and time it for when we were both there? And then the hit at the hospital. Okay, people knew we were at the hospital. Easy target, but why use amateur-hour Cambodian hitmen? Same with this latest attack. No one knew I was there. Except Chai. The only common denominator was Chai. But that didn't make sense on a couple of points. One, I knew beyond a shadow of doubt Chai's loyalty was solid; we'd been together since I was five years old. And two, he could kill me anytime he wanted.

I dropped down onto Rama 9 and did a U-turn, driving past the cultural center on Ratchadapisek. I took a right into Thiam Ruam Mit Road. Pulling up the ramp into Peep Inn, I slowed to a crawl. The parking boy with his red waistcoat jogged ahead of me and pulled a heavy red plastic curtain aside. I swung the Audi into the parking slot and got out. The boy tugged the curtains closed behind the car. I gave him a couple of thousand. His eyes grew big.

"I'll be here till morning. Keep the rooms either side of me empty. Wake me in the morning no later than six and I'll give you another thousand."

The boy waied, nodding his head. He backed out through the edge of the curtain, closing it behind him. I waited. Heard him move away. Collecting my bags from the car, I went in. A vulture on a perch peered into the window out the back of the room. Peep Inn's specialty was theme rooms with an exotic bird zoo. Ostriches, eagles, and in my case, a vulture outside a room themed as a nurse's station. Very fucking appropriate.

I hung my suit bag on the back of the door and pulled the chair over from the built-in make-up table, pushed it under the knob until it held. I got a glass from the top of the fridge and balanced it on the chair. I was tired, knew I'd sleep deep. A thin blanket on the bed, Bangkok's short-time motels aren't a place that people usually come to sleep. I pulled it over me and took a Glock out of the bag, putting it on the bed beside me. I flipped the switch next to the headboard. The lights went out. My cell phone beeped. An SMS from Chai "@home". I hit reply, "K".

I lay on the bed, looking up at the ceiling. It had been a while since I'd had to kill. I'd killed five people now. I killed two when I was fifteen, on my birthday. It happened in Trat, a province next to Cambodia. Por was driving a pickup truck with Joom in the passenger seat in front, and me on the small bench seat in the back. We'd gone to the market, Por buying a pig to roast for my party. We stopped at a red light. A motorcycle pulled up next to us, and the pillion rider shot at Por. He missed, the bullets hitting steel and breaking glass, but not hitting bodies. Por pulled his gun out, but then a bullet hit him in the arm. His gun flew onto the back seat next to me. I still see it perfectly in slow motion. I picked the gun up. Joom had me on the range when I was ten. I check, safety's off, rack a round into the chamber, bring it up, breathe out, center the sights on the target, the shooter's black visor, and squeeze the trigger. He crumpled, sliding off the bike. I see as I move the sights to the next target just like on the range. The driver panicked and stalled the bike. He was kick-starting but had flooded it. I shot him in the back twice. Twenty-four hours later, Por had us all on a beach in Mexico. They treated me differently after that. The whole family did. Apart from Por and Joom, I was the only one who had killed on the family's behalf.

I got up in a rush and made it to the toilet before I puked. I grabbed a bottle of water from the refrigerator and looked out of the window. The vulture was staring at me.

Big Tiger

A white Lexus SUV with black-tinted windows stopped in front of me, and the door slipped open. A serious adrenalin spike, and then I saw Pim, a smile on her face, in the backseat. I got in, heart thumping. It could have been a hit. I ought to be more careful.

"Chai, Big Tiger's place."

"How was business in Singapore?" Pim asked.

"Good. Everything is lined up. I need Joom to sign a few documents, but we have the collateral to put up against the loan for Uncle Mike. That's the good news. Bad news is if we don't find Uncle Mike in the next couple of days, we're going to be wiped out financially."

"You too?"

"Yep. Everything is on the line."

"I have some money. Not much, a few million baht.

We won't be poor, and you can get a real job."

Not what I needed to hear after three hours of flying and immigration. She meant well. I breathed out.

"Sorry."

"That's okay, I know what you meant. Just let me get us through this, and then I'll clear things with Por and Joom."

She reached across and put her hand on top of mine.

We took the outer ring road, avoiding the curfew checkpoints on the route into Bangkok. Army Humvees were stationed on high ground, and trucks filled with soldiers armed to the teeth sped along the empty expressway. Bangkok was at war. Twenty-two people killed in street fighting in the last two days, and over one hundred seventy wounded. Sounded like Lebanon more than Bangkok. Twitter was the main news source, and it told of a Bangkok with running street battles and more dead. Pim told me the army had put up razor wire around the protest site downtown, signs hanging off the razor wire, "Live Fire Zone".

Chai handed me a ringing cell phone – Mother.

"How was Singapore?"

"Good. We're all set."

"A couple of guys tried to lean on Tong for protection money."

"Crazy Tong – Jesus – when did this happen? Are they still alive?"

"Earlier this evening. One escaped, and we've got the other at the farm. He's not said anything yet, but he's Cambodian, same as the others."

"Okay, I talked to Ken earlier today. I'm expecting

his call, but we should be moving the cash tonight. Is everything set?"

"All fixed. We're using the warehouse in Lat Krabang. There's too much shooting going on down in Klong Toey."

"Okay, I'll let Ken know. Transport?"

"Fixed. The same colonel who helped with your trip to Phuket. Careful with Ken. He's nicely polished up, but take away the suit and he's a cold-blooded operator."

"I know, Mother. I'll be careful."

She clicked off.

It was very quiet for a Saturday night, and we parked easily near the pier. Big Tiger owns a seafood restaurant out in Bang Pu by the sea. Big Tiger's, originally named, "Big Tiger's Seafood Restaurant", was on the end of the main pier.

I'd sent Pim to Joom's home to stay there. Chai stayed with me. I wasn't sure what I was walking into, but then I wasn't here for me. I was here for Por. Last thing he'd told me was to keep my eye on Big Tiger and that he needed to repay a favor. I was here to repay the favor and look into Big Tiger's eyes.

We walked up the concrete pier, Chai on the cell phone ordering a new set of wheels for us. Joom owns two luxury car dealerships in Bangkok and one in Chiang Mai. Chai used the cars sent in for service, or the second-hand cars in the lot, fake plates on them all.

The restaurant was big enough to seat a thousand, bigger than most Government Halls. There were barely a hundred on the tables outside, and fewer inside in the air-conditioning. Urban warfare will do that to a business. I'd been told by Mother on the way in that Big Tiger was on the second story on the outside balcony. We took the stairs two at a time.

I was nearly at his table before Big Tiger or any of his boys realized we were in the place. A look of panic flicked across his eyes. Deer in headlights, I thought. He relaxed when he saw our hands were empty. What's got you so jumpy?

"Big Tiger, sorry for arriving late. Por sent me. Said you needed me to do something for you?"

He seemed confused. I kept a pissed off look on my face, focused right on his. His second in command, a guy called Daeng (all mafia gangs in Thailand have a guy called Daeng, it's mandatory) didn't like the look I was giving Big Tiger. Chai went over and stood next to Daeng. Daeng modified his behavior.

Big Tiger stood up, spreading his arms wide, and walked around the table. The girl eating with him, dressed in a university uniform, was trying to make herself invisible. You could've boiled a lobster in the atmosphere. Big Tiger stood close to me. Hand on the back of the girl's chair, mouth open, shaking his head from side to side.

"Chance, what a shock. Well, fuck everything. If that isn't the best, then I don't know what is the fucking best. You're alive. I didn't know what to fucking believe. First you're dead. I went to your fucking funeral, then we hear you're not, and today the fucking photos in Thai Rath from your girlfriend's phone, showing you're fucking dead. And now you're here, standing in my restaurant. Well, fuck me." Big Tiger used exclamation and question marks at the end of every sentence he spoke. Mouth and eyes wide open, hands wide, shoulders hunched. "Well, isn't this a fucking miracle!?" Eloquent.

He stood, shaking his head. And then he waved at the table. "Sit, sit."

I took a seat in front of him. He told the girl to go wait for him downstairs and invited Chai to sit with a gesture of his hand. Chai shook his head slightly and stayed next to Daeng. Big Tiger flicked a glance at Daeng, and getting the message, he sidled off to sit with Chai, at a table just out of earshot. The waiter came over and asked what I wanted to drink. A whiskey soda, tall glass, lots of ice, in front of me later, Big Tiger waved the waiter away and leaned in close. Now we could talk in private.

"Look, Chance, that thing I needed you to do. Don't worry about it. I'll take care of it some other way, and tell Por that I send my best wishes."

I looked at him, not responding either way to his probe on Por.

"He is okay, right? I mean, same as you, the two of you being dead, just a trick, right?" He laughed.

I gave him a tight smile, took a sip of my drink, paying out rope. Letting him talk. I looked out over the railing to the gulf, fishing boat lights off in the distance, catching the squid that lends its smell to many a Bangkok sidewalk.

"So who do you think has been trying to kill you? Do you know the motherfucker?" He closed his mouth, finally.

"We've got a good idea. What was it that you wanted me to do?"

"What?" He looked confused, hanging out his lower lip for effect. It didn't work, I knew he wasn't drunk.

"The favor Por was repaying. You wanted me to help

you with something. Now, what was it?"

He sobered up fast at the hard bite in my tone, tonal nuance a language all its own in Thailand. I can bring the full weight of the family to bear on a sentence with the slightest alteration to the way I say something.

"I've got a deal going, in Australia, and the party over there wants to meet me. Here, Monday, he flies in. You know me. I don't speak a word of that dog-fucking miserable language. I was hoping you could handle it for me."

Plausible enough. It was true. Big Tiger was renowned for his inability to speak anything other than Thai and his ability to curse.

"What's the deal?"

"Counterfeit stuff."

"Money?" I wouldn't touch counterfeit money. Countries are serious about that stuff. All kinds of the wrong heat.

"No, no. Levi's, watches, bags, that sort of thing. We get in China, truck it down, and ship through Singapore. He's got a contact in customs on the other side."

"How much?"

"He reckons he can move about three million a month. He's got a network through all the major cities, the local markets…"

"What time Monday?"

"Dinner at eight, the big room upstairs." Big Tiger's restaurant had a large air-conditioned function room on the top floor with a balcony running around it.

"Okay. I'll be here. Then you and Por are square, right." It wasn't a question, and he wisely nodded, raising his glass to me.

"So Por's still alive, then. Fuck me! He's a tough fucker, that one."

I didn't answer the question in his eyes, just polished my drink off, stood up, and walked out.

Back down the pier, I stopped and leaned my elbows on the edge. I lit up a smoke. Chai went on ahead. Looking down, the muddy brown water reflected my thoughts. I was nowhere in finding out who was trying to kill me. I had been half-convinced it was Big Tiger, but his reaction and answers told me otherwise. It wasn't him. Whoever it was, their information was good. Either they'd been following me for some time, and done a very good job because I hadn't seen them, or they had someone on the inside. Horrible, but logical.

The other thing I didn't know. Was it an attack on me personally or was it an attack on the family? It amounted to the same thing in the family's eyes, but it meant the source would be different. I thought back over recent business deals, as Chance, and as Harper. Nothing I'd done was worth killing over. At least not to me, but then I'd recently read in the Bangkok Post about a Cambodian guy killing his neighbor because the neighbor stole his melon. I breathed out. It was stressful knowing that someone out there wanted to kill you. The smoke tasted good. I smiled. It was going to be hard to kick these again if I survived.

Cambodians – why had I just thought of that? Because so far everyone who had been sent to kill me had been Cambodian. Work with what you have. I threw the butt into the sea. Time to go to work.

The Count

Ken called as we were entering Bangkok.

"I've got the money, but I want to move it now."

"Where do you want me to send the guy who'll bring you to our warehouse?"

"Send him to my place in Thaniya. We'll take it from there."

"Okay. Aim to be at a warehouse near the airport no later than midnight. Can you do that?"

"No problem." He hung up.

I called Mother to tell her we were on our way to the warehouse. We had to count the money and counting one hundred million dollars takes time and space.

"Chai, the Lat Krabang warehouse, but take your time." It was only twenty-five kilometers to the airport. Chai used the back streets. It was quiet. Very quiet. We had to move the cash to Phuket. I was sure that the kidnappers would want to make the exchange at sea. If they didn't, then I was going to persuade them it was their only option. I wanted them to stay with that boat.

And then. There were two sides to every coin. I didn't trust Ken. One hundred million was a lot of money, enough to tempt anyone. Ken had got the cash for us by going to his board. The deal had been approved in Tokyo, so he was covered for the action. Stealing it back from us would be a big temptation.

Moving one hundred million in cash is no simple thing. There're eight hundred kilometers of road and seven provinces between Bangkok and Phuket. Each province has its own police force, army, and "families". Nothing moves in or out without being at risk that one or more of those parties will take an interest in it. If it was something normal, like an errant son who'd killed someone and needed to leave the country for a while, clear passage could be obtained by connecting the dots between the "owners" of the province. Cash or favors the typical currency. But a hundred million USD in cash was too risky. The value was so high. So we had to move it "under the radar".

Thirty minutes later, we pulled into the warehouse, one of the boys, an AK47 on his back, wheeling back the chain link gate. Chai parked in the loading bay, next to the caravan Mother had organized for transport to Phuket: two black Toyota Land Cruisers with windows tinted black and a VW van to match, all covered in military badges. Very subtle. I guessed the colonel's son could go for a doctorate.

We went into the warehouse. At least ten of our boys were on the loading bay, armed to the teeth, strolling around, joking. I nodded and smiled my way through them.

Joom had put forty women at tables in the area just behind the loading bay. Thirty of them had counting machines with counterfeit inspection scanners built in on the tables in front of them. The other ten were for moving. The women were all wearing the same gray one-piece track suit. Made them look like some weird bunny rabbit pantomime. Joom was in the office in the back of the warehouse. I walked past the girls, all smiles, round faces and white teeth.

I waied Mother and sat down.

"You look tired", she said, tapping her pen on the paper in front of her.

"I'm okay. How's Khun Por?"

"Still in a coma, but all other vital signs are okay."

"This hospital he's in, in Cambodia, you're sure he's safe, right?"

"Yes. He's in an army base. Aunt Su's cousin, a general in the Cambodian army, organized it. Why?"

"Everyone who's been sent to kill me has been Cambodian."

"They're the cheapest gunmen around. All that tells us is that our enemy is operating on a tight budget."

"Maybe. Maybe not."

"I have to stay here, keep an eye on things. It'll take us at least half a day to count. Why don't you head back to the farm and see what you can learn from the idiot we caught today."

"Okay. Call me when we're ready to move."

"I will, and Chance?"

"Yes, Mother?"

"Don't be soft with the guy. Pit 51, the crocs haven't been fed for a week. Take him down there. He'll talk."

"Yes, Mother."

She smiled, and her phone rang. I left.

Thirty minutes later, Chai and I arrived at the Crocodile Farm, the largest in the world, with over one hundred thousand crocodiles. It had two faces. The public face with the shows, the zoo, and the private face, with the disposal business. The "day" staff knew what happened at night, but everyone came from Pak Nam and knew when to look the other way.

Two of the boys were waiting for us in the staff parking lot.

"Pichit, where have you got him?"

"He's in cold storage boss." Cold storage was behind the unloading bay. We go through a lot of supplies, so we'd put in a full docking/undocking facility last year.

"Shit. How long's he been in there?" I didn't stop moving, and Pichit fell in step with me. Proactive adjustment of a process, initiative in the chain of command, is not a Thai strongpoint. We usually deal in dead bodies, so cold storage was the first place they end up, before processing and organic recycling. We are proud to promote The Crocodile Farm as a "green" business.

Pichit was scurrying to keep up with my stride. He looked at his watch, a worried expression on his face.

"About four hours, boss."

Outside the cold storage door, another of our boys, Somboon, was having a smoke. He snubbed it out on his boot and then put the butt in his pocket. No littering at the Farm. Pichit went to the door and took the padlocks off the deadbolts top and bottom. Somboon then opened the main door handle. Cold air billowed out in a white cloud. The walk-in cold storage room door big enough to drive a forklift into. The room itself was ten meters wide and thirty deep. We kept the frozen chicken for the crocs here.

At the far end of the room, tied to one of the cheap black swivel chairs that we used in accounting, was the Cambodian. Slumped over. Not moving. Shit. I covered the distance to him in a nano-second. Even the rope tying him to the chair was frozen. He was as stiff as a board.

"What temperature is the room?" I asked Pichit.

Sensing an opportunity to shift the blame, he turned to Somboon and asked him in an angry tone, "What did you set the temperature at?"

"Minus fifteen degrees, boss," Somboon said to the ground, not daring to look at me.

"Christ, why did you set it so low?"

"Wanted to soften him up a bit."

"Come on, feel him, feel how soft he is."

Somboon looked at Pichit. Pichit and Somboon, both paler than the guy in the chair, stood heads down, waiting to be tongue lashed. I sighed.

"All right, what's done is done. Put him through processing and recycling, and stay with him till he's croc food, understand?"

"Krup Pom, yes, sir!" they shouted in unison, standing at attention.

"Come on, Chai, let's go."

We got back in the Jaguar that one of the boys had

delivered to Chai at Big Tiger's Restaurant. Chai raised an eyebrow at me.

"Back to the warehouse?"

I was starting to get seriously pissed off. Then the SIM that had been in Lilly's mouth and was now in a new phone rang. Lisp. Shit. I checked the time, ten past midnight, Sunday.

"What?"

"You have my money, yes?"

"I want to talk to Mike. Put him on the phone. I want proof of life." I've seen the movie with Russell Crowe, the one with Meg Ryan – that's where I got the proof of life thing.

"He is sleeping. You can talk tomorrow. You have my money?"

"I have my money, which I'll give to you after I have received proof that Mike is okay."

"You get proof tomorrow. Tuesday, you give me money. I tell you where tomorrow." He hung up.

I immediately dialed back and dialed Mother on the other phone. She answered instantly.

"Yes."

"Mother. The number I gave you from Lilly. Can you get your contact to check the routing on the call I just made. I'm dialing the number now. It is now twelve after midnight exactly."

"Yes. Where are you now?"

"On the way back to you."

"What did you learn?" She sounded anxious, not like her.

"Nothing. The boys put him the deep freeze and

95

turned down the thermostat to the lowest level."

"Oh. Well, I'll talk to them tomorrow at your funeral. Cambodians aren't very good with the cold." That was more like Mother. I'd forgotten about the funeral I was having.

"Chance."

"Yes."

"Have you seen the Thai Rath newspaper tonight?"

"No." Now I was worried.

"Um, late edition, the paper has made the connection between Samuel and Chance." That was bad. Really bad.

"Does it give the reporter's name?"

"No. Just says 'by staff reporters'."

"Okay. Do we know anyone at Thai Rath?"

"Yes, I've already spoken to her. She'll find out what she can tomorrow."

"Okay, I'll see you in a bit."

"All right. Ken is still here. We're unloading now."

Mother hung up without saying goodbye, something she did with everyone she was close to – a little signature of hers. So, Sam Harper and Chance had been linked to the family name. That was going to complicate things a lot. By tomorrow, if it hadn't already made it on the "Breaking News" sections, it would be in the English language dailies, the Bangkok Post and the Nation. Apart from the fact that Sam Harper was involved as director on a host of companies – which being dead, would be positions that I would have difficulty fulfilling my obligations – there was the added complication that "my out" had just been blown, which meant that at some point in the not too distant future I was going to have one of hell of an argument with Pim.

We pulled up at the warehouse. The guy on the gate was now accompanied by a Japanese guy wearing a silver suit and shades. It was such a cliché, it cheered me up a little.

On the loading bay, the crowd had swelled in our absence. More guys in bad suits wearing shades at midnight. Ken was in the office, I could see the back of his head. The guy who'd told him Seh Daeng had been shot stood by the door to the office. Must be his number two or his bodyguard.

Chai positioned himself on the other side of the door. Between the two of them, they made the space in between look small. I walked through it. Ken turned and stood up, reaching out a hand. Mr. Smooth.

"Chance. Good to see you. I've just been telling your charming mother that she must be our guest in Tokyo."

"Sorry I'm late. Little something I had to take care of."

"Is everything okay?"

"Yeah, all cool. Shall we proceed?"

"Sure."

Mother reached down and pulled up a file folder with all the documents we'd prepared. Deeds, shares, bonds. Ken checked the documents and nodded. He pulled out the Loan Agreement and put it on the table. Mother checked it, giving it a quick but thorough reading, and passed it to me. It was straightforward enough. It listed the property we were handing Ken for collateral and the amount we were getting for it. Forfeiture of all the property if the funds were not returned within fifteen days. To be placed in escrow with Bank Tokyo Mitsubishi. I nodded at Mother, and she signed, handing it back to Ken. He signed. Now we were responsible for the hundred million.

Ken stood up and waied Mother, his wai perfect. Not many foreigners can do that. He turned to me. "Chance, or should I say, Sam?" and smiled. Shit! This guy was plugged in. He got rumors and news faster than Mustang Sally.

"So you've heard the good news, then."

"Yes. A friend of mine called me on the way here."

"Ah, well. At least I still have a choice. Life or death for Sam and Chance."

"Chance, don't say that. It's bad luck." Mother is not the most superstitious of Thai's, but she is Thai.

"Sorry, Mother. Ken, let me walk you to your car."

I followed Ken out of the office, walking past the women counting the cash. The head cashier had given the thumbs-up after checking random samples. The money was good. Ken watched as the pallets he'd brought in were being broken down and loaded on the counting tables, the machines creating a symphony of sound with the sharp flick of the paper.

"Quite an operation, how long will it take you?"

"About sixteen hours," I lied. We should be able to get it done in ten or eleven.

"So what are you going to do about being exposed?"

"Don't know. Haven't really given it any thought, yet. Play it by ear, I guess. See what tomorrow, sorry, today, brings."

We shook hands again, and he and his men pulled out. Six cars and one UPS truck. I smiled. UPS, that was original. The UPS truck went left, the cars went north. Golf somewhere upcountry, would be my guess.

A MARRIAGE PROPOSAL

16 May 2010, Bangkok, 2 am

I left Chai with Mother and the money and took the Jag, driving back to Mother's house to pick up Pim.

I stayed out of Bangkok. There were running battles in the streets around the red shirt encampment and army road blocks everywhere. Twitter reports said that the "Men in Black" were out in full force, sniping targets on both sides to stir up trouble. It was a mess. Paralleled my life quite nicely.

I drove slowly, skirting the airport, and then through the quiet sois beyond Bang Na Trad Highway. I didn't come this way often. Most times, I used the expressway or the highways. Somehow imprinted somewhere in my memory were the correct turns in the sois with no signs.

Joom's house was filled with relatives staying for the funeral. Apart from the aunts and daughters, only Chai,

Beckham and Tum knew that Por was still alive. Most thought I was dead as well, so I stayed in the soi outside and waited for Pim to come out. The air was cool. Joom's house is on the last bend of the Pak Nam side of the Chao Phraya River, just before it empties into the Gulf of Thailand. The five acres of land, a stretch along the river, now worth a fortune, had been in her family for generations.

I lit a cigarette, thinking of what words to use with Pim. How to explain. Nothing seemed adequate, or maybe I was just getting gun-shy. Last time I played this game, I got punched in the eye. I smiled. Out of the darkness, an old man on a bicycle, wobbling. He started singing. Drunk. He passed under the light twenty meters from me. Joom's gardener, Goong, back from an evening's drinking. I was too slow, he saw me. He kept pedaling in slow motion. His mouth dropped open as he looked at me. I smiled and gave him a little wave. He screamed and took off like Lance Armstrong going for the finish line. He threw the bike on the ground in front of Joom's wrought-iron gate and bolted through the little side door just as Pim came out of it.

"He saw you, right?" she said, smiling, as she walked over and kissed me. She smelled great. I buried my nose in her neck and breathed in deep. I kissed her on the neck.

"Whoa boy, slow down, don't you think we ought to get out of here before you freak out the rest of the neighborhood?"

I held the door open for her, her skirt shorter than a taxi driver's change. I got us out of the back roads and onto the old Sukhumvit Road headed east.

"Where are we going?"

"Well, I'm not sure any of the houses are safe, and downtown is a war zone and about to be put under curfew. I thought we'd head up to Bang Pakong. There's a little place on the river there. We can eat, get some sleep, and I'll bring you back before lunch, and then after a little business here, I'm off to Phuket."

"Can I go with you?"

"No."

"Will it be dangerous?"

"Probably. Either way, I need you to be at the funeral, playing the grieving girlfriend tomorrow."

"For Chance or for Sam?"

"Oh. You heard."

"Yes, a friend mentioned it on-line."

"Oh." I focused on driving. "Oh" seemed to be working. At least, I hadn't been punched in the jaw yet, and we were still talking.

"Have you got anything more to say other than 'Oh'?"

"Oh oh." That earned me a slap on the leg and a grin.

"I haven't had time to take it in. It's my fault for suggesting we play dead, and I hadn't really thought it through."

"Thought it through, right. You'd been blown up a few hours before. Perfectly reasonable to make mis-takes. You were suffering from concussion."

I glanced out of the corner of my eye, doing a quick "sarcasm check", but no, her profile was as straight as could be.

"What's your family going to think?"

"I honestly don't care. This isn't about them. So their

only daughter married a gangster, worse, a Farang. They'll get over it. Anyway, my mother married a corrupt cop from the south, hardly the social triumph of the century. Much as I love him, he is what he is."

I looked across at her.

"Keep your eyes on the road."

"So we're getting married? When did you decide that?"

"Yes. Today. At your funeral." There was something ominous about that, but I couldn't put my finger on what.

"You shared this good news with anyone else?"

"No. Of course not. Why? You do want to marry me, don't you?"

You're not allowed a long time to think about that one. Not when the question is asked. You have to respond, very quickly, or else the response will be made for you. Just some friendly advice. Fortunately, I had thought about this one. I had thought about it on the flight to Singapore and the night before at the motel. I had gone to sleep thinking that I had to give this life up because I didn't want to give her up.

"Yes, I do want to marry you, and thank you for asking."

"Asshole." She grinned at me and reached across, stroking my chin. "You need a shave."

"There're a few things I need. Shaving isn't at the top of the list."

"If number one on your list is shagging me, then you'd better re-prioritize that list of yours."

"Okay, shaving's moving up the list."

"Shagging wasn't number one on your list?"

"No."

"Oh." We drove in silence for a bit.

"What was number one on your list?"

"Getting a blow job."

"Well, forget that. Not until you shave. What's good for the goose. I don't want a rash from your stubble. Besides, I shaved. Look." She lifted up her skirt. I nearly crashed the car.

"What made you change your mind?"

"About what?"

"Getting married."

"I didn't change my mind. I've known I was going to marry you from the second day we met."

"Just the day before yesterday…"

"Chance. I've always been going to marry you. It was just a question of when. Do you know how weird it is to be at your funeral? Listening to everyone talking about you. Even the aunts are in on it. They spend all their time talking about you. More than one has said, in private, that if I don't marry you, they'd be happy to have their daughter take my place. One has even suggested trying hers as a minor wife."

"Who?"

"I'm not telling you. All I have had since last Thursday is a complete recapping of your entire life, as seen by them. All the scrapes and things you've done since you were kid. Mother's been chipping in too."

"What did Mother say?"

"Just telling stories about you. She took out the family album at one point, showing me photographs of when you were eight. You were really cute, by the way. When they take on a role, they really act the part. Sometimes I have to pinch myself to remind me that you're not dead. That you're off somewhere, doing whatever it is gangsters do. What is it you do?"

"A lot of driving around and yakking on cell phones. Talk a lot mostly, lunches, dinners, drinks in bars at late hours – that's it."

"Not to mention meetings in massage parlors. Doesn't sound very exciting."

"Yes, and sometimes meetings in massage parlors, usually in the restaurant, but you're right, it's not exciting, most of the time."

"It's not the most of the time that worries me. It's when it gets exciting, that's when you're in danger. That worries me. Don't you get scared?"

"Honestly, yes. Before and after, but when it's going down, there's no time. You're just doing whatever it is that needs doing. No time to think. The thing that scares me most, apart from the thought of family or you being hurt, is the thought of going to prison."

"Mere Joom told me about when you first came to the house. She and Por had been trying to have children. She said, 'a boy,' not children, but hadn't had any success. The other wives kept producing daughters, and she'd been to specialists and tried everything, dragging Por along when needed. This went on for years. There was no medical reason why they couldn't have a child. It just didn't happen. Nothing worked. She came to the conclusion it was in Buddha's hands. She went to Erawan, the four-faced Buddha, late one night. She made her offerings, and then with the boys surrounding the outside area so no one could look in, she danced naked around the statue nine times. The next morning, Por showed up with you."

"I've never heard that before."

"Her eyes shine when she speaks about you. You can hear the love and pride in her voice."

"Have you said anything to her about me leaving the family business?"

"No, nothing. That's for you to do when the time is right." She stroked my cheek. "Now is not the right time. Now you have to find out who's doing this. And Chance?"

We had reached the little resort on the river. I drove into an open slot in the car park and turned to face her. "Yes."

"When you do find them. Kill them all."

SPECIAL DELIVERY

16 May 2010, Bangkok, 11:45 am

Later that morning, having caught up on all the S's, I dropped Pim back at Joom's house and drove back to the warehouse. The situation in Bangkok had worsened. Sniping and firefights with automatic weapons were flaring up all over central Bangkok. Smoke, from burning tires marking the demarcation lines separated by live fire "no-man's land" zones, hung over the city like a dark gray cloud. It looked like the movie Blackhawk Down. Only it wasn't. It was real. Surreal more like it.

Back at the warehouse, the caravan was ready to roll. Four guys in the VW with the money, five guys in each of the Landcruisers, Mother standing on the loading bay, still wearing the same clothes from yesterday.

"Mother, please go home. I'll handle it."

She offered her cheek, and I kissed her.

"I'm fine. I slept earlier this morning. Don't worry."

She stepped down from the loading bay, giving final instructions to the drivers. Beckham handed them each pre-programmed GPS devices. A quick time synchronization to get everyone on the same page. Last minute instructions from Mother – speed not over one hundred and twenty, if pulled over everyone stops, if you need to piss use the bottles in the car, if you need to shit, jump out. They all laughed. They'd heard that one before and were waiting for it. They waied her and got in the vehicles. The caravan pulled out.

The women who'd done the counting started filing out. Giving Mother a wai, they all climbed into the air-conditioned coach Mother had brought them in on, tired but happy and smiling. Five thousand baht each, about a hundred and sixty US dollars, for twelve hours work counting paper. They didn't think of it as money and were sworn to secrecy on pain of being covered in chicken blood and tossed into a crocodile pit at night. Joom had told them it was counterfeit. It was easier for them to think about it that way. Much easier than them thinking they had just counted three billion baht's worth of United States dollars.

The warehouse, fifteen minutes earlier a hubbub of activity and noise, was now quiet. Mother watched after the coach as it drove away. Beckham and Chai stood near the gate, Beckham having a smoke. Mother joined me on the loading bay.

"I found out about the tip to Thai Rath. It was sent in anonymously. Photo of Samuel Harper compared with the photoshopped photos of you dead, from Pim's phone.

They un-photoshopped them and compared the two. The note just said that Samuel Harper and Oh were the same person. Of course, they want an interview."

"What did you tell them?"

Joom smiled, her hair and clothes immaculate, despite having been awake and on the move for over twenty-four hours.

"I told them, sure, anytime. Tell the reporters I'm waiting for them at the Crocodile Farm. I do have to get back. We've just received a 'special delivery' at the farm. Some people are using this little war as a way to settle scores and clean house. I can see we're going to get busy next week."

"Special delivery" was code for dead bodies. No questions asked, one hundred thousand a body, discounts applied for more than ten at a time. No children. Having a hundred thousand crocodiles twenty kilometers from Bangkok was Por's idea. Growing it into an internationally known show business, that was all Joom.

"Try to get some rest, Mother. Have you heard anything from Malaysia?"

"I will, and no, I haven't heard anything back yet. My usual contact is on a safari in South Africa. So far no luck getting ahold of him. Aunt Ning is trying through one of her connections in the army. I'll tell you as soon as I get something." She looked tired. I waied her and walked her to her Benz, Beckham in the driver's seat.

The "chase" cars should be arriving in Phuket at about eight. We'd arranged two "chase" cars and two to bring up the rear of the caravan. The chase cars were to keep ten kilometers in front of the caravan and the rear cars ten behind. All were connected with radio and phones on. This wasn't the first time we'd done this. The unknown element was the State of Emergency that the government had imposed on Bangkok and twenty other provinces. Most of these were in the north, but the army was on a heightened alert status everywhere.

I had to entertain Big Tiger's Aussie business partner at eight, and some time before then, I expected Lisp to call. I hoped to speak to Uncle Mike. I had to hope that Aunt Ning's or Mother's connections would come through and we could get people working on tracking down the yacht. I had four guys working on it, but that would take too long. Was taking too long. I was running out of time. Sometimes you have to be patient. There's no choice. When you've covered all the bases, dotted the i's and crossed the t's, you have to be able to let go. If you don't, you start second-guessing yourself. Just the nature of the beast.

Suddenly, it occurred to me. I hadn't covered all the bases. The blast must have done more damage than I realized. They might have chartered the boat. The boating, "yachtie", community in South East Asia (SEA) is a tightknit one. Each has an eye on the other, watching what the competition is doing. There aren't that many companies chartering yachts, and those with a Hatteras 53 were even fewer.

I called Pim.

"Search the net for charter companies in our region, start with Singapore, Phuket, and Malaysia."

"Hang on a second. It's a bit noisy here, hold on…" I could hear the noise of monks chanting, chatter of women in the background.

"Okay, what did you need?"

"Search the net for charter companies in our region, start with Singapore, Phuket, and Malaysia."

"Okay, got it."

"Once you've got a list, call them. Tell them we're looking to charter a Hatteras 53, must be a Hatteras 53. If they say okay, say you want it immediately. If they say okay, then talk to them about where the boat is and talk about price. Whatever price they give, say you'll think about it. Any hits let me know, right away."

"Okay."

"Thanks. I'll call you when I get to Phuket, if I don't hear from you sooner."

Chai closed the gate after Mother and joined me. It was hot now, just after noon. The loading bay was in the shade, the concrete warm, the air dusty. I walked back inside to the office. The air-conditioning too cool, I eased the thermostat up to twenty-four Celsius. It reminded me of the Cambodian freezing to death.

I put the phones on the desk, along with my guns. I felt lighter. The chair was comfy, overstuffed with a high back. I kicked off my shoes and put my feet up. I noticed the headache I'd had for the last few days was gone. Chai followed me into the office, a bottle of Johnny Walker Black, two glasses, and an ice-bucket in his hands. He put them on the desk and shut the door of the office. He poured us both two fingers and dropped some ice into each glass. The warehouse was silent except for the sound of the air conditioner in the office.

"Cheers. Good idea." I raised my glass to Chai and

took a good swallow, the whiskey burning its way down my throat and hitting my stomach with a warm wash. I took another sip, a smaller one this time, and let it rest on the back of my tongue.

"Where do you think Ken will make his move?" Chai asked.

"Chumphon would be my guess, halfway between here and Phuket. Time enough to get set up. He's got the tracking devices to follow so he knows where they are. Our guys know what to do, right?"

"They know what to do."

"I don't want anyone getting killed over this. Nice and easy."

"They'll surrender the money without a fight, but if the Yakuza come in shooting, they'll defend them-selves. Okay?"

"Sure. I hope it doesn't come to that. Although it is a risk. That, and Ken just having them executed after they surrender."

"He won't. Stealing the money is one thing. Killing a bunch of our guys another. He doesn't want a war, he wants the money."

We were both operating on the assumption that Ken would try to steal the money. Ken had put tracking devices in the smaller bundles. X-ray had showed them up. Otherwise nothing would have detected them. They had only just now started transmitting. We had kept one. Wafer thin, Japanese technology.

"You heard anything about Uncle Mike?"

"Nothing. We've got feelers out, but nothing's pinged back yet. I tell you, Chai, I can't figure out what's happening. The bombing, the attacks, the kidnapping. None of it. I've got no idea where it's coming from or even if it's connected." My gut screamed at me – it's connected, don't be a fool. And I knew my gut was right. I just couldn't figure out how.

SHELLS BY THE SEASHORE

16 May 2010, Bangkok, 3:45 pm

I'd dosed off, the chair, whiskey, and lack of sleep combining to put me out. I woke up with a stiff neck and a mouth made of sandpaper.

The light on Lilly's phone was blinking. A missed call, "Unknown Number". It must have just rung. Something had woken me up, and Chai was nowhere to be seen. It rang again. I took a swig of the whiskey now heavily diluted by the melted ice. It tasted terrible but did the job of removing the sandpaper.

I answered the phone.

"Don't fuck around with me. Don't forget I hold your Uncle's life in my handsth."

"Is he there?"

"Firsth, we talk exchange." His lisp was really annoying me. I forced myself not to pay attention to it.

"All right. Talk."

"Wednesday morning in Phuket. You have money with you in two wooden boxes. Each box must have a hook and lifting straps attached. On Wednesday morning, before eight, I will call you with further instructions. You understand this?"

"Yes."

"Now your Uncle Mike will say hello to you."

"Chance?" His voice sounded weak and scared. I had never heard him like this. Guilt crashed over me. If only I had answered his call and gone to see him.

"Uncle Mike, are you all right?"

"Yes, Chance a bit seasick, but otherwise fine." His voice normal, bouncy, with a grin in it, cheeky. I immediately heard sounds of a scuffle and Uncle Mike crying out in pain.

"Stop it," I yelled down the phone.

"Your Uncle is all right. Don't worry." He sounded out of breath. I was going to kill him. He continued talking.

"Wednesday. You will see. He will be alive. You follow my instructions exactly. You bring the money."

"Wednesday morning, I'll be there."

He hung up. So they were on a boat. Most likely the Hatteras, and most likely they had stayed at sea, avoiding marinas, knowing I'd search them. If they stay at sea, they're almost impossible to find.

I walked out of the office. Chai was sitting cross-legged on a mat just inside the loading bay, a stripped Uzi beside him. I cleaned up in the washroom and went out to him.

"Wednesday morning, Phuket. Uncle Mike sounded okay. They're on a boat."

"Boat is tricky." He didn't look up from cleaning the gun.

"Yes, it is. We'll think of something. Let's make a move. I want to get to Big Tiger's place early." He nodded, picking up the barrel and sliding it into the stock. Efficiency born of familiarity, his movements.

We were dressed for the occasion. I had a pair of Tomcat Berettas in my boots, and I'm pretty sure I saw Chai sneak a few grenades into the backpack on the floor at his feet. After the last few days, we'd settled on a fortress mentality. Trust no one, check everything, and be prepared, always. We were in a taxi, Chai driving, me, the foreigner, in the back seat. "Tamada" – normal. We took the back streets.

The little war in Bangkok was still going strong. The fight had left the stage, the conference rooms, the boardrooms, the parlors of the powerful, and hit the streets with a vengeance. The CRES had just announced that Monday and Tuesday would be public holidays, to give them a chance to deal with the situation. I read that as, the army would be hitting the red shirt encampment at midnight on the eighteenth. It's the way it works. I was glad I'd be out of town.

By the time we reached the pier, it was dusk. We parked a few hundred meters away. Chai went first to scout it out. I looked out at the Gulf. The sea here is a muddy brown, where the effluent of the Chao Phraya pours out. Seagulls swirled above the calm sea, squawking, their work would soon be over. A few couples, some with children, walked the promenade, if you could call a pavement lined with convenience stores and restaurants, such a thing.

My cell phone rang. Chai.

"Clear."

I walked to the pier. As I reached it, a white Toyota Urvan pulled up at the entrance, about ten meters away. I made direct eye contact with the driver and saw that he recognized me. I looked up the pier to see Chai already moving. Still walking, I quickened my pace up the pier, looking back at the van. The door of the van slid open. Daeng climbed out, saw me, a look of surprise, and startled, as he looked at something behind me. I spun around, five meters from me, a man with a double barreled shotgun coming up, pointed at me. I won't be fast enough flashed through my mind.

I dived, watching the twin barreled mouths swing with me. A chunk of the man's head flew off, and he fell sideways. Chai fired more shots, the Uzi clacking, spitting out shells. A couple walking arm in arm on the pier not comprehending what was happening, looking puzzled as, his back to them, Chai crouched and stalked forward. They couldn't see the weapon in his hands, but then the woman saw the guy with a big chunk of his head missing, and she screamed. Chai did a complete 360 turn, his eyes sweeping over me, as I now crouched looking around to see if there were any other threats. Chai flicked the muzzle of the Uzi at the woman and held a finger to his lips. The woman stopped screaming.

Chai dropped the muzzle on the silenced Uzi and showed the woman his fake police badge. He told her and her boyfriend to get out of there. They nodded and took off. He called to Daeng to get his guys to throw the body in their van and take it to the farm. Daeng told his boys to do as Chai ordered, and called up to the restaurant. I lit a cigarette, my hand shaking. I looked around, but everyone was busy, no one noticed. Then I saw Chai watching me. He'd noticed. As Daeng's boys picked the body up, Chai walked over and quickly rummaged through the pockets, finding nothing. The killer could have been Thai, Cambodian, or Laotian, but I would have put money on Cambodian and I'm not a gambling man. Chai picked up the shotgun, broke it, and took out the shells. He gave the shotgun to Daeng's boys, telling them to file any numbers off it.

Chai handed me the shells. Triple-aught. At fifteen feet, one shot would have blown a hole in me you could put your fist through. Two would have cut me in half. I let out a long slow breath. That was close. Adrenalin cooling, I felt like I wanted to puke. I sucked hard on the smoke. Daeng was on the phone, Chai standing near me. A boy and a woman arrived on a motorbike, the woman sitting side-saddle on the back, holding a bucket and a mop. Daeng showed her where to clean up.

"Let's get out of here," Chai said.

"No. Let's go have dinner," I said, putting the shells in my pocket.

Big Tiger was waiting for us at the entrance.

"Fuck my mother, but believe me, I had no idea that was going to happen, Chance. Fuck, you have to believe me."

"I believe you, Tiger. Has the Aussie showed up yet?"

"No sign of the fuck yet, but he's due very fucking

soon. Let's get off this fucking pier. The heat is enough to kill a fucking camel."

Big Tiger took us to the elevator. The door held open by one of his "dek-serve", a waiter. I wondered if Big Tiger and "Heaven" shared the same designer.

Tiger had cleared the top floor. The girl from the other night was sitting waiting at the table. Obviously we wouldn't be talking business. Tonight she was wearing a T-shirt and a pair of shorts. Very short, shorts. Chai took a seat at a different table with Daeng, and I sat down with Big Tiger and the girl.

Tiger had "Hotel California" by the Eagles playing on the room's speakers. Apart from that, it was like eating in the middle of an auditorium.

"Tiger. Can I make a suggestion?"

"What?"

"Let's move outside, where we were the other night. This is too formal. Keep it light."

The girl smiled. Tiger scowled at her and gave me a pissed-off look.

"What's wrong with here? Outside is too fucking hot." His hand waved around the scarlet-red-papered walls interspersed with tall white columns. Folded up tables ringed the empty space around us. You could hold an Olympic ice-skating competition in the space we were in the middle of.

"Just trying to help. I am the Farang here, right?"

He thought about that. I watched the thought move behind his eyes. He reminded me of one of our crocs. An old, fat one.

"Well, fuck me. What's the fucking difference, right?

Let's go eat the fuck outside. Why the fuck not?"

He got up. The girl rolled her eyes in my direction. I kept my face expressionless. Sorry, babe, not playing your game. She adjusted focus and scuttled after a muttering, cursing Big Tiger. I could tell this was going to be a barrel of laughs.

While Big Tiger went off to berate a dek-serv, I chose a table at the corner of the balcony, with my back to the sea, facing the door to the restaurant. Chai sat down at a table between me and the door. Only two other tables on the deck were occupied.

Big Tiger came back with the Aussie couple. The guy had arrived with a woman in tow. In their late thirties, early forties, at a guess, they looked like Ken and Barbie, only worn and a bit wrinkled. Big Tiger shouted out to me from the door.

"Tell him to sit next to you so he can have a view of the sea. Then I can sit next to this beauty. Look at the fucking tits on her." Big Tiger's Uni girl got a serious pout on. Her lips came out about an inch.

Dinner and deal done, Ken and Barbie, actually Bret and Sheena, were now in the white Urvan on their way to Samui, courtesy of Big Tiger. Smiles all around. He was salivating at the thought of seeing Sheena in a bikini. Already planning a trip to that "fucking resort of mine, on that goat-fucking, miserable, monkey-infested swamp of an island", his name for the island of Samui.

Big Tiger hadn't noticed his Uni girl had taken off with Bret and Sheena. Flirting in English throughout the meal, Uni girl had talked them into a threesome for ten thousand baht. She gave me a smile from the back of the Urvan.

I turned to him.

"So the favor with Por."

He turned to me still smiling. "Yes?" Looking confused.

"This was it. We're even now."

"Sure, sure. Don't even think about it. And thanks for your help, Chance. I'd have been fucked without you. Didn't understand a fucking word when you guys were talking in English. Might as well have been fucking kangaroos for all the sense I could make out of it." He looked around. "Where the fuck did that girl of mine go?"

Holy Road Trips

17 May 2010, Bangkok, 5 am

I had forty-six hours left to find Uncle Mike. Or to figure out how to get him back and not lose the money. Worst-case scenario. We lose the money.

Ken surprised me. He hadn't attacked at Chumphon. He waited until the money was in the warehouse in Phuket and stole it from there. One of our guys got a nasty bump on the head. They trucked it out of Phuket that night and took it to Nakhon Si Thammarat. Ken's car had a GPS transmitter on it from when he had been in the warehouse at Lat Krabang. We had tags on them all the way. We got everything on tape. Ken looked especially cool – a nice profile shot of him, Mild seven packet in hand, shaking out a cigarette, the forklift carrying the money into the warehouse behind him. He had a smile on his lips. Chai won our bet – he'd said they'd steal it in Phuket.

The trick had been making it look real. Cheep had chosen a warehouse in Phuket that had a wall at its back. We'd protected the front heavily. The clever Japanese had broken in through the back. Even the guy with the bump on the head wasn't supposed to be there. He'd sneaked off for a piss. Ken had pulled the lend and steal move before – SOP for him. Ken had seriously screwed up. But he didn't know that yet.

Big Tiger had also made his first mistake. No one other than him, his crew, and Chai knew that I was having dinner there. The shotgun guy on the pier could only have learned it from him. We weren't followed – not possible. So it was Big Tiger.

I lay in bed, hands crossed behind my head, thinking about how I was going to take him down. I still couldn't figure out how Big Tiger knew my safe houses. If he'd been planning this for a while, it was possible he'd had me, or Pim, followed. Big Tiger tells Por he needs me, knowing Por will ask to see me in person. He tries to take us both out with a bomb. Fails. He then hires some Cambodians, cheap ones, because he's a tight bastard, and because they're cheap, they fail. Thinking about Por, losing his leg. Pit 51. The young, hungry, horny croc pit. Starve them a little. Dip Big Tiger's feet in cow's blood and drop him in the pond. Alive. One problem solved.

So the uncle Mike kidnapping is a coincidence? It seemed unlikely, but I couldn't see Big Tiger pulling it off, simply because there were foreigners involved. He'd hire Cambodians – he can curse at them – but he had an abiding shyness of dealing with foreigners. On the other hand, he had made a deal with Bret and Sheena. So why not Lisp and Natasha?

I got up and ran Big Tiger's cell phone number against the numbers we had from the phones we'd tracked in Phuket. No matches. Didn't really mean anything. I used different phone numbers all the time. So it was possible that Big Tiger had hired Lisp and Natasha or at least was working with them. But somehow it didn't gel. If Big Tiger knew of the plan to kidnap Uncle Mike and knew Lisp, he would have known I was alive. And he hadn't known. The look on his face when I showed up at his restaurant was real.

So Big Tiger and Uncle Mike's kidnapping were separate events but possibly connected. It was looking increasingly unlikely that we could find Lisp and Natasha before Wednesday morning. That meant we had to plan for passing over the cash. At least we had it. The real cash that Ken delivered went on the air-conditioned coach to Phuket, after spending the day at the Crocodile Farm. Mother had done the switch at the warehouse, unpacking, scanning, repacking with counterfeit and Ken's transmitters.

Showered, having breakfast, the cell phone rang. It was Mother. She was up early.

"Chance, how are you?"

"I'm good, Mother. Just having breakfast."

"Good, you need to eat. Keep your strength up. Now, some good news. Aunt Su came through with her contact in Malaysia. None of the passports have entered Malaysian territory, and a preliminary scan of the foreigners entering the country hasn't drawn a match."

"That is good news. Can we get anyone in the

coastguard to check the area north of Langkawi? But we only want them to look not approach."

"Already asked and explained. They'll get back to us sometime later today."

"Great. How is Por?"

"Good. Still in a coma, but his vital signs are improving. He's over the worst. Thomas is sure he's going to make it."

"The attacks are coming from Big Tiger."

"Are you sure? I didn't think he had the courage."

"Sure. He's the only one it could be. Yesterday someone tried to cut me down on his pier. Luckily, Chai took him out before he got the shot off, and Big Tiger's boys aborted their hit. Seeing Chai with an Uzi in his hands is a strong deterrent. The only people who knew I'd be there were him and his crew."

"He's got to go."

"We'll talk more in person later."

"Chance?"

"Yes, Mother?"

"Remember your promise."

"Yes, Mother."

We'd stayed the night at the Peninsula. Even from there, you could hear the explosions downtown. Chai checked us out and was waiting for me in the forecourt, sitting in a green Range Rover, engine running. We had to get the money to Phuket safely. Mother had organized to send a large Buddha statue south to Phuket. Monks from the temple where it was created sat with it in the back of a canvas-covered truck. Underneath the floor they were sitting on, a hundred million, real, United States dollars. We would follow at a safe distance, and the taxi we had used last night, now with a new set of plates, in front.

We passed the truck just south of Samut Sakon. Another eight hours and we'd be in Phuket. We pulled over, filled up with gas, and waited for the truck to pass. Traffic going south was steady and heavier than in other parts of Bangkok. People getting out of the city. No army to be seen. Normal life, if life can ever be called normal.

In view of the press interest, Mother had decided to cut my funeral short, and I was to be cremated, along with Por, at 4 pm that afternoon. We'd worked out a plan. It was sad, complicated, and final, but Samuel C. Harper had to go. Where it gets complicated is that in Thailand I have two "birth" certificates: one for Ohgaat and one for Sam Harper. Mother had handled the paperwork. Dr. Tom had put Ohgaat on the death certificate attached to the body. Mother had the paperwork switched, and Dr. Tom signed the new papers. Ohgaat lives. Sam Harper dies. Mother had a plan how to handle the "case of mistaken identity" is how she described it.

Pim called at ten.

"I've got a hit. SS Marine, a Singapore boat charter company, has a Hatteras 53. They chartered it with a crew of two to a party in Langkawi last Tuesday for a two-week charter. The customer paid cash. Was a Russian but didn't have a lisp. Everything was normal until last Friday. Since then, they haven't heard from the crew, and the crew is supposed to check in every day."

"That's it. That's them. What is the company doing about the boat and crew?"

"They've told Singapore Police and Malaysian Coastguard and Police."

"Good work. How did you find all that out?"

"It was online. An article that came up when I searched Google. I called SS Marine and pretended to be Malaysian police following up."

"Nice work. Let Mother know. I'll call you when I get to Phuket. Call me if anything else develops."

"Love you."

"I love you too."

We were just passing Meuang Prachuap Khiri Khan, making decent time. Highway four, straight south to Nakhon Si Thammarat, and then across to Phuket. About another five hundred and thirty klicks to go. Six hours give or take. That would put us into Phuket at four fifteen, four thirty, something like that.

An hour later, Cheep called. He was laughing. I could hear his boys laughing in the background.

"How did it go?"

"You'll hear on the news. A surprise red shirt protest and riot. Commercial buildings burnt down. Police say arrests are imminent."

"Everyone get in and out okay?"

"No problems. We're in the clear. We had time to break the blocks down and leave no trace."

"Ken's boys?"

"We used the army to move them away during the protest. When they came back, the fire was already burning good."

"Nice." I chuckled. "See you this evening. We need boats, fast ones, seagoing. Can you organize?"

"How many?"

"Three should be enough. With drivers who know

what they're doing but not showboaters."

"Can do. Have you got a lead?"

"Maybe. Talk more when I get there."

I was guessing Lisp would be at sea somewhere between Langkawi and Phuket. I had to find them before the coastguard did. If the Malaysian coastguard, not connected to us, caught them for ripping off the yacht, I was worried they'd kill Uncle Mike. The cruising speed of a Hatteras 53 is about 13 knots, using about 90 liters per hour at that rate. Fuel tanks hold about three thousand liters. That gave them a cruising range of about five hundred and fifty miles, assuming they didn't carry extra fuel in drums. No one at the marina could remember filling any up, so I assumed they didn't have any.

Langkawi to Phuket is about a hundred and eight nautical miles. Assuming they'd stay within fifty nautical miles of the coast, that made a search area of over five hundred square nautical miles. I figured the eight am thing was a ruse. They'd either drive around in circles or want the exchange to happen at dusk, figuring, with radar, they could slip away in the dark. That's what I'd plan on doing.

Passing through Chumphon, we heard on the news about the red shirt protest in the Democrat stronghold of Nakorn Si Thammarat. Ken would be wondering why I hadn't called him to tell him the hundred million had been stolen. Or maybe he'd be wondering about the money going up in flames and how he was going to explain that to the bosses back home.

The monks stopped for a pee break in Chumphon. We took the opportunity to eat. "Khao Mok Ghai", spicy chicken in rice at a roadside stall. It was delicious. Break over, we got back on the road.

At Surat Thani, we cut across the isthmus of Khra and entered Phang-nga province. The sun hung mid horizon on my right shoulder. Our route, Highway 4 to the 402 and then Phuket. So far it had been a smooth trip. No surprises.

The cell phone rang just as we entered Meuang Phang-nga. Mother.

"Malaysian Police have found two bodies, suspected to be the crewmen of the Hatteras. A fisherman caught them in their nets and reported it in."

"Where?"

"North of Langkawi. But the bodies could have floated with the current. They were fairly badly chewed up. They'd probably been dead for a few days."

"Okay, thanks, Mother."

My bet was they were planning on running to Indonesia, probably down the western side. They wouldn't want to deal with the Malacca Strait. I spread the US Navy and Thai charts I had of the area out on the back seat. I'd been over them all before, the creases in the folds familiar. With calipers, I marked off the areas on the chart where I wanted the boats to wait. I was pretty sure we'd have to make the exchange. I was sure the exchange would be at sea. Somewhere just on Thai borders at dusk. Then, I was sure they'd run for Indonesian waters.

We delivered the Buddha statue and the monks to a Wat just past the bridge. The abbot was a happy man with the statue and the million baht donation from Mother. We drove into Cheep's resort, just as the sun was setting.

Cheep's resort surprised me. I was expecting your basic bamboo A-frame huts at the end of the steep dirt road. The bungalows were well-designed, tastefully hidden behind jungle, with pools of water beside each. The main building back from the beach, understated, white stucco, with high ceilings. A cool breeze helped by ceiling fans cooled the air. In front of me, the Andaman Sea. Somewhere out there, Uncle Mike.

Cheep had closed the resort. His boys and ours occupied the restaurant, looking out over the beach. Camouflage trousers, black T-shirts, Sak Yant tattoos, and fake Ray-Bans surrounding whiskey bottles, ice-buckets and soda bottles. Not an image you'd want on the front page of your website. The mosquito zapper lent a flare and a crackle to the atmosphere. Far away from the seedy bars of Patong, where girls, boys, and everything in between can be had for fifty bucks, here, cicadas played solo and chorus, rising crescendos that harmonized with slow, lazy rolls of the waves.

I sat apart from the boys. I wasn't in the mood for socializing. A woman skirted the long table where the boys were, a tray in her hands. She came to the table I was sitting at. I recognized her. Cheep's second daughter, Nong Wan, which means "Sweet". She set the tray on the table, smiled, waied and started putting ice in a tall glass, all in one fluid motion. Her actions reminded me of Chai stripping a gun.

"Sawasdee, Pi Bao," she said. "Pi Bao" was southern Thai dialect for elder brother. Cheep was from Bangkok, but he'd married a Phuket woman.

"Hello, Nong Wan. It has been a couple of years since

I've seen you. How old are you now?"

"Fifteen, ka, pi, Chance." She was gorgeous: big eyes, white teeth, dimples in her smile. I bet she would give Cheep many sleepless nights in the future, if not already. Cheep walked across, smiling at Wan. He ruffled her hair and told her to go do her homework. Another wai and she was gone.

"She's growing even more beautiful, Cheep. One of the great mysteries of our time."

"What mystery?" he said, grinning.

"How someone as ugly as you could produce a daughter as beautiful as that."

Cheep laughed. It was a joke of Uncle Mike's. We'd all shared it many times. We sat and watched the sea darken, as the sun lay down its final display for the day. Comfortable to sit in silence.

THE BEST LAID PLANS

18 May 2010, Phuket, 5:30 am

Strong, hot, sweet, black coffee and an onshore breeze are enough to lift anyone's spirits. I was enjoying both on the balcony of the master suite that Cheep had given me. The sun had not yet risen, facing due west it was dark, but the far horizon to the south already showed a dark purple sea, with a fringe of scarlet and orange.

Someone knocked on the door. It was Cheep, an excited look on his face.

"Last night, midnight, the Hatteras came back to Yacht Haven." Cheep was practically quivering with the news, fingers like claws, flexing in and out.

"Anyone on board?"

"So far only one Farang has shown his face. He paid cash in the office for two days mooring in advance, and he booked fueling for this morning. I've got guys watching

131

the boat. They'll call us if they see anything."

Back to Yacht Haven? I thought. That was dumb. Or maybe not. I began to see Lisp's plan. I turned to Chai. Chai had been a Thai Navy Seal for five years.

"We need to get a transmitter onto the boat. Somewhere it can't be found. Maybe just above the waterline by the rudder. If possible with a back-up. He's not going to swap money and Uncle Mike. He's going to swap boats."

Chai nodded.

"How about those boats? Are they ready?"

"They're ready."

"Radar?"

"Thirty mile radar installed on three meter poles. They worked on it all night. It's done, working."

"Good work, thanks." I spread the charts I'd worked on yesterday and more last night. "These circles here are where I think they'll make their escape. The way I think they're going to do this, is to have us load the money on the Hatteras. Then we'll drive out to sea, probably south, the route under the bridge to the north is dangerous without local knowledge. Once past the southern tip, we'll head southwest towards the west coast of Indonesia, until we get out of Thai territory. Then the guy on the Hatteras, which also has thirty-mile radar, will check to see what is around and call Lisp. Lisp will come in on another boat with Uncle Mike. We then swap boats, Uncle Mike staying on the boat he's on and the money on the boat we'll be on. As soon as we've done the swap, we'll want to move in, but before then we'll want to stay out of radar range. We can stay in touch without arousing suspicion by moving in and out of radar range from different directions. Also by varying speed and changing the radar signature. Did you get the aluminum foil?"

Cheep nodded. "We've sent a fishing boat with extra fuel out this morning," Chai said, his finger roving over the map. "With these distances you're talking about, the boats will need to refuel at least once."

"The key thing is to stay in touch but not be seen."

"I got it, Chance." A flash of annoyance crossed Cheep's eyes to accompany the bite in the tone. I put my hand on his arm.

"I'm sorry, Khun Cheep. I'm just keyed up. Worried about Uncle Mike."

He nodded and smiled back. Feeling awkward that he'd let his emotions show. He was as stressed as I was. Cool heart, "jai yen", is fine when it isn't blood on the line.

The Hatteras was moored at the end of a pontoon on the outside of the marina. We had a dredger and a pile driver working twenty meters from the Hatteras driving a pile into the seabed. I could hear the thump of the huge ball of iron as it struck the concrete piling from where I was. According to the range finder in the binoculars, that was three hundred and eighty three meters away.

It was just after one thirty in the afternoon. I was on the third floor of an office building, watching the boat from the shore. Tum, holding a Barrett .50 sniper's rifle, was with me, and one of Cheep's guys, called Sak, shot photos with a Canon digital with a huge telephoto lens. Chai was underwater somewhere between us and the boat.

I switched views and looked at the far end of the pier. Two of Cheep's boys were there, drill and wood in hand. The guy on the Hatteras came out of the cabin into the cockpit area and looked down the pier at Cheep's boys. They ignored him, focused on drilling the piece of wood. Chai surfaced in the shadow of the hull near the rudder. He worked quickly, head and hands barely visible, then he was gone. Two antennas sticking up just above the waterline marked his passage. Cheep's boys packed up and walked off the pier. Lisp's man went back into the cabin. Ten minutes later, Chai surfaced in the dock of the shipyard. Job done.

Later in the afternoon, we tested the GPS devices, turning them on and off for brief periods. They worked. We wouldn't turn them on again until I was on board and we were under way. We reckoned they'd scan us for transmitters. It was unlikely they'd find the pair now attached to the boat, but better not to take the risk. All we could do now was watch and wait.

Lilly's phone rang at exactly 8 am. A shake of the head from Cheep told me it wasn't the guy on the Hatteras. He was watching the Hatteras on a notebook, courtesy of more Japanese technology. We were back in the resort. Last night no one drank alcohol. It was a quiet dinner. Now it was all business. We were "Go".

I answered the phone.

"Yes."

"You have the money packaged how I ordered?"

Arrogant little prick, I thought. "Yes, I do."

"Good. You will leave now. Alone. You will drive to the Yacht Haven, you have thirty minutes. Take this phone with you."

The line disconnected. We had already mapped out the fastest route to Yacht Haven. Thirty minutes was ample time. I felt hot under the shirt, bulletproof vest and T-shirt under that. That was why I was sweating. I breathed out.

We had all the bases covered. Chai would be with one of the two boats on the southern route. That was the most likely route they would take. If the signal was lost, all three boats would converge on the last signal at thirty-five knots. On the southern route, that would put them only five minutes away at any time. I ran through these details once more as I checked my weapons.

Cheep grabbed my arms.

"Good luck."

"Thanks, Cheep. See you soon."

Cheep, Chai, Tum and the rest of the boys filed out. They would join the boats at different locations and be in radar range of the Hatteras within fifteen minutes. Two of the cars would check the route until the main highway, when one would branch off east and one would check the route north.

The rain from last night had burned off, and the morning was bright and clear, a hint of the heat that would bake at noon tempered by a cool sea breeze and a blue sky. I climbed up into the cab of the seven-ton truck. Painted as a food delivery vehicle, and grubby looking, the engine was top grade and the tires new. I over revved and then settled down, getting the feel for the clutch and accelerator.

After a jerky start, I got the truck running smoothly, heading north, a running commentary via the encrypted comms channel of the team's progress in my ear. Past Nai Thon beach, the road empty, I picked up the speed. The 4031 would take me to the 4026, which cut north and then east, then I would join the 402, straight north. But on Thai roads, anything can happen, so make time while you can. Now that I was alone, I could wipe my sweaty palms on my trousers. I passed a couple of kids on a motorbike, but otherwise there was no traffic on the 4031. Through Sa Khu, I turned right onto the 4026 – six and half kilometers and just another four to the main dual carriageway.

I eased off the speed as I came around the sharp left corner, too late to stop for the spikes lying across the road. The front tires blew out. The truck slewed across the road as the back tires blew, a huge plume of sparks in the side mirror. In front of me, a container truck blocked the road. Braking hard, I stopped with a meter to spare. Static in my ears. They had blocked radio signals. The ticking over of the truck's engine, the air conditioner in the cab, all the sounds I could hear. Quiet.

Glock in hand, I climbed down from the cab. A glance at my cell phone confirmed the blocked signal. I was on my own. A spike of pain in my leg – I looked down – a dart with a bright orange cap hanging out of my leg. My legs went out from under me. I lifted the Glock in the direction of the bush, but it was too heavy. Vision blurred. Thinking how long before Chai and the others would realize. I've screwed up…

A Crazy Plan

I woke up in darkness, lying on a metal floor, a hood over my head. It stank, stale sweat and wool. It itched. An itch I couldn't scratch. My hands were bound behind me with what felt like a cable tie. My feet the same. I was naked. The hum of tires, muted bumps, metallic thumps, and echoes. I guessed I was in the back of the container that had blocked the road. Moving, the metal ridges of the floor digging into my shoulder blades as we hit bumps in the road. I pushed with my feet and jerked my body, looking to sit up. My fingers felt swollen and painful, but I used them to try and get purchase. I pushed and jerked and hit something with my head.

I turned my body around. No mean feat, when you're bound arms, hands, and feet. My fingers were my eyes, feeling. Hard plastic, rough wood. The money on the pallet.

137

I fell over countless times. Enough that I taught myself how to brace for each fall. My knees, face, shoulders, everything hurt. There wasn't a part of me that wasn't protesting. I was like Bangkok. Bruised, battered, with every part fighting against the other. Thirsty, breaths coming with a rasp, the smell of my sweat now a close cousin to the hood's previous owners.

I had searched the container. Old frayed rope, cable ties, a metal ramp, a forklift, and one hundred million dollars, the fruits of my labor. Not bad for an hour's work. I was exhausted, but there was more work to do.

They'd driven the forklift straight in with the money. Its rear to the doors of the container. They could only be opened from the outside. I'd searched higher parts by running my face, particularly my nose, over objects until I could picture them in my mind. I was thankful for the hood and hated it as the cause of my suffering.

I had a plan. It was a crazy plan, but as far as options go, it was the best of what remained. Sometimes that's all we have – the best of a bunch of bad choices.

I paused, a quick task and sanity check – this is fucking insane! I went to work. I'd watched MacGyver as a kid. The frayed rope I tied one end on a knob of the forklift's steering wheel. The other to the frame of the forklift. To start the forklift I had to use my hands, which meant they weren't free for steering. I reasoned that the wheels must be straight now, so tying the steering wheel would work. I hadn't been able to raise or lower the lift and that meant the pallet would drag along the floor of the truck. I had one shot at this. It would probably take too long to get the gear in forward and control braking if the doors didn't open on the first hit. But that was plan B. There was no plan C.

I climbed up into the cab and felt around until I found the metal circle that the starter button was encased in. Kneeling on the driver's seat, facing the doors, the tone of the truck changed, and I heard the gear shift down. My body tilted back a little. We were on a steep hill. I waited. The truck with its light load gathered speed in the lower gear. Five minutes passed. My thighs burned. The tone changed as the driver shifted into a higher gear, my body tilted forward, cresting the hill. I hit the starter button. The starter whirred and then caught. I immediately twisted around to sit in the driver's seat. Lying sideways on the seat, I pressed my feet hard on the accelerator pedal and used my hands to throw the gear into reverse.

The forklift shot backwards. I braced myself as best I could, feet hard on the pedals, shoulder into the back of the driver's seat. I hit the doors with a massive bang that echoed in the metal chamber, but I was stopped. The wheels of the forklift screeching on the metal floor to no effect. I took my feet off the pedal and put the gear back in neutral, listening. The noise from outside had changed. I could hear the container trucks tires on the road surface more clearly. The echolike quality of the container had changed as well. The truck braked hard. I was thrown against the steering wheel, the knob hitting me right between the shoulder blades as I heard the tires skidding on the road.

The forklift slid forward, as I struggled to keep myself upright. We slammed into the far end of the container, and again I was thrown against the steering wheel. We had stopped. The forklift motor had stalled. I pushed with my chin on the seat and pushed until I got my thumb onto the starter. I heard the doors of the cab slam shut outside. The starter motor caught. I threw the forklift into reverse. My knees slipped, and I missed the pedal. I heard footsteps running outside. I got my feet on the pedal and pressed down hard.

The forklift must have skewed when we slid because I crashed against the side of the container, but as the money hit, it straightened and picked up speed. I hit the door and heard it wrench free of the container. A man's scream cut off. The forklift dropped off the container and landed with a bone-jarring crash. It tilted, and for one moment, I thought we were going over, but then the front thumped down. I was on the floor near the pedals. I pushed the gear lever into reverse with my hooded head and used my knees on the pedal.

The loud crack of a pistol within feet of me, the bullet smacking into the metal by my head. The forklift was moving. The crack of the pistol further away. I pressed down, listening to the running feet, the shots, the sound of the wheels and pallet on the road. I could feel rain on my body. The forklift picked up speed, the motor howling. I'd crested the hill. What sounded like, "Stop," shouted further away – no way. Escape.

The forklift tilted alarmingly, what sounded like gravel crunching beneath me, and then we hit something. I was airborne. Dead, I thought, flashing on Pim talking about my funeral. I hit the ground hard. Could hear the crashing of the forklift near me. Rolling, hitting hard objects, head over heels and then airborne again. A long drop and I landed hard. Silence. I opened my eyes. Dark purple sky. It was snowing red spots. I passed out.

When I came to, it was cool. Night. It was a struggle to breathe. My throat's sides stuck together, both looking for a drink. The hood was bunched up beneath my nostrils. My hands touched rock, I'd only just missed it. Or had I landed on it? I didn't know. I found an edge. Desperate to be rid of the hood and free, I started working the cable tie against it.

I worked and passed out several times, my arm muscles burning beyond endurance. My mind found that special place where a space is reserved for observing the absurd things you are doing to yourself, a space marathon runners know well. Finally, the cable gave. I lay on the ground, my last moments with the hood on, darkness, listening to my breathing. My shoulder joints screamed as I lifted my hands up and took off the hood. Darkness. Tree trunks, rocks, leaves. I found a rock, and putting my feet on the slab of rock that I had narrowly missed, pounded the cable tie into a quick surrender.

I woke up as dawn was breaking. Above me, the cliff I'd fallen down, and a little further up, the forklift and the money at the base of a clump of gnarly old trees. I was on a ledge in a steep gulley, the ledge about ten meters wide. The tops of trees were parallel with the ledge and a steep slope ran into an ever narrowing space. I was sure I'd cracked a couple of ribs. Breathing hurt. I hoped there was no internal bleeding.

I've watched Discovery Channel, seen the Man vs. Wild shows but this ledge didn't offer much of anything, least of all hope. Walking over to the forklift, the walls of cliff steep enough that everything was in shadow, the morning air cool, I listened but couldn't hear any running water. Occasionally I heard the hum of tires on the road up above. Otherwise birdsong and the chattering of monkeys were my playlist.

I was sure they'd be back. One hundred million dollars is too much to throw away. They'd be back with climbing and lifting gear. It wouldn't take much, and the equipment was easy to get. I had a couple of hours at best.

Going up was out of the question. Sideways was practically a straight drop to another ledge forty feet below – didn't think I'd survive that. Staying here, I was an easy target. Down was the only option, the best of a bunch of bad choices. It had been like that for a few days now. I went and looked over the edge. A bit wobbly on my legs, I stayed well back from the edge. The tops of the trees spread out such that I couldn't see the ground beneath them. Difficult to judge their height. They were thick, though, and entwined. At one point, the earth on the ledge had slipped and created a step that jutted out. The step was about four meters lower than the rest of the ledge and about two meters away from the tops of the trees.

I looked around and sighed. Pause, task list, pray, run, jump and sanity check – we should skip the insanity checks from now on. I got into a sprinter's crouch – my body had given up protesting and turned to laughing hysterically instead. Thighs quivering, I breathed out and sprinted.

At the point where the ledge had slipped, I thought – this is really fucking crazy, but I hit the slab at a good speed, without tripping and made a huge leap.

I hit the branches, caught one, but it was too thin, dropped through, arms flailing. And hit another one hard, bouncing sideways until I fell right across one with my stomach, nearly flipping over it but holding on. If I didn't have cracked ribs before, I did now. I looked down. Still couldn't see floor.

Two hours later, I walked into a clearing, a DTAC cell phone base station tower in the middle of it. A pick-up was parked next to the tower's iron fence. Inside the fence, a man wearing coveralls had his head inside the gray metal box he was kneeling next to. I walked up to the fence and called out hello. All that came out was a garbled croak. My voice having a little laugh at my expense. The man turned, and his eyes went big in fear, then closed. He grabbed his amulets hanging at his neck and lifted his hands in prayer.

I swallowed, forcing the Velcroed sides of my throat apart.

"I'm not a ghost. I had an accident. Fell down a cliff. I need a cell phone."

The man opened his eyes and dropped his hands. Standing up slowly, he looked wary as he advanced crablike around the fence. He walked over and touched my forearm, pulling his hand back quickly. Relief flooded his features.

"You scared the shit out me," he said, laughing and removing the pakama he had tied around his waist, giving it to me. I put it on. He took me to his truck. I sat in the passenger's seat. It felt cool and soft. He handed me a phone. I called Mother on her home phone – the only number I could remember.

Ba Nui answered on the third ring.

"Ba Nui get me Mother." I heard a scream, and the phone dropped. The man handed me a bottle of "Red Bull", cap off. I gulped it down, feeling the sweetness pouring energy into me – the best thing I'd ever drunk.

"Where are we?" I asked him.

"Bang Yai," he said.

"What province?" That caused his eyebrows to go up.

"Ranong."

"What's the number of the base station?"

"Ranong-Bang-Yai-31."

"Chance?"

"Mother."

"Thank Buddha, you're alive. Where are you?"

"At a DTAC base station Ranong-Bang-Yai-31."

"I got it. I will send help. Can a helicopter land there?"

I looked over the car park.

"Yes."

"Stay there. What's your number?"

I turned again to the guy.

"What's your number?" I held the phone to his mouth. He spoke his number. I put the phone back to my ear.

"I got it. Thirty minutes. Don't move from there." She hung up.

A Lucky Break

Mother was true to her word. Twenty-five minutes after we'd spoken, an army helicopter landed in the car park of the base station. It flipped Pi Sila's pick-up over. He hitched a ride with us. I told him I'd buy ten more pick-ups.

In front of me, a detailed survey map showed the area of Bang Yai. I worked out, judging distances from the road and the base station, roughly where I had crashed over a cliff. I showed Colonel Paisarn, alongside me, the younger brother of a general married to Aunt Malee's cousin from her second younger aunt. His skin was the color of cognac, stocky, hair clipped short military style, greying at the temples, a green beret on his head.

"You reckon here, Khun Chance?" His finger prodded the map.

"Yes. No doubt."

145

"Okay. I'll put a team on the road. How long will they need to be there?"

"It'll be about four hours until we can get our people there." Chai, Cheep and the boys were on the way, but it'd take them time to get there by road from Phuket. Mother was trying to arrange, with the help of the army relatives, a helicopter from Surat Thani. Either way, it would take at least a few hours.

"Consider it done."

"I'll be joining them. When are we leaving?"

He seemed surprised and a little disappointed. He wanted a look at what we were protecting. "But, Chance, you're badly hurt, dehydrated. You should rest. Don't worry I'll take care of everything."

"The general would be disappointed if I didn't go…"

He straightened up, his eyes angry, but obedience training and a quick calculation, no doubt, of the powers of leverage, prevailed.

"Of course, Khun Chance. We must do what we can for the general."

We took off in the Bell 206B-3. Designed to carry four passengers, it was holding five: a lieutenant, a ser-geant, a radioman, a private and me. It took us thirty minutes to fly to the spot, the soldiers all armed to the teeth. This was very close to Burma, and border incursions by Burmese soldiers hunting Mon rebels were not unknown. The colonel, at my request, had loaned me an US army issue Colt .45 and an M-16. A large part of me was hoping that Lisp and his gang would be at the site of the crash.

They weren't. The road was too narrow for the helicopter to land. We had to jump the last ten feet. It hurt. I checked out the crash site. The broken, twisted end of a metal barrier, the work I'd done the previous evening. From the edge of the cliff, a drop onto a steep slope of about ten meters. No wonder I hurt all over. The whole area was quiet. I checked the GPS coordinates and sent an SMS to Chai. Further up the road, we found a shady spot, and the soldiers set up camp. I eased my back against a tree and fell asleep.

About three hours later, I woke up. The lieutenant and sergeant were asleep next to me, the private boiling water over a fire. The sun was almost directly overhead. It was baking hot. The soldier threw a packet of Mama Noodles into the pot. My mouth watered. I heard vehicles and looked up the road. They were coming from the direction of Thailand. To the west of us, the Burmese border. I picked up the M-16, checked that the safety was off and it was on full automatic. The soldier gave a wistful glance at his noodles and picked up his weapon.

The vehicles pulled up fifty meters away, and Chai got out of the driver's side of the Cherokee Jeep, holding up his arms. I dropped the muzzle of the gun and nodded to the soldier. He smiled and went back to his noodles. Priorities.

Weariness hit me like a wave. I leaned back against the tree as Chai and Cheep walked over. Chai squatted on his haunches in front of me, studying my face.

"You look like hell," he said.

"Don't worry. I feel a lot worse than I look," I said and smiled.

He handed me Lilly's phone. "It's rung five times since late morning."

"Checking to see if we're back together. Any sign of them?"

"The guy on the Hatteras was hired four days ago in Pattaya and joined the yacht by speed boat from Krabi. They told him they had urgent business and asked him to drive the boat to Yacht Haven to wait for them. Paid him in cash. Russian, he thought, but wasn't sure. The guy asked to be called Alex. No sign of Uncle Mike or the woman. The cops found the truck in Kra Bhuri. They could have crossed the river and be in Burma."

"Possible. Possible that they've been here all the time. So far my guesses as to their actions have been fairly off-base. I'll just play it step by step for now. First step is to recover the goods. See down there, where the railing is torn away. That's where I went over with the forklift. There's a steep slope for about ten meters, then another fifteen meter drop, then there's a ledge. The goods are on the ledge."

The lieutenant and sergeant had woken up. They were pretending to look out over the gulley, but their ears were pinned back, listening.

Cheep moved off, shouting to his boys. The road was sectioned off, and the soldiers put on guard duty. Cheep's boys hooked up and climbed down. Within minutes, shouts came up that they had found the goods. The first of many bright blue thick plastic bags was hauled up using the winch on the front of the Cherokee. I sat and watched from the shade, Chai by my side. He handed me a packet of Marlboro red. Chai doesn't smoke, doesn't approve of me smoking; what friends are made of.

I drew in deeply, watching as a blue bag bumped its

way over the cliff and was dragged a short distance before the winch stopped. A guy untied the cable and dropped it back over the edge for the next bag.

"Do you know how much shit Mother gave me in the last twenty-four hours? No one has ever made me feel so bad about myself."

"I'm sorry, Chai. It was my fault. I underestimated them."

"No. Joom is right. What you do is your business. What I do is protect you. That's my business. That's what Joom and Por trained me for. Not to listen to you," he turned sideways and grinned at me, "and your crazy plans." He shook his head slowly side to side. "You really are crazy, you know. Driving a forklift out of a moving truck and over the edge of a cliff. I haven't dared tell Mother that part yet. Anyway, I've learned my mistake. From now on, my only job is making sure you stay alive. Okay? I don't want Joom talking to me like that again – reminded me of when I was five."

"When you were being bullied and Joom told you to fight and stand up for your name or she'd cane your legs till you bled to death, if you didn't die of shame first? You mean that time?"

Chai stared at the ground, squatting, tapping his combat booted foot on the tarmac. "Yeah, that time."

"Wow. I'm sorry, Chai. That's pretty scary." I tried but couldn't keep the grin out of my voice. He smiled at me and punched me on the shoulder. It hurt.

Last to come up were the guys who had climbed down, pulled up by the winch, the last man all smiles. Money loaded. Ropes pulled up. Cables tied away. Barrier on the road taken down, and the soldiers put in the front two vehicles. Time to move.

I walked over to the gap in the safety barrier that I had flipped over in the forklift, Chai by my side like a shadow. I had the feeling the shadow would always be watching my back.

"You know how far you fell? The boys told me it's at least forty meters to the ledge. One hundred and twenty feet. Your amulets are going to be worth a fortune."

I smiled. It was true. The only thing I was wearing, the whole time I was in the container and on the run, was my amulets, the three of them given to me by Por, Joom and Uncle Mike. I sat in the back seat of the Cherokee, Chai next to me, Uzi on his knees, and we looked out of the window as we wound down the mountains towards Chumphon.

There was one thing that puzzled me. Why hadn't Lisp just taken the money? Why did he need to take me? Was he planning on running the same kidnap routine on me with Mother? It didn't fit. You've got the money, you put a bullet in my head, and you're home free. Why go to all the trouble of a tranquilizer gun and more kidnapping? One hundred million was more than enough for anyone. It didn't fit. Just another fragment of a mosaic where none of the pieces fit, and the picture remains unclear.

On the outskirts of Chumphon, Lilly's phone rang. I answered it.

"Who is this? Who is this?" Lisp was excited.

"Chance."

"Ah, so you're alive."

"No, they have cell phones in hell."

"Don't get funny."

"Funny – I thought we were going to make an exchange – that is, until you decided to get funny."

I heard a woman say, "Leon", in the background, and the sound from the phone cut off. Silence for a few seconds. I looked at the phone, signal strength strong. Lisp spoke again, his voice quieter, almost calm.

"You want your Uncle Mike?"

"Yes. I want Uncle Mike, and I want to speak to Uncle Mike."

"You can talk but not now. You go to Koh Kong, on Cambodian border, have the money with you. Keep this phone with you. When you get there, you can talk to Uncle Mike, and we make exchange. Straight exchange this time, no tricks. You go now."

"Not today. I broke my arms, I need treatment. It'll be tomorrow."

"Tomorrow." He hung up.

Leon. What sounded like a woman had opened a door and called Lisp, "Leon". A break, a lucky break. A lot can be done with a first name. Assuming, of course, he was using his real first name. Something nagged at me about the woman's voice. That feeling you have when you leave the house and know that you've forgotten something but ignore it – and you get halfway down the street when you realize you've left your wallet at home.

SHADES OF GRAY

19 May 2010, Pak Nam, 6 pm

We stayed out of the city and disembarked on the Samut
Sakhon side of the river. Mother owned the land opposite
her and Por's house. Her boat, a Bertram 42, was waiting
for us. Even from here I could see the pall of black smoke
rising above Bangkok.

The redshirt encampment had been stormed by the army
about the time I was waking up on the ledge. In the early
afternoon, the stage where the red shirt leaders were making
their last speeches was reached and some were arrested and
some escaped. A foreign journalist and at least ten others
were killed in the day's fighting. Over forty buildings had
been set on fire, and looting in the department stores next
to the redshirt encampment had been widespread. Pockets
of resistance held out and a curfew, at six pm, had just gone
into effect. There was trouble in other provinces in the north

and northeast. Muted whispers circulated of the potential for civil war, mostly from Farang, posturing from pseudo-intellectual backgrounds who didn't know shit about what was happening on the ground.

I learned all of this in the backseat of the Cherokee, using Twitter and the net. On the cell phone, I learned of deals made behind the scenes. Only naïve CNN and BBC reporters pitched this as a battle between rich and poor, the elite versus the downtrodden. Even the dumbest Thai knew it was a lot more complicated. Elite versus elite, each with a tapestry of past and present favors and feuds, captains and foot soldiers, all with their own agenda, to be executed with a weather eye on the way the wind was blowing. Shades of gray.

Money, cold hard cash, close to the amounts I'd just hauled around Thailand had been spent and made. Bosses putting their boys on the street for a payment to a Swiss bank account. The fight on the street had been fierce, close, and was ongoing. Points were being made, scored, and tallied. This phase, the phase of a medieval fortress in the middle of downtown Bangkok, was over, bar the curtain being dropped. The Fat Lady had sung.

There was little need to play dead now that I knew Big Tiger was the force behind the Cambodians trying to kill me. He was high on my list of priorities, but my first task was resting up and getting Uncle Mike back safely.

Mother and Pim came across in the Bertram. Standing in the cockpit, Pim a good few centimeters taller than Mother, it struck me how similar they looked. Not in looks, but in stance. The boat boy maneuvered in, and the boys waiting on the dock gathered in the lines, tying the boat off. Mother and Pim stepped off, and the boys immediately made a human chain, the heavy blue plastic bags in a pile by the dock.

Mother walked over and stood in front of me. I saw a look of shock flash across Pim's face as she got close enough to see mine. I smiled. Pim looked even more horrified. Mother reached out, held my jaw, and turned my face left and right. I had a flashback to when I was eight. She looked in my eyes – we shared the flashback. Thais are conservative by nature. We avoid "overt" public displays of affection, such as kissing or hugging. Mother hugged me, squeezing me tight. She stood back and shot a glance at Chai. It lasted a second, but froze the far side of the river for a while. Chai shuffled his combat boots and studied the ground between them.

"It wasn't Chai's fault, Mother. He was just following me." The flashback merged with the present, to the word.

"I ought to give the both of you a good spanking. What the hell did you think you were doing driving around on your own with that kind of money? You ought to know better." She rounded on Chai. "and since when did you think that you were to follow his orders?" Chai wisely, did not answer this, and did not grin. I was not so wise.

"And what are you smiling about? Your father's in a Cambodian hospital with his leg blown off, your Uncle Mike is in the hands of a sadistic madman, and you're driving a forklift truck loaded with a hundred million off a cliff. Oh yes, don't look surprised. Of course I know what happened. I had a full report from the colonel before you left for the site." Pim's mouth had dropped open. Fifteen grown men stood perfectly still, me included, and

I got rid of the grin. Mother was pissed off. She turned to face the others.

"Get busy loading the money," she said quietly.

There was a mad scramble to load money and be spared the wrath of Mother. I thought about joining in but decided against it. Looking at the way Chai was sneaking sideways glances at the boat, I could tell he'd had the same thought. Mother turned her attention back to us.

"Since it appears that you have forgotten, let me remind you both. Your job, Chance, is to make sure this family is safe and healthy, and your job, Chai, is to make sure he is safe and healthy. Are we clear on what our jobs are?" She had her hands on her hips. Pim was grinning. I fought the urge. I'm not suicidal.

"Yes, Mother!" Chai and I said in unison. She turned her back on us and stalked off to the boat. Chai and I shared a grin. For all the times we'd been there. Then Pim climbed in.

"What are you two grinning about? This isn't fucking funny. Did I hear Mere Joom say you drove a forklift off a cliff? With all the money? And you were on a boat waiting for him. While he drove around Phuket with a hundred million in cash. Is that it?"

"Well, no, it wasn't exactly like that, and it wasn't a very high cliff."

"I have to go help Mother." Chai grinned at me and escaped. Coward.

"Pim, it's done. It's past. It was a complete fuck up, but no one got killed, and we still have the money. Well actually, one guy might have been killed, but he was on their side."

"You mean you've killed another person? That's three in a week." Her mouth was hanging open again.

"Let's talk about this later. Now's not the time. Okay? It looks like Mother's ready to head back." I nodded at the boat, the last of the bags on board, and Mother standing in the stern.

Pim nodded, the news of my latest killing quieting her questions for the moment. In the space of a week, the Chance side of my life had pretty much wiped out the half she thought Samuel Harper had been. She looked like she was trying to figure out if what remained was the half she wanted.

Despite Joom's mood, the river was not frozen over, and we made swift time to the opposite shore. Ba Nui, who'd answered and dropped the phone, looked at me with terror. Mother stopped and assured her I was not a ghost, and encouraged her to take a feel of my arm to be sure. It looked as if Ba Nui was not convinced on the first and declined absolutely on the second, grabbing Mother's hand bag and taking off up the path to the house.

As we reached the top of the path and walked around the pool, Mother turned.

"You're staying here tonight. I've prepared your room. Pim, of course you will stay again tonight. The guest room is yours for as long as you need it." It wasn't a request or a suggestion.

"Yes, Mother." There was no way that Mother would let Pim and I share a room in her house if we weren't married. Never spoken, but understood by all. Cultural rules telepathy. Thailand is a very male dominated society. Run by women. We all know that.

My room was on the second floor at the back of the house, overlooking the river, down the hall from Mother and Por's room. Pim was in one of the guest rooms on the third floor. My room had a window seat. It was my favorite place to read. I hadn't been back there in ages. After a long hot soak, I lay in the window seat, lights reflecting off the river. I looked around the room: a silver gun Mother had bribed me with to get me to go to the dentist when I was six; my degree on the wall – the joy in their faces when I looked out for them in the crowd after receiving it; the .22 air rifle – Por telling me never to point it at anything I didn't mean to destroy. The movie of my life played scenes cued by the objects in the room.

I thought of Pim. Her intelligence, beauty, strength of character, and I thought of the choice I had to make. I felt guilty that my planning to leave the family had brought this bad luck upon us. Irrational I know, but only if you're a Farang. If I left the family, Mother and Por would be heartbroken. If I didn't leave the family, Pim would leave me. The look on her face when she'd learned I'd killed again, a look I didn't want to see again.

There was a soft tap on the door. Pim. She sat down on the polished teak wood floor next to the window seat, didn't say a word, looking out at the river, her right ear waiting for words from me.

"I don't enjoy killing."

"I know."

"Only when it is a matter of life and death. Yes, I've killed. Last one was an accident. He was behind the door of the container when I crashed it with the forklift. He may have survived, but I doubt it. If someone came to harm you, I would kill them before they had the chance, if I could."

"How many people have you killed?"

"Six including the last guy."

She nodded. A tear swelled up from the eye I could see and rolled down her cheek, making a spot the size of a one baht coin on the white cotton of the seat's cushion.

"I killed a kitten once, in London, outside my flat in Kensington late one night. We'd just come back from the pub. The kitten was in the gutter next to the pavement. It had been run over by a car, its back and hind legs crushed. It was crying in agony. I was the designated driver, only had one glass of wine all night. Stone cold sober. I drove my mini over the kitten. I still feel the bump the car made when it ran over the kitten. I still think about it. How do you live with it?" Her voice was barely above a whisper. She laid her head on my thigh. I stroked her hair.

"It's done. It is the past. They were situations. Me or them. Karma. I carry the faces of all of those I have killed, and I've thought countless times about each one. Could I have done it differently? I can live with it be-cause I am alive. It's the only answer I've come up with."

A Mickey Mouse Exchange

20 May 2010, Trat, 8:30 am

It was a three hundred and seventy-five kilometer drive from Mother's house to Hat Lek, Little Beach, in Trat province. We left just after five in the morning, three black Lexus RX350s, each carrying 33 million dollars. Red siren lights and two BMW police cars led the charge. We made the distance in just under three hours.

There were nine of us, excluding the cops, all we could fit in the vehicles. Chai, Tum and me traveled in one, Cheep and his boys in the other two. The rest of our crew was on full alert back in Bangkok, as rumors of a redshirt protest surfaced. When I left, Mother was telling organizers of both red and yellow shirts that if anyone came to her district to cause trouble, they'd be getting a beating. So far no one had shown up. The red shirts might take on the army and the government, but Mother was a whole new level.

Pim and I had shared a muted goodbye, a strange dreamy look still in her eye. It kept surfacing in my mind all the way to Trat. We had pulled over before the town of Trat and removed the sirens from the vehicles. Now we were just a caravan of "Poo Yai" – big shots – on our way for a weekend's gambling at the Koh Kong Casino. Next to the casino was "Safari World", with its crocodile show. We'd supplied the crocs and the training for the show. But all that was on the Cambodian side of the border, where gambling was legal.

Hat Lek is one of the quieter border crossings with Cambodia. A seaside town, more fishing than tourist boats, with most buildings single story and made of wood. The main road split the heart of the town in two, continuing right to the border crossing. A trickle of tourists, bent double with backpacks, made their way to the border crossing. We had taken over a small restaurant about three hundred meters from the border. The restaurant backed onto the sea. I sat at a rear table with Chai and Cheep. The view looked out over the Gulf of Thailand. On the table in front of me, Lilly's phone, signal strong. Silent.

Three cups of bad coffee later, the phone rang.

"So you made it. You don't look as pretty as you used to. Maybe your HiSo girlfriend will find another man."

"Let's skip the bullshit, and get to the point. Where and when?"

"Right now, Koh Kong Bridge."

"That's in Cambodia. We'll never get across with all this cash."

"One vehicle, two people, already cleared. Thai and Cambodian checkpoints. Just drive through." I hadn't expected that. Lisp or Leon had more clout than I'd imagined. "But leave now." He hung up.

I picked up the phone, nodded at Cheep.

"Get everything loaded in one car. You stay here and stay on the comms. If we change route or have an issue, I'll call you. Chai you come with me."

The car was over its maximum payload so Chai was taking it easy. We crawled through the Thai and Cambodian checkpoints, the officers turning the other way as we passed. Koh Kong Bridge was seven and half kilometers from the border. Driving in Cambodia – anywhere, but especially Cambodia – with a hundred million in cash was not a low risk proposition.

Keyed up, talking to Cheep and keeping him informed of our progress, Chai's and my eyes moved left and right to see any threats, keeping the speed low. A couple of taxis overtook us, but apart from that, we were alone. We reached the bridge fifteen minutes later. Chai lifted his Steiner 7 X 50s.

"There's a car parked about three hundred meters up. Three people inside. One's wearing a hood. The others have caps and cartoon masks on."

Lilly's phone rang.

"Looks like the guy in the car is talking on a phone."

Chai answered Lilly's phone and held it to my ear. We guessed they might be watching us, and I was wearing the plaster box I'd had made last night. It fitted up to my shoulders and could be broken apart with a twist of the wrist. Inside was just big enough for two Berettas. It was heavy and itched, but might give us an edge.

"Get out of the car, and I'll get out of mine. We will

start walking with your Uncle Mike. You give me your car keys and the money. I give you my car key and Uncle Mike."

"You take the hood off Uncle Mike." Chai swapped hands with the phone and the binoculars. Watching. There was a delay.

"They're taking the hood off. It's Uncle Mike. He looks okay. They've put the hood on him again now."

"So now you see. You walk. We walk. We pass each other on the bridge. Simple." He hung up.

"We walk across. Swap car keys in the middle."

Chai nodded, did a quick weapons check and climbed out. He walked around and opened the door for me. I climbed down.

"Cheep, can you hear me?"

"Yes, Chance. I can hear you."

"We're making the exchange now. Keep the line open."

We started walking. They started walking. My eyes strained to see Uncle Mike's condition, but he was too far away. We walked, fast, long strides, the plaster box bouncing against my stomach. As we got closer, I was sure it was Uncle Mike. I'd recognize his rolling gait anywhere.

"Yes, it's Uncle Mike for sure. Cheep, they'll be taking the Lexus from the Thai end of Koh Kong Bridge."

"Got it, Chance. Be careful."

When there was a gap of about twenty meters, the taller of the two Mickey Mouses held up a palm and shouted, "Stop." It sounded like a Thai person speaking English. He pointed at me and dangled car keys. He pointed at Chai and held up a palm. Clear enough.

I walked forward, gesturing with the plaster box at

Uncle Mike. The tall guy hung back as the shorter Mickey Mouse brought Uncle Mike towards me. As he passed me, he threw a set of car keys to Chai and then pushed Uncle Mike. He grabbed me, twisting me around to face Chai and sticking a gun in my throat. He snatched the keys, and I felt him toss them to the taller Mickey. He was bending me backwards, dragging me by the throat. I was off balance. I watched Chai pull Uncle Mike behind him. I could hear running and figured the tall one had bolted. As I risked a glance behind me, the gun pushed harder into my throat.

Chai was running and pulling Uncle Mike to the other car. He'd taken Uncle Mike's hood off. I could see his light brown hair. I stumbled against the guy dragging me. He staggered, released his hold on my throat, and grabbed me by the shoulder. He still faced back to Chai, but had turned me to face the Lexus. Tall Mickey reached the Lexus and climbed in. Short Mickey glanced behind and, releasing my shoulder, took out a box with a switch and an antenna. Shit! A bomb, I thought. He held the gun on me and watched Chai and Uncle Mike at the same time, glancing from them to me.

Behind us, tall Mickey got back out of the Lexus and shouted something. It sounded like Cambodian. Short Mickey turned to face him, and I lunged at him. My wrists twisted uselessly as the box held together, trapping my hands, but I kept going. He pressed the switch, and I watched Chai and Uncle Mike blown backwards as the pickup on the bridge exploded. The shockwave and sound reached us almost simultaneously. He sidestepped and smacked me on the side of the head with his gun.

Dropping the device, he grabbed me again, forced me around, gun at the nape of my neck, walking fast. I looked back. Chai and Uncle Mike hadn't moved. I was filled with rage, arms twisting inside the box trying to get the damn thing open.

I heard a cough and a thud behind me. I turned. Short Mickey was lying face down, bullet holes in the back of his denim jacket and a bloody mess at the back of his head. A wave of relief. Chai, kneeling, weapon pointed. I smashed the box on the ground, turning around. Tall Mickey took out a gun and fired. The front window of the Lexus exploded. He looked at the space where it had been and took off running. Berrettas in hand, I went after him.

I went past the Lexus, arms pumping, adrenalin surging. I was gaining on him. In the shadows, I spotted a motorbike fifty meters from me. A rider on a motorbike. Tall Mickey jumped on the back, and the bike accelerated away. I steadied myself. Aimed and fired a group of three. The range was too much for the little .25 gun. They sped off over the hill.

I ran back to the Lexus, a spare set of keys in my pocket. Chai had the other. I jumped in and hit the starter button. I gunned the engine, shoved the gear in "drive" and pushed hard on the accelerator. The Lexus jumped forward, wind in my face from where the window had been shot out.

I pulled up alongside Chai, Uncle Mike smiling. Chai pushed his way into the back with the money, and Uncle Mike jumped into the passenger seat.

"Chance, man. It's good to see you."

"Same here, Uncle Mike, but we got to get going."

I nodded to the Koh Kong end of the bridge, a police car approaching. Chai leaned between the driver and the passenger seat. Before I could say no, he fired, spent cartridges flying past my ear. The police car stopped and started going in reverse.

I threw the Lexus into reverse and looking back, hand holding the wheel steady, drove as fast as I could. The cop car, discouraged by the burst from Chai's Uzi, kept its distance. I flung the wheel hard right spinning us around and slamming the gear into drive at the same time. Thinking fast. There was no way we'd get back across the border in the Lexus, not with a blown out front window, along with what had happened at the bridge.

I drove fast. Uncle Mike put his seatbelt on, giving me a worried look. The overweight SUV slid around corners barely holding the road, but we made good time. Five minutes later, I pulled into the parking lot of the Koh Kong Resort. I ran into the lobby and up to reception.

"Hi. Is Sonny at the resort?" I asked the girl behind the counter. I'd sold Sonny Wong the crocodiles for the show at Safari World. He was the general manager of Safari World. Hong Kong Chinese, born and bred, Sonny wasn't above lining his pockets when the chance arose. The chance had arisen.

"Let me check for you, sir." She gave me a sweet smile, fiddled with some papers on the counter…

I could hear sirens racing past outside on the main highway. They didn't turn in. They would be responding to the call from this end.

The girl spoke in rapid fire Khmer and handed me the phone.

"Sonny, it's Chance. Can you come see me? I'm in the lobby."

"Chance, great to hear from you. Get yourself a drink. I'll be there in a moment. Wow, what a surprise."

I gave the phone back to the girl and went to the entrance, looking out. Everything seemed normal, but we didn't have a lot of time.

Sonny came bouncing down the steps, hand extended, a big smile on his pinched face. I grabbed his hand and pulled him away from the receptionist.

"No time to talk, Sonny. I need your boat, and I need six guys to load it. There's a hundred thousand and a new Lexus in it for you." I watched Sonny's eyes as they darted to and fro, calculating.

"When?"

"Now."

He turned to the girl at reception and told her something in Khmer. She picked up the phone and said something into it.

"Show me the Lexus."

Fifteen minutes later, we were standing on the beach, the Lexus being covered in a tarpaulin by two of the six guys who had helped load the boat. Sonny was smiling, a hundred thousand lining his pockets. If he guessed what had been loaded, he didn't show it and didn't ask.

"Send the boat back safely okay?"

"Sure, don't worry. Just a little trip to Hat Lek and it will be back. Not more than an hour. Don't worry."

I called Cheep and told him what had happened. We climbed on board, and Chai nudged the throttles to full power, pushing the boat boy out of the way and taking the helm. We rounded the long pier to our right, and Chai kept the wheel over and the throttle wide open. I could see the restaurant through Chai's Steiners, Cheep and his boys waiting.

"Wow – what a rush, man. That brought back memories. Phew, man, that was close." Uncle Mike laughed, putting his arm across my shoulder. I hugged him tight. He shouted in my ear. "Thanks, Chance. I never doubted you'd come to get me." He reached over and punched Chai in the shoulder. "You too, man." Chai grinned.

I hugged him tighter.

UNCLE MIKE'S STORY

20 May 2010, Pak Nam, 9:30 pm

We sat in the sala, pergola to you Farang, at the bottom of the garden. The sala was raised a meter off the ground for a view of the river, but surrounded by bushes and trees, giving privacy to the occupants.

Occupying the sala were Joom, Uncle Mike, Cheep and me. Pim was up at the main house. Helping the aunts tidy up after the dinner that Mother had organized to celebrate Uncle Mike's safe return. We were drinking whiskey sodas, and Uncle Mike smoked a joint, Mother disapproving, but reaching over and lighting it for him when he couldn't find his lighter. Uncle Mike loved Mother like a sister, would have loved her as a wife, had she not been Por's woman. I think the feeling was mutual, and over the years, it had developed into something pure and selfless. A deep friendship based on unconditional love.

We sat cross-legged on reed mats laid on the teak floor of the sala. It was hot and humid, but fans with cooling air kept a steady cool breeze wafting our way. "Yaa Gun Yeung", mosquito repellant, their green spiral coils hung from the tops of empty soda bottles, their scent mixing with the scent of jasmine from the bushes nearby. Uncle Mike passed me the joint. Mother frowned. I grinned at her and took another hit.

"I don't want to spoil the mood, Uncle Mike, but if you're cool with it, can you tell me more about what happened?"

I passed the joint to Cheep, but he waved his hand, and I handed it back to Uncle Mike. He took it and lifted it to his lips, sucking the smoke in deep and holding it. He held it and then blew a little towards Joom. She sniffed in, smiled at me, and then waved the smoke away.

"Yeah, it's cool. It was heavy, though. I went out to meet a chick at the airport and, as I came out of the house, I got shot by a dart. The next thing, I woke up in the back of a van wearing the hood. Then they injected me with something, and when I woke up again, I was in the cargo hold of a fishing boat. It was hot as hell in the day, but they fed me water and rice." He reached across and touched Joom's arm. "Dinner was yummy, by the way. Then, I think it was the Saturday or Sunday, I spoke to you. I didn't know that then, but I've worked it out since."

"It was Sunday."

"Yeah, Sunday, and that Farang, he wasn't there long. Just for the call. I heard him leave shortly after. We weren't that far off a beach. I could hear shouts of people playing, and jet skis. Then about two days ago, we started moving again. Then I was brought ashore, and after a short trip in the pick-up, I saw you and Chai."

"So you must have been on the Gulf side the whole time? That whole business with the Hatteras was just a diversion."

Mother started getting up.

"I must go up to the house and see how the girls are getting on. You need to talk with Pim. Don't smoke too much." She gave me a hug – we were among close family – and kissed my forehead. She held the back of my neck and looked in my eyes.

"Job's not done yet. You have to find who did this to us." I nodded. She stroked my hair and kissed Uncle Mike giving him a hug. "So glad you're safe. You will stay with us for a few days, until we can find who did this."

"Yeah, sure, babe. I'd like to see Por if I can."

"We'll see if it can be arranged. But tomorrow you must rest more and follow Dr. Tom's advice."

"Okay, darling. Good night. See you tomorrow." Mother left us alone.

"Did you hear anything else?" I asked Uncle Mike.

"No, not till this morning. Jesus, just this morning. Feels like a lifetime ago now. I heard the guy call someone when we were on the bridge. It sounded like he was getting instructions. I don't speak Khmer, but it sounded like he was saying 'yes' a lot."

"Makes sense. Right up until I heard them shout in Cambodian, I thought at least one of them would be Lisp."

"Lisp?"

"Yeah, my nickname for the guy. He had a lisp."

170

"Yeah, I noticed that. Funny though, he didn't say a word apart from talking to you."

"Wasn't he the one who beat you?"

"No, that was one of the others."

"It's weird. I can't figure it out. Both times when they could have taken the money, they screwed up by trying to take me. Why would anyone do that? Why not just take the money or kill me?"

Uncle Mike let out a long plume of smoke. "That's simple, dude. They wanted you and the money."

"Sure, but why?"

Cheep took our glasses and began the top up. A glass of whiskey is seldom finished. We just drink heavily diluted whiskey until the bottle is empty.

Uncle Mike was very stoned. So was I. He sat up straight and put his hands on knees, breathing in deeply. He held the breath and then released it slowly, until I could see him push his stomach muscles in to squeeze that last bit of air out. Then he lifted the joint to his mouth, the joint held between the second and third fingers of his right hand. The left hand joining the right, thumbs together with a small hole to draw on. He sucked deep, making a sharp whoosh sound with his cupped palms. The joint flared a bright orange that grew in length. He held the smoke for a count of thirty, slowly releasing it in a long, thin stream. It floated among us like a fog on a river.

"I was kidnapped before you and Por were bombed. The bomb attack and the kidnapping are two separate events. The kidnapper has proven, twice, that he doesn't want you dead. You weren't meant to survive the bomb attack."

"I'm not so sure about that. There was CCTV on the floor. I'd just left and was entering the lift when the bomb went off. If anyone has tapped into their CCTV, or just watching it, they would have seen that I'd left. We won't know more until we get the police forensics report."

"Shit, man. That was more than a week ago."

"Forensics is busy with all the shootings and other bombings."

"You know maybe it wasn't about you and Por."

"What do you mean?"

"Maybe it was the chick."

"Por's new girl? 'Ice'?"

"Yeah. Sure. Why not? I've lived here a long time, longer than you have by a stretch. Most of the time someone gets killed or shit happens, it's about a woman. Think about this. What would have happened if the bomb hadn't gone off?"

"Por gave me a hard time for not calling you."

"Yeah, I spoke to him earlier in the week."

"Your house was bugged. I assumed they did it when they kidnapped you, but you told me they took you outside on the road. Why then did they have to kill Lilly?"

"Yeah, fucking sad, man. Just animal behavior. I can't believe she's gone. Thanks for taking care of the funeral, Cheep. I heard it was a good send off."

"No problem, Mike. It was my duty."

Uncle Mike raised his glass. "To Lilly. May we always remember her fighting spirit and her good heart."

We drained our glasses. There are exceptions to every rule in Thailand. Cheep gathered the glasses in and started the process of filling each again: blocks of cubed ice to the top of each glass. Each lump was selected and placed with short metal tongs. Then the whiskey, a hand-poured measure into each glass, stronger now that the night was growing to its full strength. Then the soda, fresh bottles required. The cap of one was used to lever open the cap of its twin. A loud pop, and then each glass filled to the brim. A quick stir with the metal tongs for each glass before it was placed in front of its owner.

Uncle Mike put his hand on my knee.

"I called Por, and we talked. I think it was on the Monday. I mentioned that I hadn't seen you for a while. He said he hadn't seen you for a while either. He told me you were getting serious about Pim. She's a keeper by the way. And that you were spending most of your time with her. But he was cool about it, and so am I. No big deal. Just missed you, that's all. He did say he would talk to you to call me."

"So they knew that Por was going to tell me to call you. I call. You don't answer. I come to Phuket. If the bomb hadn't gone off, same thing would have happened. Por would have sent me to Phuket."

"With the hundred million. Sure, I know. And Por would have stayed here until he knew what was going on, and then he'd make his move. That's his style."

"So whoever kidnapped you expected me to bring the money."

"Right. And look at the first time they tried to grab it. How did they know you were on that road?"

"It's the fastest route between Cheep's resort and Yacht Haven."

"Yeah, but how did they know you were there?"

"My guess is they used the Hatteras as bait and followed us back to Cheep's."

"Actually, Chance, Uncle Mike owns the resort. I just manage it for him." Cheep smiled and raised his glass in toast. He had the "happy look" in his eyes, "da wan" – sweet eyes in Thai. Stoned.

"The reason they wanted you is leverage. If they had you, they could use you to stop Joom or Por retaliating, which means they assume that you'll find out who kidnapped me. Makes sense?"

"Makes sense, but allow me to revisit this when I'm not so stoned. I've got to head back up to the house. Great to have you back, Uncle Mike." We shared a hug, and I left the sala. I checked my shoes for scorpions and slipped them on. I heard another sharp "whoosh" sound and chuckled. Uncle Mike and Cheep would be chatting till the wee hours.

I stumbled up the path, thinking I'd go take a shower before I spoke with Pim. Sober up. As I reached the turn by the pool, I saw her sitting on one of the loungers nearby. Mother was giving her a hug, stroking her hair, and it looked like Pim was crying. I stopped dead still. It seemed they hadn't heard me. Joom took Pim's head in her hands and said something. I couldn't catch it, and I didn't want to eavesdrop. I just didn't want to intrude upon them.

Mother got up and walked into the house. Maybe she had heard. I walked out of the bushes, making enough noise that Pim could hear me. She sat up and quickly wiped her cheeks, sitting with her hands in her lap. I sat on the beach lounger next to her, reached out and took one of her hands, holding it in both of mine.

"What's up? You don't look happy."

She sniffed, wiped a tear, and shook her head. I didn't say anything, just held her hand. A few minutes, sniffs, and tears went by.

"When you came back all beaten up, I was shocked. It made everything real. Then you said you'd killed someone again. I love you, but I don't think I'm strong enough for you. I told you about the kitten. I'm not Joom." She sniffed again and breathed out. "Fuck, I didn't want to cry."

I got down on one knee, holding her hand.

"Pim, will you marry me. Will you do me the honor of becoming my wife, bear my name, and have my children?"

She looked at me straight, studying my face. What she was searching for I cannot say, but it seemed she found an answer. She lunged at me, grasping me around the neck. I teetered, hanging on, off balance, and then we fell into the pool. We came up gasping, coughing, and laughing all at the same time. We stood in the shallow end. Light from the back of the house cast a glow across her face, her wet shirt transparent, the lacy bra underneath an invitation.

I sunk into the water up to my neck. Taking her hand I pulled her into the deep end. The pool was in shadow here and the sala next to the pool was dark. We crept quietly into it.

A Confession in Heaven

Ken had called me three times the previous night. I wondered if his rumor mill extended to Cambodia.

A smoldering Bangkok was returning to normal, if a city made of extremes can be called normal. At least the last pockets of urban war had settled back to being just urban. Tension was high, though, in people's thoughts, about what the future will hold. A sort of national sentiment of, "what's next?"

I was having coffee in the kitchen downstairs. Ba Nui, Joom's maid, cook and boss of the house, had made me the coffee. I told her Joom's story of the case of mistaken identity that led to my funeral. She still was not one hundred per cent convinced that I wasn't a ghost.

"So Por and the Farang who looks like you, Sam, was blown up and Mere Joom didn't call you for four days

176

while you were on holiday in Bali? Is that what you're trying to tell me happened?"

"No, Ba Nui. I told you, in Bali only some places have signal towers, and I was at a dive resort on the far side. Most of the time I was under water."

She gave me a disbelieving look. "Well, even if you're a ghost, you bullshit the same as Chance did. You want your usual breakfast?"

I laughed and nodded. Ba Nui moved off, starting to prepare my breakfast. I like this time of day. Good thinking time.

We were bringing Por back home today. Mother, Beckham, and a few less than half a regiment of Thailand's finest were picking him up at Don Muang and taking him straight to the safe house. The living room of the safe house had been kitted out to Dr. Tom's specs with equipment bought, borrowed, and rented. Cleaned, stocked with food, generators filled with fuel, and all the systems checked. The house had been under guard since yesterday morning when the final medical equipment had been installed. We also kept the money there. I would move in with Pim, Mother, and Uncle Mike. We'd look after Por, and we'd stay until we'd dealt with the situation. Chai and Beckham would, of course, be with us. The aunts were scattering with the daughters: Europe, America, Australia, and Korea. The choice of Korea sparked a pool on who was having what done, mother or daughters. With everyone safe and being on home turf, we could shake the bamboo and see what came out.

It was time to go on the offensive. But first I was going to have breakfast.

Ken lived in a walled compound off Thonglor, in one of the small sois leading to Soi 49, just like a few thousand other Japanese executives. This whole part of Bangkok had been occupied by the Japanese. Every street from Soi 33 to Ekamai has Japanese restaurants and book shops. Entire shopping complexes, rows of shop-houses, shop on the ground floor, storage on the second, living on the third and fourth floors, mostly built by the Chinese, catering to the Japanese.

Ken was out. We had watched him leave a few minutes ago. I nodded to Chai. He spoke into his cell phone. We were parked about a hundred meters from Ken's front gate, in front of a row of shop-houses. Tum drove up and parked right next to Ken's wall, Pichit and Somboon in the back. Tum jumped out, climbed on the back of the pick-up, and helped them lift the package over the wall. Pichit jumped over the wall. A few seconds later, he was pulled back over by Somboon and Tum. They scrambled back into the pick-up and drove off. The whole operation had taken less than two minutes. Message delivered.

Bangkok's traffic was almost back to normal as we got snarled up in it on Petchaburi, heading for the Expressway. The army was still keeping a strong presence on the streets, but things were generally quiet. We passed the Humvees stationed at the top of the on-ramp and headed north.

Jutumas Sangponcharoen, otherwise known as "Ice", had lived with her parents in Nonthaburi, just past the Bangkok Remand Prison. A sign at the front of their soi read "Welcome to Bangkok". Their house was one in a row of town homes, three-story houses built exactly like shop-houses, but with a door instead of a roll-up iron gate.

I pressed the doorbell on the wall outside. I could hear a small dog barking inside, and then the door opened. An older man dressed in a white T-shirt and black trousers came out. I waied him.

"Excuse me, Elder Uncle, but I am looking for the home of Khun Jutumas."

He nodded and bit his lip. "Yes, this was her home. I am her father."

"I am very sorry for your loss. I saw her just before the explosion."

"You did. You were there?"

"I passed her in the hallway, just before."

"Come in, come in. It's too hot to sit outside. Tell your driver to come in, too," he said nodding at Chai, sitting in the car, engine running, with the air-conditioning on.

I nodded to Chai, and the man opened the gate. We walked to his front door, I slipped off my shoes, and we went inside. Chai stayed outside, better to keep an eye on the road.

The furniture was Chinese, black lacquered, inlaid with mother of pearl. He indicated I should sit on the bench seat and sat down next to me. A woman dressed in black, I guessed her mother, brought a glass of water, and set it in front of me.

"My wife, Fern's mother. My name is Sompong," he said, looking at her and softly smiling. He had tears in his eyes, but they stayed there. He reached up and brushed them away with his wrist. Her mother walked back into the house.

"She was our only daughter. Fern's mother was advised against having any more children after she gave birth to

Fern. So I had the snip, you know. She was twenty-four. Just finished university. Good grades, good university. She was happy, doing well. I warned her against going out that day. I knew all that trouble in Bangkok was getting bad."

I took a sip of the water. He wanted to talk about her. I wanted to listen. His pauses were filled with the sound of the fan vibrating in the corner of the room each time it reached the apex of its arc.

"She was a smart girl. Stubborn and willful too. She wanted a car her first year at university. I thought she was too young to be out and about at that age. Bangkok is a big city and a dangerous city for a young girl. But she told me that she could take care of herself, and she could get her own car."

"She lived here with you."

"Most of the time. Sometimes she stayed with friends. Sometimes she said she was going on a trip with her friends. She was grown-up. You can't keep them with you all the time. You have to let them go." A tear swelled and escaped from the corner of his eye.

"Was she seeing anyone special?"

"Oh, there were boyfriends. In her third year, she was away a lot. Exams and studying, she said. But each time she came, she was driving a different car. This friend, that friend, she said. I never said anything, but it made me and her mother sad. We just hoped it was a phase she was going through. But there was no one special, at least, she never mentioned anyone. There was one boy. Came around here one night. He was angry with her about something. Yelling and carrying on in the street about how he loved her. This was just before she went to Korea."

He got up and walked over to a sideboard that ran along one wall and took down a photo. He handed it to me. A smiling "Ice" at her graduation ceremony, flanked by her parents looking stiff and awkward, but proud.

"This was Fern before she went to Korea. She told me she was with a friend. When she came back, she looked different. She'd had her nose and her, you know, her breasts done." He looked embarrassed as he talked about his daughter's boob job. "I asked her where she got the money to do it. It's not cheap, you know. She just said a friend had lent her the money, and she could pay it back whenever she liked. I argued with her. She told me I didn't understand. She was right. I don't." He bit his lips, and the tears rolled freely now. He turned away to hide them and took a tissue out of the box on the table in front of me.

I sipped the water and gave him a moment to compose himself. He sighed and then sat back in the seat.

"How about you, young man? Were you injured in the blast?"

"Only very slightly. I was protected by the elevator. This boy, the one who shouted at her from the street, how old was he?"

"Her age, a little older perhaps. He had one of those modified cars, low suspension and loud sound."

"Do you remember what make it was?"

"Yes. It was a Honda Civic. I have one. Mine's not modified, but the basic shape is the same."

"Did you hear his name?"

"She called him 'Pi Um' I think. But I'm not sure. Like I said, that night they were shouting and screaming at each other."

"Did you see him any time apart from that one night?"

"Only once a couple of weeks before. He parked up the soi. Didn't even have the decency to say hello to us. Do you think he might have had something to do with this? The police told me it was an argument between Poo Yai, big shots, and they were investigating. Of course, I don't hold out any hope they'll catch who did it, but that's what they told me."

"I don't know what happened, but I'm trying to find out. If you remember anything else, can you call me on this number?" I gave him a card with a cell phone number on it. He looked at it for a while. The well of tears had filled again. Finally, he put the card on the table in front of him.

I waied him and stood up. He showed me to the door. I slipped my shoes on, and he walked me to the gate. Chai had turned the car around. I turned, waied him again, and got in the car. As we left, I looked in the rear mirror. His face was in his hands, shoulders heaving.

It didn't sound like Ice had anything to do with the bombing. Just an innocent bystander, wrong place, wrong time. I'd check the jealous boyfriend with the modified Honda Civic, but I reckoned Uncle Mike's hunch was wrong. We went out the back way. There was heavy security around the prison. From the Chaengwattana Expressway, we cut left onto the flyover to Ratchayothin and then onto Ratchada. We did a U-turn just before Huay Kwang, and Chai cut across three lanes of fast-moving traffic to make it into the soi that Heaven was in.

Having narrowly avoided death, we parked in Heaven's car park. Chai put on his shades. I tried to get my heart to slow down. The doorman, who doubled as valet parking, did a double take when he saw us and hurried inside the building. By the time we reached the door, he was back to open it with the manager bent double in a wai.

We walked into the cool marble-floored foyer, the walls decorated with quasi-roman statues of naked women. Here and there, little boy statues peed. The manager now straightened up a little, but still kept his head bent low.

"Khun Oh, please do accept our humble apologies for what happened. We assure you we are doing our utmost to find out who could have done such a cowardly thing. Of course, we would be happy to host you, and your guest, anytime free of charge."

I smiled at him. I gave him the one I'd copied from the crocs.

"Don't worry. I'm not here to kill you. Not today. I would like to talk to you in private. Is there somewhere we can do that?"

The manager was looking from my eyes to Chai's to see if I was joking. Then he processed the second part of what I'd said.

"Oh yes, yes, of course. Please come this way." He took us through a door under the stairs marked "Staff", down a corridor, and through a door that had "Manager" written on it. I guessed it was his office. We sat down. Chai stood by the door.

"Khun Oh, how can we be of assistance?"

"When and how was the suite booked for the meeting?"

"It was booked that morning by his driver, Bank."

"Who knew that we were here? You did. Did you

perhaps tell someone? Let it slip? Tell us truth. It will all come out in the end anyway."

"I swear on my mother's life that I didn't tell anyone. You can take me to any temple and ask me to die on the spot if I lie to the Buddha. I swear I told no one about the meeting."

"Okay, I believe you, but was there anyone else who could have known about the meeting?"

Wringing his hands, staring at the table in front of him, he licked his lips and looked at me, then looked at the table again.

"Who? Don't fuck around. I'm not in the mood."

He jumped, weighed options and made the right choice. "The owner."

"The owner knew that Por and I were having a meeting. Why should he know?"

"Because he wanted the room for himself, and I had to explain why he couldn't have it."

Chatree, the owner, was a minor mafia boss with a small crew. He made a lot of money smuggling oil and put it into property on Ratchada. Not a major player but I'd met him at a few functions. The manager was looking increasingly nervous. He was sweating, but it was cool.

"The owner's here, now?"

His eyes darted to the door, hit Chai, widened in fear, and came back to me. I used the crocodile smile again. His eyes widened further. He nodded, vigorously.

"Where?"

"Suite 501 on the fifth floor, first door on the left out of the elevators. We've closed the sixth and seventh since the bomb."

"Show us."

The manager used his key card to unlock the door and then scuttled away. I opened the door and stepped in. Khun Chatree was in the tub. Judging by the angle of the girl, he was getting a blow job. I walked quietly over to the edge of the tub and sat down. His eyes opened, and he started. The girl giving the blow job sat up. Her dick was bigger than his, and she didn't have a hard on.

"What the fuck? Who the fuck do you think you are? Get the fuck out of here."

"Khun Chatree. I only have one question for you, and I need an honest answer – now. So either you get smart and answer me politely and honestly, or I'm going to tell Chai to stick his Uzi up your ass and pull the trigger. Do you understand?" Chai was at the other end of the tub, screwing the fat tube of the Uzi's silencer on.

Chatree nodded.

"Did you tell anyone that I was meeting Por here that day?"

He nodded, his eyes on Chai's Uzi.

"Good. Thank you. One more question. Who did you tell?"

"Sor Sor Sankit, you know, Police Colonel Sankit."

I did know. I knew very well. He was Pim's father.

ANIMAL PLANET

21 May 2010, Bangkok, 1:30 pm

It seemed Uncle Mike's hunch was right. It was about a woman. I'd just figured on the wrong woman. I told Chai to drive around for a while. I needed to think.

Pim's family had been opposed to me since we first started seeing each other. After a couple of visits enduring frosty silences and baited words, we gave up on cozy family get-togethers. When Pim told her parents she was moving in with me, her father had threatened to cut her off. He hadn't done it, but he'd threatened to. I still couldn't figure out how he'd got the bomb in there at such short notice. Nothing showed on the CCTV, and Chatree wasn't stupid enough to agree to kill Por in his own place, never mind lie about it.

I tried to think back to the week before the bombing, trying to remember Pim's movements that week, if she'd visited her parents or not. She usually saw them at least once a week, but I couldn't remember anything special about that week. I couldn't ask either. Not right now. She'd pick up on it in an instant. I wondered if he was behind the Cambodians as well. Missed with the bomb so sent in the backup.

Chai pulled into a gas station, stopping at the restrooms. He jumped out and disappeared. I got out of the car, a break from the air-conditioning, and walked over to the smoking area. Yes, we have smoking areas in our gas stations – stops people smoking at the pumps while their cars are being filled.

Last night, after we'd made love in the sala, we'd talked more. Pim was excited, eyes large, shining. We'd agreed to break the news tonight at dinner. I looked at the cell phone. In another four hours. We'd also agreed to wait for Por's health to improve before having the engagement party. The way Thai weddings work, at our level, is that once the happy couple have decided to tie the knot, they turn the whole process over to the respective families. The groom's parents visit the bride's parents and "Sing Sodt", the dowry payment, is negotiated – almost always settled between the mothers. One loses a daughter, one gains a daughter. A down payment, usually in gold, is made once suitable compensation has been agreed upon, and the engagement party is arranged. After that Monks are consulted for an auspicious wedding date. Although the males make all the speeches, the reality is, weddings are women's business.

Thinking about it, the bombing was a pretty smart move by Colonel Sankit. It was win-win. If he succeeded, problem solved. If he didn't, he could claim, and he'd be right, that living with me was dangerous. Chai came out of the restrooms, looked around, saw me, walked over and sat beside me on the bench.

"We keep this to ourselves, okay? For now, anyway."

He nodded, staring at the forecourt of the gas station, gas fumes and shimmering heat distorting the view. It was a hot day and humid. Good. Ken's house had a pool. It was his habit to take a swim when he got home. Usually he got home late, between eleven at night and one in the morning. If he missed his night swim, he never missed a morning swim.

"I can take care of it, quietly. An accident."

"No. At least not yet. He might be behind the Cambodians. I want to know if he is, then we'll decide."

Chai looked at the space between his boots.

"What?" I asked him.

He glanced at me out of the corner of his eye, head twisted sideways. It looked like he was going to say something, but he shook his head, got up, and went back to the car. I followed him. A young guy sitting in a new "red plate" white BMW, parked behind our car, beeped his horn. Chai got out.

"Forget it. Let's go," I said.

Then the young guy leaned out of his window and shouted, "Get a fucking move on, Uncle," and beeped his horn again. The girl sitting next to him giggled. Chai, who had been about to get back into the car, looked across at me. I shrugged.

Chai moved. The young guy panicked, closing his window fast. Chai whipped out his K-Bar and smashed the driver's window with the butt end of the knife. The laughing girl screamed. I glanced around at the pump attendants. They all looked away. Chai reached in. The guy climbed up his seat like there was somewhere to go. The hood popped open, and Chai walked around, reaching under, releasing it. He grabbed the top with both hands and kept pushing, climbing onto the grill, bending the hood over the front windscreen of the car. When the hood touched the roof, he jumped off. He squatted down until he was looking directly in the young guy's face.

"With mindfulness, a person always prospers." Chai, spreading the Buddhist word, a walking contradiction in a city of extremes balanced on the edge of chaos.

I tapped a spoon against my wine glass and stood up, clearing my throat.

"I have an announcement to make."

They were all there. All the family, except Por. Uncle Mike was filling in for him at the head of the table. I sat at his right hand, Mother opposite and Pim next to me. Further down, the aunts were arranged in order of seniority, then the daughters, those with husbands first, until my youngest sister-in-law at the far end of the table. At another table, set a short distance away, were Beckham, Chai, Tum and a few of the most trusted boys, their eyes now all focused on me.

I looked at Pim sitting by my side, dressed in a simple white shirt, one of mine, and jeans. I held my hand out, and she took it.

"I have asked Pim to be my wife, and I'm happy to say, she said yes."

There was a burst of applause. Uncle Mike stood up and gave me a hug, Mother doing the same with Pim, and by then, the aunts had crowded around us.

Mother gave me a hug, whispering in my ear, "Has Pim told her parents yet?"

I shook my head.

"Have you fixed a date yet? If not, I'll ask Por Luang Soong for you. He's the best. Every marriage date he's fixed, the couples live happily," Aunt Su said to Pim.

"What about the doctor that brained his wife with the golf club?" asked Aunt Ning.

"He didn't do that one. They ignored his advice and went to another monk chosen by the doctor."

"Are you pregnant?" Aunt Malee said in a voice that was meant to be a whisper but was heard in the far-thest corner of the room.

"No, but we're trying every chance we get." Pim smiled sweetly, her answer bringing a smile to Mother's lips and a faux scandalized gasp from the daughters. If there was a virgin among them, I'd walk across Pit 51 naked and covered in buffalo blood.

Behind the smiles, and they were genuine, I saw the calculators go off. There had just been a tectonic shift in the plates on which the family's foundation rested. No matter that they all loved me, and I knew they did, they were all jealous of Mother. In varying degrees of course, and as time had passed, and they realized Por would never leave Joom for any or all of them, the jealousy had waned. I was the son they never had, but I was not their son. I was Joom's. Yesterday, the sons of their daughters still had a shot at the title. Today they were "could've been". It's the way we are.

Later, the men at one table, the women at the other, and the youngest of the daughters sent to bed, Chai leaned across to me.

"Now I have two lives to protect." His way of saying Pim was okay by him.

I squeezed his breeze block of a shoulder. "Thanks Chai, that means a lot to me."

We touched glasses and emptied them. A phone rang. It was Ken. I looked at the time, 10:45 pm. I left the table and went to the patio doors. Sliding them open, I slipped outside. It was quiet, warm, and a mosquito buzzed my ear. I answered the phone.

"Yes, Ken."

"Ah, Chance, I've been trying to get ahold of you. You haven't been answering my calls. Is everything okay?"

"Sure, Ken. Why? What's up?"

He sounded like he was in a car. So he hadn't got home yet.

"Oh, nothing. Just wondering if everything is okay on your side. Got to keep an eye on my investments."

"Sure. All good. How about you? You sound like you're out and about."

"Yes, I'm heading home. Been a long day."

"Anyway, Ken, if there's nothing urgent, I've got some stuff I have to deal with."

"Stay in touch, Chance."

"I will Ken. You'll be hearing from me soon, I promise."
I hung up. Let him think about that while he's taking a

swim. I went back inside and sat down at the table with the boys.

"I have another announcement to make," I said, cutting through the talk of football, politics, and loose women. The buzzed eyes turned to look at me.

"The show is on. Now. Mother's entertainment room." There was a cheer and a mad scramble for the best seats in Mother's mini-theater entertainment room. They left the center sofa for me. Pichit and Somboon brought the whiskey, ice, and soda with them. Chai worked the laptop, the screen flickered blue once, then filled with an image of a garden and a pool. Ken's garden and pool. We'd set up a camera on the rear wall hidden by a tree. Chai had zoom control from the laptop. Tum jumped up and turned the lights down.

Headlights showed, visible through the glass walls of the entrance of the house. Ken had arrived home.

Chai zoomed in. The door opened and someone came into the house, male, wearing a suit. Lights turned on in the house, illuminating the area by the pool.

Crocodylus porosus – salt water crocodile to you, Farang, are ambush predators. They are opportunistic feeders but prefer to hunt at night, near water. Of all the crocodile species, they are the most aggressive, prone to charge, especially the females, and especially during the egg laying season, October to May.

"Ten thousand even odds he gets killed in the pool."

"I'll take a piece of that."

"Two-to-one, five thousand, he loses an arm but escapes."

"Five to one, he gets out without a scratch."

I turned in my seat. "Who offered the 5-1?"

Beckham ducked his head at Tum.

"I'll take it. Ten thousand."

"Shush, he's coming out…"

We turned to watch. Ken, wearing a white bathrobe, had opened the sliding door to the patio. We still couldn't see the croc, then Ken reached up, turned on the pool and the garden lights.

"There, there," someone whispered. It was in darkness at the end of the garden, its eyes glowing red. The croc would be pissed off. This morning it was looking after a clutch on a sandy bank in Samut Prakarn. It had been lassoed, manhandled, blindfolded, and thrown in the back of a pickup, then dropped over a wall separated from its eggs. Maybe pissed off was an understatement.

Ken took out a pack of cigarettes, tapping one out. He tapped the cigarette against the pack, tamping it down. Then he stuck in the corner of his mouth and lit it. He took a long hit, put the pack and lighter on the table. He exhaled. We could see the cloud of smoke drift lazily across the pool.

One of the boys behind me giggled. That set everyone off.

"Shush, shush…" from Chai, a rare smile on his face.

Ken was taking off the bathrobe. His arms tanned, his body pale. Yak tats covered his body except his arms. White Speedos, I cringed. He took another drag of the cigarette and snubbed it out in the ashtray on the table.

"Oh, fuck me. He's going to use the diving board." I don't know who said it, thought it might be Pichit, but he was right. Ken walked around the pool to the side closest to the house. He climbed the diving board steps and stopped. The room went quiet, everyone held their breath.

Then Ken started swinging his arms around, and the room breathed out. The croc hadn't moved. Ken stopped swinging his arms and bounced a little on the board. The croc moved forward about a meter and stopped. A loud cheer erupted. A flurry of bets made. Crocodiles have excellent hearing and eyesight. A particular strength is the ability to judge distance exactly, aiding in the ambush attack. On land, for short bursts of speed, they can outrun a human. In water, it's no contest.

Ken stopped bouncing and took two steps forward, diving into the pool. The sound of a splash in water is a sound hardwired into a croc's reptilian brain. From the sound, they determine speed, weight, velocity, and make a decision whether or not the splash is prey. Ninety-nine percent of the time it is. Tonight was no exception. The croc moved forward to the edge of the light in the garden, about four meters from the edge of the pool. Ken swam freestyle, smooth, long, steady strokes. He touched the end and turned back to the house. If he kept to his usual routine, he'd do this another nineteen and a half times: twenty lengths of the pool.

Crocs are patient hunters. They'll wait, often missing opportunities, until they're sure of their kill. Our croc watched no less intently than us as Ken swam to the far end of the pool and turned. The audio wasn't that good, just a small directional mike, but we could hear the splashes he made as he swam. Ken reached the turn, the room held its collective breath, and the croc didn't move.

"He'll strike now, for his legs. I've seen them do it that way." It was Beckham, his gravelly voice an echo of Ken's. At that moment, Ken's bodyguard, the guy from his club, with him at the warehouse, came out of the door near the diving board. He was holding a phone, saying something in Japanese. Ken stopped at the end of the diving board, taking the phone from the guy kneeling down handing it to him. The croc covered the four meters to the pool in the blink of an eye and slipped in with hardly a ripple.

And there was a knock on the door. We froze. The door opened, and Pim stuck her head around.

I jumped up from the sofa seat to block her from coming in. Chai had the presence of mind to freeze the screen.

"Hey, what's up?" she asked, smiling.

"Oh, just watching a show with the boys."

"What are you watching?"

"Ah, Animal Planet, Bad Animal Attacks. The guys love it. They're sick, always rooting for the animal."

"Ah, okay, look I'm going up." She leaned forward and whispered in my ear, "Mother said we could share the guest room." Kissed me on the lips, gave me a naughty look filled with promise, and a little wave. I closed the door and locked it.

Chai unfroze the screen just as the croc struck. The croc uses its all-muscle tail to propel itself, up to its full body length, out of water when it strikes. Ken's bodyguard reeled back in shock as the croc took Ken at chest height. The pressure of the crocodile's bite is more than five thousand pounds per square inch. If this bite, the strongest on the planet, doesn't kill, the prey usually drowns as the croc takes its victim into a death roll. The death roll serves two purposes; the first is to drown the victim; the second, to tear off whatever they've bitten.

Ken's bodyguard made a big mistake. He pulled out his gun and leaned over the edge of the diving board to take a look. Brave but stupid. The croc launched itself and got his arm. He tried to hold onto the diving board. The twenty-year-old croc weighed three hundred kilos. The pool changed color. The thrashing stopped. The waves in the pool smoothed.

How Much For Your Daughter

22 May 2010, Pak Nam, 3:30 pm

There were still eight days left before the escrow account would be triggered. They'd check the account for a deposit from Samuel Harper and when there wasn't one, they'd move to transfer the assets. There was only one problem, well a hundred million of them actually. The documents that Ken had carefully inspected were copies of the real documents. Mother's signature was false, and Sam Harper, the witness to her signature, was dead, complete with Death Certificate, issued three days before he'd signed the documents.

This alone wouldn't prevent a war with the Yakuza. We were hoping that could be avoided by the email we'd sent them with the tapes of Ken stealing their money attached. Along with the link to YouTube where Chai posted an edited version of the video, "Crocodile Pool

Attack", complete with Animal Planet logo.

Our gamble was that they had no idea Ken was operating his "lend and steal" scam in Thailand. It was a risk but a calculated one. And the reason Ken had to go in such a way.

It was Por who first came up with the idea of using crocs to scare the bejesus out of enemies, and occasionally allies, who needed firming up. He got the idea after watching the first Godfather movie, the famous scene with the horse head. Uncle Mike could act Por very well. Had him down pat, the time when Por told him of the idea, being a favorite scene.

Uncle Mike would adopt Por's calm, emotionless face. Crossing his arms and stroking his chin, like Por did when he was thinking about buying a piece of land or a car, he'd drop his voice, mimicking Por's English.

"Mike, you know, I've been thinking. You know, Mike, a horse's head is nothing. Send it down to the cook, prepare it for lunch. But imagine waking up to a live crocodile. We'd have to sedate it, just enough to knock it out while we get it in the bed. We could experiment on weights and measures…" He'd go on for hours, everyone, including Por, in stitches. Thinking about it made me think of Por. I missed him. Missed his weight around the place. Our anchor.

"What are you thinking about?" Pim asked, putting her hand on mine. We were in the backseat of Mother's Benz, on the way to Pim's parents' house in Phuttamonton, west of Bangkok.

"I was just thinking about Por. How I miss him. Wish he was here."

Mother turned around in the front seat, Beckham driving, trying to keep up with Chai in the vanguard.

"I've arranged for Por to come home on Sunday. Thomas says he is stable enough to travel, and it will be better for him to be here with us. His vital signs are strong, and he moved his fingers last night. Thomas said it was exactly at the time that you announced you were getting married." And of course Thomas would never make such a thing up.

"That's great news. He'll stay with us at the house?"

"Yes. Tomorrow morning Thomas is coming with all the equipment and staff for twenty-four-hour shift work. I've turned the guest house over to him. They're doing some work today, backup electrics that sort of thing."

"I'll go with you to pick him up."

"No, I think you should stay out of Cambodia for a little while. I've arranged military transport either side. It'll be fine, and Moo will be with me." Moo was her name for Beckham. Ham is moo as pig is moo in Thai. When Beckham told her he was changing his name from Opart to Beckham, Mother was talking on the phone. All she heard was "Ham", and Opart became Moo.

It occurred to me that these little jaunts down memory lane might be my life slowly flashing before my eyes as I proceeded to an untimely death. I doubted Colonel Sankit would kill me, not with Mother there, but when Mother told him I was going to be marrying his only daughter, who knew.

We pulled up outside their gate. The house set well back from the road surrounded by a high wall. Chai pressed the buzzer by the gate, and the gate immediately opened. We drove in and parked on the white gravel.

Pim's mother and father came out of the house. They'd been told we were on the way. Though no one had said why, you didn't have to be a rocket scientist to figure it out. Neither of them looked happy. Pim squeezed my hand and got out. Beckham raced around and got Mother's door.

Pim introduced Joom, formally, to her mother and father. Of course they had previously met, and knew exactly who she was, but we have a way of doing things, form, and function.

Pim's mother, Khun Suchada, led the way, Col. Sankit stepping aside. As I reached the steps, he held his hand out towards the house, indicating I should go in before him. I smiled politely.

"No, Khun Por. Please, after you." My wai kept in place as I said this. As son-in-laws, we call our wife's father, Father. Khun Por was more formal as befitting a prospective son-in-law. It caught at the back of my throat. I followed him into the house, clearing my head. It's just plain wrong to be thinking about shooting your father-in-law in the back on your engagement day.

We filed into their living room. De rigueur standard issue hiso Louis XIV chair and sofa set was parked in front of an enormous oil painting portrait of the happy couple; he in full police uniform; she in traditional Thai costume. I thought the artist had captured the naked ambition on her face very well. Small talk ensued while the maid brought water, and everyone agreed tea would be lovely.

One of Mother's special talents, and she has many, is her ability to charm people. Whatever the social station, be it construction worker or Khunying, Mother's ability to push the right buttons never ceases to amaze me. Of course her spy network, from which the CIA, Mossad, and MI6 could all take lessons, is second to none, feeding her with all the facts, but outlining and coloring in with juicy gossip and tidbits of information gleaned here and there. Mostly out of the mouths of maids and hairdressers. Ask Mother a question and you'll have an answer within twenty-four hours, at the latest.

Khun Suchada was the driving force behind Colonel Sankit's career, one foot always lifted for the next rung up the social ladder. She'd driven Sankit from police inspector to police colonel, and then to member of parliament. Her next ambition was a ministry, preferably something to do with highways and roads. Having a son-in-law known to be associated with a mafia gang was a definite obstacle on the path to the dizzy heights she dreamed of. She also knew that Mother was not a person to be treated lightly. Khun Suchada, no doubt, would also have her spy network. I doubted it was as sophisticated as Mother's, but it wouldn't be trivial. No self-respecting hiso Thai women's spy network is trivial.

Mother, bringing the full force of the information armada to bear on the right flank, turned, smiled sweetly at Colonel Sankit, and fired the first broadside.

"Colonel, these must be tough times for an MP from one of the smaller political parties."

The colonel, who'd obviously seen these types of early skirmishes before, smiled and drank his water.

Khun Suchada swiveled her fleet to match the thrust of the attack, hackles visible, a sweet demure smile.

"Oh, Mere Joom, you know how it is, when big dogs fight, the pork is kicked into the small dog's mouth..."

Tea arrived. Pim rolled her eyes at me. Mother put her handbag on the seat beside her and reached across for the tea offered by Khun Suchada. Mother gave her a sweet smile and gently placed the cup of tea on the table in front of her.

"Yes, you're right, but when the big dogs stop fighting, and the pork is eaten, the big dogs look at the little dog and think about lunch. But a small dog today might acquire a big dog's bite. When the winds of change blow, there is always the opportunity to grow. Change is coming. Soon there will be elections. With the election will come opportunity..."

I wasn't sure how the not-so honorable Colonel Sankit felt about being obliquely referred to as a little dog, but it was his wife who had started the analogy rolling.

Khun Suchada's arguments as to why the son of a gangster would not be marrying her daughter had come unmoored and were adrift on the shores of her ambition. Thrashed and tickled by Mother with just a few words, her eyes had a shining quality. She knew Mother's word was good, and sensed that this was a watershed moment.

She cast a stone into the forest, to hear the sound of where it may have fallen.

"A ministry..."

"A ministry... one of the minor one's at first, of course. I think the Ministry of Happiness and Wellbe-ing..."

"There is such a ministry..."

"Not yet, but who's to say. When cabinets and prime ministers are chosen and there are more ministers than there are ministries. Who's to say that a few more essential ministries might not be created? What could be more essential than happiness and wellbeing?"

"Yes, I see. I think. What do you think such a ministry would be responsible for administering?"

"I would imagine its responsibilities would lie somewhere between the Ministry of Tourism and Sport, The Ministry of Culture, and the Ministry of Human Development and Security. A little bit from each, would be my guess."

"And when do you think such a thing might happen?"

"I can't see elections before next year. This current mess is going to take a bit of clearing up."

"Early next year, perhaps…"

"Early next year, for sure."

"I see. And to what do we owe the pleasure of this visit and your excellent advice."

"As you know, dear Khun Suchada, Colonel Sankit, my son, Chance, has fallen in love with your beautiful daughter, and today we have come to ask your blessing and permission for them to marry."

Khun Suchada, to her credit, managed to act surprised. Sankit maintained the same toad-like expression he'd held since we walked through their front door. Any moment I expected his tongue to lash out and latch upon a fly.

"Dear Chance. Oh, what a lovely surprise. Pim, my only daughter. Such a match, surely a match made in heaven. We must have a large wedding, in Bangkok, over a thousand guests I would think. It will be expensive, but I am sure the colonel will be happy to sponsor the event. And what should we say the amount of Sing Sodt was?"

Mother turned to me.

"Chance, why don't you take Pim for a walk in the garden. I have much to talk over with Khun Suchada and I am sure you will be bored."

I gave Mother a smile. Pim and I retreated. I gave the colonel a smile.

In the Sing Sodt calculation, everything would be weighed, haggled over, and adjusted to fit a number satisfactory for all. The amount leaked to the press would give no indication of the "finer details" of the deal. The press would simply report on how many million. Even the amount leaked to the press might be false, inflated, or deflated depending on the circumstances. Mother was right to ask us to leave. It was the usual practice, when mothers get down to the nitty-gritty detail.

We went and sat outside in the sala by their fish pond. On the pond, a dragonfly played with the surface tension of the water. I watched it fly, settle and fly again. A flat slab of rock made me think of the colonel sitting there, of a night, zapping dragonflies as they skated on the surface.

"What are you thinking about? You've seemed pre-occupied today, staring off into the distance. Is everything okay?"

A picture of Ken's dragon tattoo, sliced in two by the croc, flashed across my mind.

"Yeah, sorry. Just been … yeah, big day. I guess I'm just nervous with how that's going in there."

Pim made a sound somewhere between snorting and laughing.

"What?"

"Joom has got my mother licking the hairs on her

shin." I grinned. Pim continued, "She's so hot for father to be this or be that, it's got nothing to do with him. And it's not money. They have enough from when he was a cop. It's her. She wants to be called, wife of colonel, wife of MP and now, wife of minister. It's pathetic. I don't understand her at all."

"Pim, I've got to tell you something." She turned at looked at me. I was going to tell her. I was. But it was just too heavy. Whatever happened between Joom and her mother, this was her official engagement day. I wasn't going to ruin it by telling her, her father had tried to kill me a few days ago.

"I don't care what happens up there. You're going to be my wife. That's it. All the rest of this, it's for others, not for us."

She smiled, her arms snaking around my neck, her lips close. My luck astounds me at times.

MEN IN BLACK

The deal was done. Mother called us back inside, telling us that Pim's parents had granted their permission. Wais to the parents; we called them Por and Mere now. For one moment, when I was waiing Colonel Sankit, he had raised his hand as if to give me a paternal pat on the head. He saw something in my face that stayed his hand, hovering in mid-air. He had turned it into a little wave, saving face. Irrespective of him trying to blow me up, he hadn't given me the time of day until Mother had shown up with a ministry in tow.

When we got back in the car, once clear of Sankit's house, Mother twisted round in the front seat to talk to Pim.

"Your mother drives a hard bargain." Mother paused, grinned, and added, "But I'd have paid ten times more."

Pim smiled, but the tension of the day and Mother's words put a tremble in her lips, and a tear rolled down her cheek. She leaned forward, hugged Mother, and said, "I'm so happy."

"Welcome to the family, my daughter."

The sun hung low in the rearview mirror as we came down Sathorn Bridge. I called Chai driving a Porsche Cayenne, in front of us.

"Pull over at the Shell gas station." I hung up the phone.

"Beckham, pull over at the Shell station near Rama 4." He nodded. I turned to Pim.

"I've got some stuff I have to do. I'll be back late. Don't wait up."

Mother and I got out at the station, standing by the car.

"Have you got anything yet from the forensics on the bomb?"

"Other than it was about half a kilo of Semtex, with a mobile timer, and went off somewhere around the door to the master bedroom, no."

"That's great, when did you get that?"

"While I was talking with Khun Suchada." She held up her cell phone. "Don't worry about Pim. I'll look after her. You go and take care of business."

I nodded, gave her wai, and headed over to join Chai. We had to move fast. We had a few places to go and the nine pm curfew in Bangkok was still in force.

First stop was an apartment off Suthisan in the Ratchada area. It had taken all of a day to track down Pi Um, Ice's angry boyfriend. I was pretty sure, dead certain, that Pim's father was behind the bombing, but loose ends aren't ends at all. Chai took the expressway off Rama 4. Traffic was much lighter than normal, and in five minutes, we were at the Suthisan intersection.

Waiting for the light to change, I looked across the intersection, noticing a white, low slung, modified, Honda Civic. The driver looked a lot like the photo downloaded from Ice's Facebook page. I touched Chai's sleeve and pointed at it. The Honda pulled away from the intersection heading back up Vibhavadee Rangsit Road. Chai drove through the red light, straight at the oncoming traffic, and just before I thought we were going to crash into a bus, he pulled a hard right and got us onto Vibhavadee Road about five cars behind the Civic.

"Nice driving."

"Thanks."

"Could you warn me when you're going to do that? You never warn me. You just do it."

"Think. Act. Analyze." Chai said. A hangover from a stint of training he did with a US SEAL team. I'd heard it before, often.

The Civic stayed on Vibhavadee until Din Daeng, took a left, and headed up Rama 9. Chai stayed a few cars back all the time. Dropping down from Rama 9, underneath the expressway, we got close, just two cars behind at a red light. With the height difference between the Cayenne and the Civic, he couldn't see us. Chai snapped off a couple of pictures of his car and plate. The Civic turned into RCA, Royal City Avenue to you Farang, the nightspot for young Thais. Not many Farang here, for the simple reason that there are not that many young Farang in Thailand. And

RCA, apart from the owners who run the place, is a young people's place. But there are also motorbike shops, cafés and restaurants, and right now, with the curfew, these were open and the clubs were shut.

It was early, way too early for there to be anything other than staff. With the curfew in place, business here was dead, and car parking slots on either side of the road, usually impossible to find, were empty. The Civic pulled up opposite a little restaurant with tables outside. We drove past, nowhere to stop without being noticed. "Nong" Um – we'd only call him Pi if he was older than us, which he wasn't, being in his mid-twenties – got out of the Civic and headed across the road to the restaurant.

Chai parked behind a delivery truck about a hundred meters further up the road. We used a dark alley across from our parking slot to observe. I had the Steiners, Chai the camera. The guy Um was meeting with looked heavy. He wasn't young, mid-forties, maybe early fifties. Pockmarked, thin face, high cheekbones. Dark colored skin. Black jeans, white T-shirt, black denim jacket, big amulet, black bandana around his head. Mafia or wannabe? Something about this guy told me mafia for sure. He wouldn't dare look like him if he weren't bad.

The pair of them got up and went back to the Civic. We hotfooted it back to the Cayenne. I was hoping he would go back the way he'd come. He didn't. We waited till he got to the parking toll booth on the Petchburi Road side. Once he was through the toll, Chai threw the car into reverse and headed after him. We hadn't been there long enough to pay for parking, but the attendant was slow checking the time. We lost valuable seconds. Chai stamped on the gas and turned onto Petchaburi Road at speed, the road practically empty, with no Honda Civic in sight. Shit. Up ahead I saw a flash of white. I glanced at Chai. He nodded. He'd seen it.

Chai got us five cars behind the Civic, now on Pattanakarn and driving quickly. A glance at the speedometer showed we were at one hundred and twenty. Ordinarily that would be impossible in Bangkok's traffic, but traffic was light. At the intersection with Srinakarin, he turned left, and shortly after, got up on the Bangkok Chonburi Motorway. The only road in Thailand where driving at one hundred and twenty kph for four wheel vehicles is permitted. Naturally that means we all drive at one hundred and forty.

Chai eased up on the throttle, and we dropped back a few cars. Usually when we were tailing someone, we'd use six or seven cars, swapping them in and out. There'd been no time to set it up. Also, normally, we'd have just grabbed Nong Um, and had a chat until he told the truth. I had a strong feeling that the guy with Um wouldn't be so easy to grab. It wouldn't be easy to get him to talk either.

Before the motorway rest area, past a strip of shops selling a mix of beach stuff, food and coffee, he turned off to Chacheongsao. The light had faded to black now, street lamps and headlights lighting the way. Traffic here was heavier than Bangkok. Trucks, motorbikes and cars all hurried along on the dual carriageway. I looked at the phone, 7:30 pm. The Civic kept going, stopping at the occasional red light, but otherwise keeping to a steady one hundred, one hundred and twenty. We'd invested this much. We stayed with him.

We continued up the 304 until, about forty kilometers in, he turned off onto the inner road. This is a two-way traffic road that runs alongside the highway, supporting local traffic. We turned, and then he took a left, driving down a dirt road. A garage for trucks and a shed for keeping rice marked the entrance to the road. We turned off our lights and followed. Rice paddy either side, the road planted both sides with mature eucalyptus. I wound down the window to see better, the tinted windows not doing us any favors in the dark. We were crawling along.

After about a kilometer, a small road forked right and stopped at a farmhouse in the middle of about twenty rai – one rai is half an acre – of rice paddy. The Civic was parked outside beside a pick-up. Chai drove on straight for about fifty meters and parked behind a thick clump of eucalyptus trees. We climbed out. I was stiff from the journey. We went around to the back of the Cayenne, Chai unzipping his backpack and taking out a pair of black coveralls, one for each of us, a pair each of German-made paratrooper boots and camouflage paint. A flashback to when we were eight, making a raid on the mango trees of Joom's next door neighbor. Three minutes later, we were shadow.

All Thai farms, and a good proportion of homes, have a dog. Most have at least two. Chai always carried a tranquilizer gun from the farm. He'd experimented, using the stuff we shot the crocs with, on the boys. Chai liked dogs, and dogs liked Chai. He didn't like killing them. Never had. He squirted some of the juice out of the dart, squinting to make sure he got the measure right, and then we set off.

On the edge of the eucalyptus trees, we were in darkness. A dog barked. We froze, waiting. The dog's barking grew, and soon, we heard its feet running on the hard-packed dry red earth. When it reached us, it did what ninety-nine percent of Thai dogs will do. Stop and bark. It got out two barks before Chai shot it. The dog managed another half a bark and a whimper, then keeled over. Chai retrieved the dart, and we waited.

The house seemed quiet, nothing moving on the outside. The moon hadn't yet risen, and the rice provided good cover. We ran, crouched low, to a chicken coop about ten meters from the back of the house. At the back appeared to be a kitchen enclosed in metal bars. Chai, crouching low, scuttled over to the wall of the house, on the corner. He signaled for me to follow. I crept across, hearing my boots on the hard ground. We inched along the wall, keeping low. At a closed window, light poured out. Chai peeked up and ducked down, nodding to me. I took a peek.

Nong Um was sitting at a table, hands in lap, head looking down. The guy who he'd picked up was standing against the wall to my left. The guy standing over Um, with his finger in his face was new. Two other guys sat on the floor cross-legged, playing cards.

The guy standing over Um was pissed off.

"You fucked up. You were paid to do a job, and you fucked up. Because of you, we couldn't do what we needed to do. You made us look like fucking idiots. What did you say?" I couldn't hear what Nong Um said, but it earned him a slap around the head. The guy moved around the table. I ducked. Waited. Then the sound of more talking.

I eased my head up until I could see into the room again. The guy who'd been doing the talking had his back to me, everyone else was in the same position. He was talking, nearer the window; even though he was facing away from me, I could still hear him clearly.

"I don't give a fuck who got killed. It's a war. Us against them, and you're a soldier. People get killed in wars. Soldiers get killed when they don't follow orders…"

Chai tugged on my sleeve and pointed. Back on the road, another vehicle had stopped at the turn off to the farm. Inside the room, I heard the ringtone of a cell phone. Shit. We speed-walked, crouching, back to the chicken coop. Keeping the coop between us and the house, we ran, crouching, along a low earthen dyke separating the paddy fields. About fifty meters from the farm, we dropped into the rice paddy behind the dyke and looked back at the house. Nothing had changed. Then I heard the sound of the Honda Civic's modified engine start up. The Civic and the pick-up took off up the dirt road, men standing in the back of the pick-up, one hand holding onto the truck, the other holding what looked like AK-47s.

The car on the road drove up, passing the Cayenne. It did a three-point turn, the beam of light cutting across the green paddy field. I lost it behind the trees. The sound of car doors being slammed and automatic gunfire made me duck, but it wasn't aimed at us. The muzzle flashes highlighted the Cayenne. The firing stopped, and the car doors slammed again. Red dust thrown up, shown by their taillights. We watched until we couldn't see lights anymore.

We went back to the house, Chai checking the entire

perimeter while I waited in the paddy by the chicken coop. He came out of the back door, unlocking the metal gate in the bars. Dirty dishes in the sink, Styrofoam boxes for food, lots of them, in the trash. They were here a while. In the house, sleeping bags, the cards, discarded, some DVDs, karaoke and porn. They left the small TV and DVD player. They took what they needed to carry, and that wasn't much by the look of things.

Chai was crouching in the doorway, in darkness, Uzi in hand, looking down the road.

I might have given you the impression that Thailand is filled with gun-toting individuals, but that's the world I live in. So I would stress here that the vast majority of Thais do not go around carrying firearms. I'd go further to say, less people here, per capita, have guns than those in the USA. Not sure of my facts there, but I'd take the bet, and I don't gamble. So when a bunch of guys open up on your car with full automatic weapon fire, you don't have to be a rocket scientist to figure out you've stumbled into something pretty fucking heavy. Chai confirmed my deductions.

"I recognized one of them. Guy playing cards. Ex Ranger."

"They all looked hard."

"Military, for sure, all of them."

"Yeah, and they were all wearing black."

We crossed the fields, angled well above the Cayenne. It was shot to pieces. Flat tires and riddled with shots from the front to the rear. I opened the rear door. My shirt and shoes had survived.

"Well, looks like we've got a bit of a walk ahead of us,"

I said as I wiped the camo cream off in the wing mirror of the car.

"That's not the bad news. We can catch a cab on the main road."

"What's the bad news?"

"This car belongs to General Montri. He's expecting it back tomorrow."

A Casualty of Circumstance

23 May 2010, Bangkok, 3:30 am

Driving around Bangkok after curfew, with weapons, was an invitation to be on the front page, afternoon edition, of the Thai Rath daily. Roads to and from Bangkok, north and northeast, were heavily patrolled with army and a few police checkpoints. Three days after the crackdown, the 3 am knock on the door, "we'd like you to help with our inquiries," was running hot. A call to Mother cleared our passage with Colonel Damrong. He ordered an army Humvee to pick us up in Chacheongsao and take us back to Pak Nam. I debated telling Mother about the true condition of General Montri's car and decided I'd leave the details vague – yes, just won't start, might be a fuse. I could deal with that when the sun shone.

As we came past the airport, on the way in, I asked the lieutenant who'd picked us up how much money he earned a month as an officer. He glanced in the back, but the soldiers he'd brought with him were asleep.

"About ten thousand baht," he whispered. "Of course, I don't have to pay for food or lodging."

Ten thousand baht is around three hundred and thirty dollars. I took out ten thousand baht and slipped it to him. "Thanks for picking us up."

We did a couple of rounds of the polite thing of him refusing, me insisting, rinse and repeat, and the money fitted reasonably well in the top pocket of his tailored green army jacket. I counted out another ten thousand, and watched his eyes flicking towards the cash as I counted.

"I'd like you to do me a small favor. I need to see someone. It's on the way, but let me give you this for your trouble." I took his hand and placed the cash in it.

"Where would you like to go, Khun Oh?"

"Suthisan." I wanted to get back to Um's apartment, just in case he was stupid enough to go there. Even if he'd bolted, we might find out a little bit more than what was on a Facebook page by having a look around.

We stopped in the soi before the apartment. Chai and I got out. Chai left his Uzi in the Humvee. We just took hand guns. The lieutenant looked nervous, checking his watch. Few lights were on in the apartments above us. It was your typical local apartment building with a hair salon, laundry, and restaurant on the ground floor next to the entrance. An old man, dressed in a guard's uniform, slept, slumped on a blue plastic stool. In the entrance, behind the glass doors, were a small elevator and a stairwell, the fire door propped open with a brick.

I've learned through past experience that it's better for

me to disguise my Farang appearance rather than try to explain what I'm doing with a Thai cop banging on doors at three in the morning. Wearing a DSI sharpshooter's cap and a pair of very large Ray-Bans does the job nicely. Chai gave the old man a tap on the arm. The old man's cap fell on the floor. Chai picked it up for him and flashed his fake cop DSI (Department of Special Investigations) badge. The old man stood up and came to attention. Chai showed him the photo of Um.

"What's his room number?"

The old man extracted a pair of black-framed glasses and put them on, frowning.

"Oh, that's Nong Um. He hasn't returned. Drives a white car, expensive one. Just the exhaust cost twenty thousand. One shock absorber, ten thousand. Expensive car. Has he done something wrong?"

"We need to take a look in his room. Have you got a key?"

"No key. Most of the rooms have outside padlocks on them anyway. No point to a key."

"What's the room number?"

"He's in 511, I think. Could be 509, but anyway, on this side of the building, which is all the odd numbers."

I took out a photo of Ice and held it in front of his eyes.

"Have you seen her?" I said.

"Yes, sure. That's his girlfriend. Saw her just a couple of weeks ago. But haven't seen her for a while. Good boy that Um. Most of the boys here have girls in and out, more than there are meals in a day, but not Nong Um. Good lad."

I nodded at Chai.

"Thanks and buzz us in, Uncle."

He stepped smartly to the card swipe, swiped his card, and opened the door for us, standing at attention, a shirt tail hanging out.

The lift door opened, the door opposite said 501, and the one next to it 503. The corridor was silent. Outside a couple of doors, used dinner plates had been left for the restaurant to collect when they next delivered food to someone on the floor. As the old man had said, all the doors had latches for padlocks, but none had a padlock on them, except 509. It was an expensive, high security padlock – said so on the label. Chai took out a small can with a needle-thin spray nozzle. Two quick squirts into the lock. There was a fizzing sound, and the lock fell on the tiled floor with a clatter. Chai removed the remainder of the padlock from the door, careful not to touch the metal ends where he'd sprayed.

The gap between the door and wall exposed the normal door lock. Chai used a flat file to ease it back until the door popped open – took at least five seconds. It was a typical three meter by four meter one-room apartment. Toilet, shower, door opening onto a small balcony with an air-conditioning compressor taking up most of the space on it. There are millions of these apartments in Bangkok. It's where fifty per cent of the population live; population of Greater Bangkok, eighteen million. You do the math. All rented, the price varies depending upon amenities and location, but ranges from 2,500 at the low end, no air-con – in the boonies. This one was probably in the four thousand a month range.

The apartments come furnished with bed, mattresses, cupboard. The TV at the foot of the bed, and the computer on the work table were his. Also his, were the drawings, posters and other "red" paraphernalia that covered the walls of the room. Not football red, political "red". Not good. There was another enemy that was the worst kind – the clever fanatic.

It didn't take long to search the place. There are only so many places you can hide something in a four by three meter concrete box. In the wardrobe, women's clothing took up more than half the space. I doubted Nong Um was a cross-dresser. I reckoned the clothes belonged to Ice. I took the large central shopping bag folded on the top of the drawers in the wardrobe and shoved all the paper on Um's work desk into it. Emptied the bedside drawers in there as well.

"Take the computer. Let's go." There was nothing more to be learned from the apartment.

Back in the Humvee, the lieutenant all smiles, paying no attention to the computer that Chai was carrying on his lap, the driver taking us south, home.

Por was always good with women. Whether his own or others, treated them with respect. He did have a rule or two though, and one of them was that if you were sleeping with him, then you shouldn't sleep with anyone else. It looked like Ice had been breaking that rule. If Por found out, he wouldn't do anything about it, but the cash and presents would cease. I didn't judge Ice. Bangkok is a big, hard, hungry city. It devours innocence, rewards corruption, and destroys it all on a whim with a smirk on its face. Everything is what it seems, and nothing is what it seems.

The roads were deserted. It was eerie. I'd never seen Bangkok this quiet, not even at four in the morning. I wondered if we had changed, if the latest in this long series of political power struggles had reached in and twisted something inside us. Or maybe I was just projecting. Had I changed? It's hard to know that about one's self, and now wasn't the time go there. Now was the time for doing. Thinking and analyzing could come later.

My guess was that Ice was supporting Nong Um. Um was mixed up with some heavy guys: military, and they had the worn look of a team that'd been active recently. The "men in black" (MIB), a term used by the media to describe the so-called "Ronin warriors", a term used by the now dead Seh Daeng, fighting on behalf of the red-shirts. None of these MIBs had been arrested or killed. Or if they had been, the bodies had been disposed of and none were the wiser.

I'd been thinking about the suite in Heaven, trying to remember the layout. As far as I could remember, and I planned on going back to check, there wasn't any furniture near the entrance to the master bedroom. There would have been nowhere to plant the bomb, unless it was wired into the ceiling, but then the blast would have taken out another floor, and it hadn't. So the bomb was in the room, near the door. The bomb must have been carried by Ice. I remembered the bag she had with her, multi-colored swathes of leather, a large bag – easily large enough to carry a half a kilo of Semtex without it being noticed.

Ice was many things, but not a suicide bomber. Despite our Jihad in the South, we hadn't had any suicide bombers to date. So obviously Ice was not the first. If she had carried the bomb, and it sounded like she had, she had done so unwittingly. Either by fault or design, she was killed. She may have been intending to plant the bomb and it had gone off accidently. She may not have known what she was carrying. It would be easy to dismiss this as Ice carrying a bomb for her red fanatic boyfriend to deliver to his mercenary "friends" and the bomb accidently going off. And maybe that's all it was. Wrong place, wrong time. But that discounted Colonel Sankit and his knowledge of our meeting.

Big Tiger was off the hook for the moment. Sankit could have known from Pim that I was meeting with Big Tiger for dinner that night. I wasn't sure, and it was a bit awkward to ask, but I sort of remembered mentioning to her that I was having dinner with Big Tiger on the Monday. I may even have mentioned the restaurant. The Cambodians and Sankit were speculation, but Heaven and Sankit were not. Chatree had pointed the finger. Sankit had known Por and I would be there, and a few hours later, a bomb had gone off nearly killing us. Ice, a not-so-innocent casualty of circumstance, devoured by Bangkok. Too much coincidence.

The Humvee's driver, directed by Chai through the back sois in Pak Nam, pulled up outside the gate to Mother's house. Pichet, on sentry duty, let us in. A hot shower and sleep beckoned, tiredness hitting my legs as I climbed the stairs to my bedroom. The room was empty. Pim must have decided to sleep in the guest room. I felt a guilty surge of relief. I wasn't up to dealing with questions.

Stripped, I stood in front of the mirror in the bathroom and peeled the bandages around my ribs off. The bruises around my stomach fading into a yellow-tinged purple. The 9 on my chest still showed clearly, looked like a tattoo. I eased the plaster off my eye. Dry around the stitches, sewing together nicely. I could shower without a shower cap.

Showered and dry, I slipped between the cool, soft, heavy white sheets. My cell phone's alarm went off, 5 am. I reached across, "Dismiss".

TELL IT LIKE IT IS

23 May 2010, Bangkok, 8:30 am

In the early days of the Battle of Britain, the Royal Air Force commissioned a study into sleep deprivation. Fighter pilots were few. German bombers were many. The conclusion they came to was that the average male needs four hours sleep in every twenty-four hours to operate at a minimum of efficiency. In other words, with less than four hours sleep, you start to do stupid things.

Chai was shaking my arm, a cell phone in his hand. I glanced at the time on the cell, 8:30 am. Three and a half hours – better than nothing. I rubbed the sleep out of my eyes and looked at the number but didn't recognize it. I put my hand over the mouthpiece.

"Who?" I mouthed at Chai.

"Sankit."

I held the phone to my ear.

"Do you always sleep this late? I'm always up before dawn. Anyway, I called to invite you for a game of golf. Thought we could have a talk, man to man. Two o'clock at The Royal. You know it? Just past the airport on the Motorway to Chonburi."

"Yes, I know it."

"Good. Then I'll see you there." He hung up. Golf with father-in-law. Great.

Mother had been at the showroom when we went to pick up a new car. General Montri's Porsche Cayenne parked in the service bay. Some thoughtful person had washed it. It didn't do much to improve the look.

Chai, one hand guiding the wrist of the other in the polite Thai manner when giving something to an elder, handed the keys of the Porsche to Mother. Mother, hand on hip, dangled the keys in her other hand, looking at them. Dragging Chai's eyes with her, she looked at the Porsche, jangled the keys in her hand. She raised her eyebrows and smiled. Chai was wise enough not to smile back.

She nodded at the black Maserati Quattroporte Sport GT parked at the rear bay to the showroom. "Take the Maserati. It cost four times as much as the Porsche. The keys are in the office."

The Royal Golf Course's parking lot was crowded. There's nothing like a game of golf after a little war. Chai parked the Maserati and popped the trunk. Hadn't used the "Bag Drop". Chai had stuck an Uzi and an USAS-12 shotgun in the bag. Chai believes in overkill.

I paid the green fee. Stingy old toad hadn't even picked that up. Then I organized a cart and ordered a beer. No sign of Sankit. He was late. I took a seat at the little café next to the putting green. Been a while since I'd played golf. I'm an okay golfer. Like anything, the more you practice and play, the better you get. I hadn't had much time for either lately. I knew from Pim that Sankit was an avid golfer and played off 12. My handicap was around 18. On a good day, I'd get around in under 90. On a bad day, under a hundred.

Sankit showed up in a flurry of wais, caddies, and a disapproving glance at the beer. I waied him with just enough humility to show him that I'd play the game of dutiful son-in-law, but only so far. We communicate a lot without saying anything in Thailand. He didn't waste any time and jumped into the golf cart waiting for him. At the first tee, magically cleared before our arrival, he suggested a thousand a hole as a bet.

"I play off twelve. What's your handicap?" At least he was an honest corrupt cop.

"Eighteen, last time I checked. Probably be twenty or worse now. I haven't played in a while."

"We'll call it twenty. Give you a chance. Hmm."

He didn't ask or toss a tee for choosing who teed off first. He just went. It was hot: thirty-five Celsius in the shade, at least. Humid too, and very little breeze. Every third hole there is a drink's stop. He waited until the fifteenth hole before he got to why we were here.

I ordered another beer, as I had done at every drink stop, knowing it pissed him off. This time he ordered one too and sat down. Leaning back in the wrought-iron chair, he wiped the sweat off his face with a cool towel supplied by the waitress. He folded it carefully and put it on the table next to his golf glove. His toady eyes, accentuated by thick bushy eyebrows, focused on me.

"I heard you had a chat with my old friend from the south, Khun Chatree."

I drank my beer. No point denying or answering to it. I waited. Wanted to see what he would come up with.

Expecting an answer and not getting one, he let out a little snort and looked off down the fairway. He turned to me, leaned forward, his hands folded on the table in front of him.

"Look. I don't like you. I never have. Doubt I ever will. Back in the day, I dealt with thousands of young rich thugs like you. Killed a few, put a lot in prison. I hoped for better for Pim, but she's chosen you. After what your mother put on the table, my wife has now also chosen you." He blew out his cheeks and sighed. "I'm aware that Chatree told you that I knew about your meeting with Por that day. I did know. As much as I dislike you, I don't go around killing people that I don't like. I knew about the meeting, but I didn't tell anyone about it, and I didn't try to have you killed." This was the longest he'd ever spoken to me.

"Colonel Sankit, as you have probably worked out, I feel the same way about you that you feel about me. Just so you know where we stand, I've bribed thousands of cops like you, got hundreds on the payroll. I honestly don't care what you or your wife thinks. I only care what Pim thinks. Whatever I feel, I can keep to myself. Pim loves you as her father, and that I understand. For her sake and for the sake of our family, I can put aside our past differences. Whatever has happened in the past, I can leave it there, as long as it stays there. A bomb ended up in that room somehow. I think I know how it got there. Now I want to know why it was there."

"I can't help you with that. I've asked around people I know, but no one knows who might have attacked you. Of course, the list of people who might want to is long, but the list of who would dare to, much shorter and unknown."

A fly buzzed around my ear. I wondered if his tongue would lash out.

"Colonel, let's keep the need for family get-togethers to a minimum – you and I should get on fine." I raised my beer to him. He picked up his, and we clinked glasses. A truce sealed, based on as much trust as you'd give a Filipino money changer.

I had a shower, paid the colonel the eight thousand he'd taken off me – there's a reason I don't gamble – and headed out past the ground floor massage room. Chai, waiting with the bag at the outside café, rose when he saw me. As I walked up, he glanced my way. I stopped. He slung the bag over his shoulder and walked to me.

"Four guys waiting on the steps by the entrance."

He put the bag on the ground. We took a quick look around. No one was paying attention to what we were doing. I took out a Glock, quickly checked the mag, put one in the spout and shoved it down the back of my trousers. Slinging the Uzi butt first under his left armpit, Chai took a windcheater out of the bag and covered up. He moved the short irons to one side, easier access to the shotgun, and then picked up the bag.

We walked a couple of meters apart, Chai slightly

behind me. By the steps, four guys who looked Japanese. The Royal is mainly a Japanese golf course, a lot of members from the Japanese factories nearby. These guys didn't look like they worked in factories, nor like members of a golf club. The three standing in the car park below the steps looked like ex-sumo wrestlers dressed in badly fitting black suits. It was like a scene from the blues brothers. The fourth guy, waiting on the steps, had a better tailor, a smaller body too.

I approached, hand behind my back. Chai had one hand on the bag, another under his jacket.

The guy on the top of the steps smiled, held his hands out wide.

"Mr. Chance san."

"Who are you?"

"Susumu Uchibori. Friends call me Steve. I work with the Yamaguchi-gumi. I've come to replace Ken. Can we have a talk?" He held out his hand to shake. I ignored it.

"Sure, go ahead. Say what you got to say."

He laughed, clapped his hands together. "Come on, Mr. Chance, don't be like that. Let's go and have a drink and a talk." Smooth smile, oozing charm. What was it with these Yakuza guys? Did they have some kind of mold they stamped them out of in Tokyo?

"We'll follow you. You go ahead. Wait for us by the entrance."

He nodded and then waved at a van in the car park. It pulled up. The three sumos climbed in. Mr. Smooth followed. Then the van pulled out of the car park.

The driveway into The Royal is a long way from the entrance on the main road. It gave me time to call Mother, set up a restaurant, and check our weapons. The van was parked, hazard lights on, on the main road. Chai pulled up alongside, and I wound the window down. Mr. Smooth opened their door.

"Follow me. I know a good place." I didn't give him time to argue. Chai took off. The government had extended the curfew until Monday night, so we only had a few hours. We headed for a place in Thonglor. I figured Steve should be introduced to the other Japanese playground in Bangkok. I was sure he'd already been to Thaniya.

It would take us maybe forty-five minutes to get there, depending on the Sunday evening traffic. There were a lot of people on the motorway, heading back to Bangkok now that open street warfare had ended. The war was still going on. Just now it was a quiet war. The run and hide, snatch and grab war. A power shift had occurred. Normally kept away from the public, this time the disagreements had spilled out onto the streets. A Thai saying, "When elephants fight, it is the ants in the grass that are trampled..." That battle had been fought, won, and lost, but the quiet war was far from over.

Beckham and about twenty of our boys were in the restaurant just off Soi 13 on Thonglor. The owner was a friend of mine. We sat in a private room looking out at a Japanese-styled garden. Steve and I sat alone. Chai, Beckham and Tum were having staring matches with the Sumos.

The waitress poured us each a cold beer and left. I'd already ordered our food.

"Salute," Steve said and raised his glass.

"Cheers."

"This is a nice place. Quiet." I let the silence draw out, took another sip of my beer.

"Allow me to express my condolences on the passing of Khun Por."

"Thank you."

"The Yamaguchi-gumi board also expressly ordered that their grief at the loss be known. Your father was our respected partner and friend."

"Thank you. Please do express our heartfelt thanks to the board for their kind thoughts."

The waitresses arrived bearing food: three different kinds of sushi, sashimi, and various other appetizers. Cold sake was poured into square wooden cups, with small dishes of rock salt for the sake placed next to them. The chefs are from Tokyo, the fish flown in daily from Tokyo, everything in the restaurant is from Tokyo, excluding the waitresses.

We ate for a while. Talked about Bangkok. He'd been here a few times. His face got red with the sake, but he was sober. Reasonable. Finally, he got to the point.

"Chance, the board wanted me to tell you that they also sincerely regret any misunderstandings that may have arisen as a result of Ken's actions. They understand and appreciate the candid nature of your response. They wanted to assure whoever acted against Ken that there will be no reprisal for Ken. He acted without honor and betrayed us all." Steve looked me in the eyes, holding the look.

"I'll pass it on. I'm sure they'll be relieved."

"The board would also like to know when you plan to

return the hundred million."

"Well, that's a problem, Steve, as the tapes showed the money that Ken stole went up with the warehouse during the protest."

"The board feels that perhaps the tapes, the fire, and the ease with which the money was stolen are a convenient explanation for one hundred million in cash."

"The board sits in Tokyo. The tapes came from DSI investigating the warehouses for Ya Baa smuggling. Your guys were filmed because you arrived with a truck in the middle of the night. In case you haven't noticed, a good portion of the country has burned down in the last few days. The only way anyone knew we had the money in Phuket was if they traced it from Bangkok. We weren't expecting betrayal from our old respected friend. The whole matter has been extremely inconvenient from start to finish. However, it is what it is."

"The board is going to be disappointed. They had hoped that this was a simple misunderstanding."

"Steve, this was Ken's karma. He pushed his luck, and his luck pushed back. What happened is unfortunate, but it has happened." I held his stare. I'm a reasonable poker player. It didn't look like he was convinced, but I wasn't giving him a lot of room to play with.

"I will report back to the board what you have said. I can't imagine they'll be pleased. They were quite adamant in their belief that Ken was set up."

"It's possible that Ken was set up. I don't know what Ken was up to, and I don't know who set up Ken. What I do know is that he stole your money."

Steve didn't say anything, pushing his cigarette pack

around with his lighter. I really didn't want a war with the Yamiguchi-gumi, and stealing the money had only come to me after I decided to borrow the money from Ken. It was a two-birds one-stone thing. Ken had ripped off a couple of families from Chiang Mai and Chonburi. The amounts weren't small, and the families had been hit hard. I was pretty sure this was his doing and not the Yakuza. Bangkok corrupts everyone. He tapped the cigarette pack twice with his lighter. Turning the charm back on. Peace for now.

"Okay, Chance. I'll talk to the board and tell them how it is. I understand the situation. Can I invite you for dinner, next week? Say Thursday? I should be back by then."

"Sure, let's talk about it in the week."

I watched as Steve and the sumos filed into the van. For big men, they were surprisingly light on their feet. Something to remember.

Conflict of Interest

Aunts, daughters, assorted husbands and hangers-on were in full attendance at the house when we got back. I slipped around the back and went straight to the guest house. Pichit was sitting in a chair on the deck. He stood up as I approached.

"Por is back. He's sleeping still. Mother is with him and Doctor Thomas. There're also a couple of nurses. One of them is cute."

"Keep your hands off the nurses. We need them focused on Por not dreaming about you."

Pichit grinned at me, happy that Por was back from the dead. "Yes, boss."

I went into the house. Por was lying on a bed in the living room, Mother and Dr. Tom talking on the sofa, and I heard the sound of giggles coming from upstairs. Somboon

234

watching football on the TV with the sound turned off.

"There you are," Mother said, smiling and patting the sofa next to her.

I went over and looked at Por. He looked pale and frail. Someone had brushed his hair the way he liked it. He was so still; I glanced at the heart monitor. I didn't really understand how the scale worked, but a light was rhythmically bouncing in an arc. Come on, Por, wake up, please. I need to talk to you. I studied his face for any sign he might have heard my silent appeal. The black accordion in the glass case thumped down, causing me to start.

Dr. Tom was talking to Mother, keeping his voice low.

"Pregnant by her cousin. They're looking for a suitable husband now. Would you have any suggestions?"

"What are the chances the baby will be..."

"Challenged?"

"Yes, challenged."

"Minimal, less chance than of the baby having Down's syndrome. In Thailand, less than one in three thousand at her age."

"And the father..."

"Shipped off to the States – Minnesota. The father's sister has an auto dealership there."

"I'll need to see the girl. Make sure there's no Romeo and Juliet thing going to happen. But yes, I have some ideas. One young man in particular, good hardworking boy, could use a lift in social stature. I'll call her mother tomorrow. Chance, how was the golf?"

"Interesting. Colonel Sankit wanted a chat about my prospects."

Dr. Tom leaned over and peeled back the plaster over

the stitches on my eye.

"I think we can get these out. Hang on, I'll just get my bag." He stood up and walked over to the counter.

"What did Sankit really want?" Mother asked, lowering her voice.

"He wanted to let me know that he didn't have anything to do with the attempt on Por's and my life. I found out that he knew about our meeting. I didn't say anything because I wanted to meet him first and see what he had to say. I haven't said anything to Pim yet either."

"No, I can understand that. Delicate subject. And did he?"

"Not sure. He says he didn't, but he seemed eager to 'put the past behind us'. After the golf, Ken's re-placement showed up at the course. It is a Japanese course, so I don't think they were tailing us. Would have been hard to stay with Chai anyway."

"Is my Maserati still in one piece?" Mother had a smile on her lips.

"Sorry about Montri's Porsche. Didn't think we'd be getting into anything that night."

"Oh, it's okay. Couple of extra days in the body shop and a few engine parts. I'm just glad that neither of you were in it. What did Ken's replacement, what did you say…"

"Steve."

"What did Steve say? Did they ask about the money?"

"Yes. I'm not sure he believed me. Fifty-fifty. Said he'd report what I'd said back to the board in Tokyo."

Dr. Tom came back, a pack of anti-septic wipes, scissors, and tweezers in hand. He wiped the eye down and started snipping. There was a soft knock on the door. I couldn't turn and wasn't facing the door, but I heard Pim say.

"Hey, how was the golf?"

"It was good. Your dad and I had a good man-to-man talk."

"Ooh, what did you talk about?"

"Well, that's why they call it a man-to-man talk."

"Fuck off. Tell me."

Dr. Tom poked the sharp end of the scissors into my eyebrow. I pulled my head away. Dr. Tom hadn't been exposed to Pim's way of communicating in English and her ability to flip-flop. Switching between immaculately polite Thai and cursing worse than a trucker on a wet road, in upper-class-accented English, is one of her trademarks.

"Tom, I don't believe I've had the opportunity to introduce you to Pim yet."

"Pim and I met at your funeral. Sit still."

"Yes, of course."

He pulled the last couple of stitches out, placing them in the antiseptic towel. Then he sat back and looked at his handiwork, turned to Mother.

"The scar will blend in with the line of his eyebrow over time. The bit where it cuts through the eyebrow and runs down onto the edge here – that might be better having some more cosmetic work done."

"Thank you, Thomas, and thank you for all your work today. It's a relief to have him home."

Thomas waied Mother. If he'd had a tail, it would be wagging. "I must be going. I have an early surgery to perform."

"I'll see you out." I walked with Tom out around the main house and showed him to his car. Before he got in, I asked him.

"Tom, what is going on with Por? This coma, how long is it likely to last? What's the prognosis? Truth please, Tom, no sugar-coating."

His owlish eyes blinked a few times. "Chance, Por was exposed almost directly to the blast. You were behind a wall and in an elevator, and look what it did to you. An explosion creates intense energy. The shockwave, and the trauma that results is often more internal damage than external. I mean excluding shrapnel, of course. Your father suffered heavy trauma to the brain. Now his body is trying to heal itself. The biggest danger we face is that of secondary infection. We have to be particularly vigilant against pneumonia. We are still within a period where the statistical chance of a full or partial recovery is high. That chance diminishes greatly after about four months. There's no quick cure. Don't expect a miraculous overnight recovery. When he does wake up, it may only be for a few minutes in a day, and the likelihood is that he will be very confused. In the meantime, we have to keep him properly fed, keep moving him, and keep him aware of us through his tactile senses. Soon, I am sure, he will respond. The brain scans are clear, and he is stable."

"Thanks, Tom. I appreciate it."

I walked back to the guest house. Tom's words replaying in my mind. They were encouraging, and Tom wouldn't bullshit me on this. Pim and Mother were laughing about something when I went in.

"Come on, then. What did you talk about?"

"We talked about Khun Por and…"

"Not Dr. Tom. I mean you and my father, and you bloody well know it."

I grinned at her and took her hand, enough teasing. "You father and I agreed that we didn't like each other and that it would be excellent if we never had to meet again for the rest of our lives. We also agreed that we both loved you, and we would not let our dislike of each other to interfere with that."

"Oh, well, that's not too bad. At least he didn't try to shoot you or anything."

She laughed at her own joke. We joined in. Mother's phone rang. I heard her say "special delivery", and after she hung up, she turned to us.

"I've got to head out to the farm. I won't be long."

After Mother left, I lay down on the sofa, a pillow under my head. Pim fitted nicely into the crook of my arm, my fingers on her stomach, softly drawing circles around her belly button. She wriggled her backside further back. I whispered in her ear, "I've got to go take a shower. Why don't you join me?"

She whispered back, "Sounds like a plan." Her backside did another little wriggle.

I went over to where Por lay and pressed the nurse button. Waiting for them, I took his hand. It felt like I was holding a small bird, scared to squeeze for the fragile bones. The nurse who appeared was, I assumed, the cute one, because she was, and if the other was cuter, then she'd be a stunner and that would make Pichit a very fussy man. Still, beauty's perception is individually subjective. Pim and I went up to my room.

We shared a long, wet, tongue-dueling feast of a kiss inside the door to my room. I was all set to jump straight to Phase 2 of the plan.

"You need a shower. You stink."

A hand against my chest pushing me back, she started unbuttoning her shirt, slowly, a raised eyebrow, her tongue poking out a little, a naughty look. I must have been a virtuous hero in my last life to deserve such a reward in this one. She reached the last button of her shirt and flicked a finger in the direction of the shower. Five seconds later, I was in the shower.

I wrapped a towel around my waist and stepped into the bedroom. Pim was lying on the bed. Naked. Raging bull. And the phone rang. Lest you think me more insane than you already do, perhaps I should explain a bit about my phones. I hardly ever use the same phone for more than a day. Every day a different set of color-coded phones are dropped off, pre-programmed with all the other new numbers for that day. The only thing the phones have in common day to day is the color. Red, appropriately, is the color for Mother. If she was calling me now, it was important.

"I'm where I said I would be. You should come." She hung up. I looked at Pim. She smiled and spread her legs, leaning back on the pillows.

"That's evil. You know I've got to go." She sucked a forefinger and brushed her hand lightly down from her jaw, across a breast, she circled her nipple a couple of times ... and I jerked the pillow out from under her elbow. Giggling, she started doing sexy moans while I was trying to put on my jeans.

"I will return." She started moaning faster. I ran for the car, pinged Chai on the cell phone.

"Drive as fast as you can." I thought I saw a smile. The farm is two and a half kilometers from Joom's house on the Chao Phraya River. We were at the farm in less than sixty seconds. Mother's car, with Beckham standing next to it, was parked outside the warehouse. In the warehouse, a pick-up truck, and in the back of the pick-up, covered by a tarp, the face visible, Nong Um. Mother was standing at the back of the warehouse away from the two guys who'd brought Um in. I went over to her.

"What do you want to do?" she asked.

"We don't take it. See what happens."

She nodded, and we walked back to the two guys. I recognized both of them as the two playing cards at the farm house. One of them stepped forward as I approached, a fat envelope stashed in his belt.

"What's the problem? We've got the payment." He took out the envelope and tried to hand it to me.

"We can't accept the body. It would be a conflict of interest for us. Under the rules by which we operate, you have thirty minutes before we come looking for you."

His eyes widened, he didn't look too bright, but he got the last part of what I'd said. Then he got stupid.

"What the fuck. You too good to take our money? You know who we are? You know who we work for? You're fucking dead. You…"

The sound of a silenced weapon is something you'll probably never hear, Farang. The closest you'll probably get is when you use the air compressor at the garage to fill up your tires. The sound the compressor makes when you release it from the valve is similar, but a silenced weapon's is a bit shorter and flatter. Chai shot him twice, once in the face, just below his eye, and the other in his chest. His partner didn't move. Which was a smart move.

"Now you've got two dead bodies to get rid of and," I checked my cell phone, "twenty-nine minutes and thirty seconds before we come looking for you." I looked at him in the Glock's sights.

RONIN

The system by which people can reach out to us is also governed by the phones. Just as red was Mother's line, black was the general line. Usually Chai answered it, often just listening to whatever was said, and then hanging up. Some, a small fraction, of this "noise" he passed to me. Most he handed off to other boys in the crew to handle. The call that came in thirty-five minutes after he had shot Mr. Impolite, as he'd been dubbed by Mother, was handed straight to me.

"We'd like to meet. We think a misunderstanding happened. Is it possible?"

"Possible. Corner of Chakkaphak and Sai Luat, there's a 7-Eleven. Next to it, there's a car park, an hour from now?"

"An hour from now is okay."

"See you there, then. Two of you only. One of you should be the guy who was asking the questions at the farm. My questions are not political."

"We understand. See you there."

Chai came out of the 7-Eleven, a cup of coffee in each hand. With snipers set up around the car park, he wasn't concerned about his hands being full. He handed a cup to me. I was sitting in the Maserati, engine and air-conditioning on, door open, feet on the ground, thinking about Pim, and enjoying a smoke. At one o'clock in the morning, with a cup of crappy coffee, it tasted great. I had to quit them. I had to quit a few things, but quitting anything was on hold until I found out who tried to kill Por and me. It appeared even sex was on hold. I looked at the cell phone, 12:59 am. A Benz turned slowly into Chakkaphak, and at the 7-Eleven, the indicator came on. Game on.

Chai gave everyone a quiet "heads-up" to not move unless he or I gave the signal. I swallowed the rest of the coffee and stubbed out the cigarette. Then I stood outside the car with my hands clearly visible by my sides.

The Benz pulled up alongside me, but not too close. The car door opened, hands on the top of the door. Polite. Smart. The face that followed the hands was the guy who had been interrogating Um. His number two was the guy that Um had met in RCA. We closed the distance between us, palms open.

"Thank you for agreeing to meet."

"I appreciate the call. Always ready to clear up a misunderstanding."

He nodded. He wasn't young. In his early fifties, his

eyes jaded but honest.

"The guy who went with him, the guy you let go, told me what happened. I apologize for his behavior. He had no cause to speak like that to you or your mother. Deserved what he got. Perhaps it was his karma for killing Nong Um."

"No problem. He's dead. I'm not here for him. I'm here to find out why Um was killed."

"Why do you want to know?"

It was a fair question. If he had been doing what I think he'd been doing, then he was playing a high-risk game. Probably a very profitable game, but high risk for sure.

"Um was the boyfriend of a girl who died in an apartment when a bomb went off. My father was in the apartment."

He sighed, nodded, and seemed to reach some kind of decision. He gestured to a wooden plank on the side of the car park. Empty now, it was usually occupied by the motorcycle soi taxis waiting for a fare. "You want to take a seat? This might take a while."

I nodded. You get a feeling when someone is sincere. You also get a sense when someone is professional. We walked over to the bench and sat down. He took out a pack of Marlboro, offered me one. I took it and held out a lighter to his smoke.

"So what's the story with Um?" I asked him, glancing over at Chai and RCA guy, stood off a little, next to each other, relaxed. All calm.

"Before the riots, over the last couple of months, we used him as a driver on a few jobs. He did well. He was reliable and didn't freak out when things got messy. When Seh Daeng got shot, we had to up the ante. Toon, the guy your guy put down – nice shooting by the way." Chai's head inclined slightly in acknowledgement. "Toon spent time in the south. We all have. He was demolitions. The cell phone and the Semtex were put together by him. The army busted a load coming down from Ayuthya, and all we had left at a critical time, this was the 10th May, was what we had in Bangkok. We needed the bombs to sow a bit of terror, up the ante at the right time while the backdoor negotiations were happening. Um was keeping the bombs for us. He used the girl. We paid her to deliver them. Fifty thousand a delivery."

"Why didn't he deliver them himself?"

"He was under watch. The army and other forces had turned up the pressure by then. We were on the move constantly. Still are, but I reckon we'll be stood down soon. I hope so anyway. I've had enough of this shit." He smiled, but you could tell the truth in his words. He looked tired.

"How were the bombs detonated?"

"You just call the number of the phone strapped to it. It sends an electric charge into the detonator and boom."

"So what happened on the day?"

"I got a call. Make something happen. I called Um and asked him to deliver me the birthday cake at three. He said he would arrange for it to be delivered, but he couldn't do it until maybe six at the earliest. That was okay for me. I asked him to take care of it. The bomb never arrived. This was the first time that he let me down, but what was supposed to happen didn't. Some powerful people wanted to know why. The next day, Um called my guy over there," he nodded at RCA guy, "told us the girl had died when the bomb went off, and he was on the run."

"What time did you get the call to make something happen?"

"It was late morning, maybe lunchtime already. I think it was lunch because when I called Um he didn't answer. Called me back about ten minutes later and apologized, said he'd been at lunch. So it could have been even later."

"You said he was under watch. Who was watching him, do you know?"

"A secret section within DSI charged with hunting terrorists. They'd started operating out of 11th Infantry Regiment barracks. Let's just say that we had it on good authority." Large sections of the national police were known to be sympathetic or allied to various groups of politicians. The recent "troubles" had divided these, more recently, into red and non-red. The idea that a senior policeman was sympathetic to the red shirt cause was entirely plausible.

"Did he say who he was on the run from? After the bomb had gone off."

"No. I assumed he had help. He wasn't unknown amongst the core. I thought one of them had warned him. He told my guy a different story, but this was much later, same night you followed us out to the farm. He said someone called him. Didn't know who it was, and the caller didn't say, just said 'they were a friend'. Knew the bomb came from him. Told him his bomb had killed an important man and that he better run."

"Why was he killed?"

"Toon panicked. He took Um back to the apartment. They were going to move all the stuff out. When they got there, they saw the place had been compromised. Toon asked around a little, heard about the army Humvee and two guys – one wearing a DSI cap. Toon made a command decision to cut the connection to us. That was it. He called me. I told him to use your service, based on a recommendation. The recommendation was solid. You run a professional service."

"Thanks, although it's not me who handles that part of the business. Thanks for being straight with me. We don't have a problem."

"That's good, Khun Oh. Again please accept my apologies for the impolite behavior of my man tonight. You can be assured that if he had lived, he would have faced a severe reprimand from me, if not the same fate as your man delivered."

"Apology accepted. No hard feelings."

He got up and offered his hand. Maybe because I looked like a Farang or maybe he just wanted to test my grip. I don't know, but I shook his because we always work with sincerity. He turned to leave and stopped.

"What I heard, it wasn't only the old man and the girl who got killed. I heard it took out a couple of his guys but one guy miraculously escaped, was that you?"

"Yeah."

"I heard that the next day a number nine appeared on your chest. That true?"

"No, it was the same day."

His eyes scanning for a lie. Not finding one. "Can I see it?"

I undid the second button on my shirt and pulled it sideways so he could see the 9.

"Wow – I've seen some stuff in my time, but that's pretty fucking amazing. Could you do me a favor? I don't forget them. Take care of a loose end for me."

"Depends."

His eyes flicked to RCA guy. RCA guy saw it and started to move. Chai put his right hand on his head – code for take out the one on the right. Three bullets smacked into RCA guy. He lay flat on his back, half his head missing, brains on display, blood black in the poor light of the car park. His arm lay across his amulets, hand near the butt of the gun that it hadn't reached. We hadn't moved.

"Thanks. I'll leave the Benz with you as payment for the disposal. Papers are in the car."

"No need. He's on the house." On my earpiece I heard Chai tell the guys to come down and clear the body.

"All the same, here, take the keys."

I took the keys. He gave me a little two-fingered salute and, hands in pockets, walked out of the car park. I watched him in the light of the street lamps, fading in and out of the shadows. He disappeared as I looked. Some trick. One of the boys came out of the 7-Eleven with four large ten-liter water bottles. The body was loaded onto a pick-up and taken off to the farm. The farm was a slow five-minute drive away. Everyone was relaxed. This was our turf. RCA guy's last stand was washed down with the water.

I sat in the Maserati. Time to go home. An image of Pim on the bed stroking herself and grinning popped into my mind. RCA guy slipped in next, a surprise in his dead eyes, looking at his brains on the floor of the car park.

I wound down the window and lit a joint, exhaling through the window, the purring throb of the V8 a theme tune for the thoughts playing in my head. Late morning call, time enough, but it all ended at the 11th Infantry barracks. Getting any information out of there would be unlikely and too dangerous.

SINS OF THE FATHERS

24 May 2010, Pak Nam, 1:55 am

Security had been stepped up because of the Yakuza threat. Until that got resolved, we were "mobbed up", as Uncle Mike called it. Coming out of the kitchen with a beer in his hand, he said, "Wow, you look damn serious, dude. Everything okay?"

I had to smile. He'd been saying that to me since I was six. "Yeah, just a heavy night, morning. How are you?"

"I'm cool, man. Want to go sit down by the river?"

"Sure, that'd be cool."

We went through the French doors, onto the patio, a couple of the boys sitting in chairs by the pool. At the fork of the path to the sala, Uncle Mike suddenly stopped. Held up his hand.

"Shush," he whispered. I stopped. He turned.

"Two roads diverged in a yellow wood, and sorry

I could not travel both." Grinning now, he'd got me. I chuckled. Frost, I should have known. His favorite. He kept walking and reciting over his shoulder, as we weaved our way down to the sala. When we came up the steps, he stopped on the top step and turned, putting his hand on his heart and dropping his voice.

"Two roads diverged in a wood, and I – I took the one less traveled by … and that has made all the difference."

"Bravo, bravo!" I clapped.

He took a bow, then we went and sat by the side of the river. He handed me a Ziploc plastic bag filled with weed and papers. I took out a bit of weed and started stripping the leaves from the stem. I like the night. I like how sound travels differently when there's less interference. I like how its shadows are never the same. Chai appeared, carrying a tray: Chivas, soda and an ice bucket. He set the tray down near us and went in search of the "yaa gan yeung". As Chai was lighting the coils, Uncle Mike started putting ice in the glasses.

"You know, Chance, why I didn't bring you to live with me in Phuket? I could have. If I'd insisted, I could have laid out all the good reasons why you should be there, but I didn't. You know why?"

"No. I always just thought it was normal. You had your life."

"Oh no. We talked about it. You and Chai. Bringing you both to Phuket and letting you live there, away from this." He waved a hand at the house, but his wave meant everything in Bangkok. Our life. I looked over at Chai pouring the whiskey into the glasses.

"I'll tell you why … ah, thanks." He took the joint

I handed him and, cupping his hand around my lighter against the slight breeze, sucked in, getting the end glowing. Chai had moved on to popping the tops off the soda bottles. He turned to Chai.

"This is some great weed you got. Can you get more?"

"Can."

"Cool, we'll talk." He took a couple of quick hits and passed me the joint.

"So, where was I? Oh yeah, after your parents were killed, it was a crazy time. I was still a kid, half your age now, your mother was younger than Pim, and Por was young and tough as they come. He already had the aunts by then and, with the exception of Aunt Dao, all were beautiful and young. Thing is, all they'd produced by then were the four daughters. Your parents planned to leave you at their apartment. With money, they said. Shit, I can't believe it, even today. Anyway, Por and I said we'd take you with us. Two days later, they left, and ten days after we got the news they'd been killed."

"Por's told me this before. So have you."

"Yeah, I know, but what I haven't told you, not because I never thought about it, but because I felt guilty about it, was what happened after your parents were killed. Por had supplied the boat and the connection to get the smack to your parents. Usually he didn't deal in smack, but times were tough. The farm wasn't getting visitors, the whole of Pak Nam was at war with each other and every other province – times were tough. You'd be sitting having dinner and someone would fire a couple of shots into the house. That kind of thing. Anyway, I'd already moved to Phuket. It was a real paradise back then. No one knew about it. I was living in a shack off Kata beach, where Club Med is now. Back then, it was just a little fishing village.

"Por went after the Germans. Took him eight months to track them all down, but he got them: two in New York and two in West Berlin. He was wounded in West Berlin and came back by ship."

I took a sip of the whiskey Chai had poured. I had heard all of this before, but if Uncle Mike wanted to talk, I was comfortable to listen.

"While Por was away, you lived here. I visited on and off. Joom looked after you. Chai arrived during that time." He slapped Chai on the knee. "You got here about a month before Por's return. You were about as tall as my knee then." Chai smiled, waving off the joint Uncle Mike passed his way. I took it instead. Chai is cool with smoking a joint now and then, but not when things were hot.

"Joom collected Por from Klong Toey. He was still very weak; he'd been badly shot up. Things here in Pak Nam were hot too. The house wasn't like this back then, just a simple wooden Thai house on stilts. You've seen the photos. The crew was a lot smaller back then as well, just a few guys. Bank and Red, of course, they'd been with him since the beginning, but only a couple of others. Por asked me to take you to Phuket. Joom was dead set against it. According to her, you were given to her by Buddha and that was that. But Por was worried. You stuck out like a sore thumb and were easy to snatch. I didn't have any jobs planned for a while, waiting for the new crops. Against Joom's wishes, I took you to Phuket."

I handed him the joint, he took a couple of hits and

put it in the ashtray. The lid of the tin the mosquito coils came in.

"When Por came back from Germany, he had a hundred thousand dollars. He took it off the Germans, their payout for the smack. It doesn't sound like much today, but back then you could buy a good chunk of downtown Sukhumvit for that kind of money. Two months after I took you to Phuket, one of the Germans kidnapped you. Por missed one, the brother of the guy who killed your parents. We still don't know how he found me or you, but he did. Course, we didn't know that right away. All I knew was that you were gone."

I had never heard this before, neither had Chai. We'd been smoking and drinking, but the buzz fell away. Even the river seemed to pause. Like Uncle Mike's soft voice was the only sound in the world.

"Joom hated me. I could tell she was going to kill me. Not for the ransom money, that didn't matter. For losing you. She fucking hated me. Would have killed me, but Por ordered her not to. They'd left a ransom note when they took you, for a hundred thousand. Por and Joom brought it with them from Bangkok.

"I was truly freaked out, losing you. Only time I ever heard Joom swear, 'fucking useless Farang' she called me. I felt it too. Por, he was my best friend, still is, and he never said a word, just went about the business of finding you. Like I said, I was useless, freaked out. You know me and the whole violence thing just never met. I was lucky. And then I'd lost a little kid. It freaked me out. I got stoned, really stoned, and dropped some acid. Then I went for a sail. I swam out to my yacht, hauled up the anchor and the sails. I have no idea even now what I was thinking. I've tried to remember, but it's all a bit of a blur. It was past midnight, but there was a full moon. I remember the moon perfectly. Lit up the sea like it was day.

"I hadn't been sailing long, but it felt like years, and then I saw another yacht moored off a few bays up. And I don't know, man, I just got this whole feeling of evil about the boat. I swear the rest of the sea shone silver, but the sea around the yacht was all black. I looked for a cloud and saw none. And the sea talked to me, whispering, telling me that you were being held in the yacht. I wasn't so out of my gourd that I did anything except turn the boat around and sail back to Por and Joom. It turned out a few bays over was Patong beach. They saw the yacht in the morning. The next day we were supposed to deliver the money. Por and Joom went that night. Used a rubber dinghy. Rowed it in after darkness. I held the dinghy steady while Por lifted Joom onto the bow. The fore hatch was cracked halfway open. Joom is small and light. She was in and out with you in less than a minute. She whispered to us that there were two men on board. We guessed the German's brother and a friend." Uncle Mike picked the joint up, and I relit it for him. He took a long drag, holding the smoke in.

"Joom whispered that the guys in the boat seemed to be drunk, Mekhong whiskey bottles over the floor of the yacht. Por climbed back on the boat, put the spinnaker pole over the fore hatch and shoved a screwdriver into the latch of the rear hatch. He called down to Joom in Thai, my Thai wasn't that good back then, but I knew the words for petrol. I handed Joom the twenty-liter spare tank. She passed it up to Por, and he doused the boat with it. He climbed off, bringing the can with him.

"We could hear someone had woken up inside because the rear hatch rattled. Por lit the ransom note they'd left and tossed it into the cockpit. Within seconds, the boat was on fire from bow to stern. I started the outboard and drove off, but Por put his hand on mine and twisted the throttle back down as soon as we were out of the light. He said, 'No one will come.' I stopped the engine. We could hear banging and then screams. None of us said anything. You were still asleep. We think they'd drugged you to keep you quiet. We watched. Por was right. No one came. After a while, the banging stopped, the screams stopped. The flames worked their way into the boat, the deck peeled off. The mast came down and smashed a section of the burning deck and hull open. The fire burnt the yacht to the waterline, and she slipped under, stern first.

"When we got back to Kata. Joom took you back to my hut. I sat on the beach with Por. Later, Joom came out, sat with us. She reached over, put her hand on my neck, and pulled me to her. Gave me a kiss the like of which I'd never had. I can still feel it. Told me she forgave me, and she would love me forever for what I'd done. And then she said they were leaving in the morning, taking you with them."

A mist hung low on the river. A dog barked, setting off others on the far bank. An ice cube rolled over in a glass. Apart from that it was silent.

"Why did you decide to tell me this now?"

"I was talking with Pim earlier today. She told me about your talk with the Farang who kidnapped me. When you told me about it, you didn't mention the bit about 'Leon'. You know, when a woman came into the room and said, 'Leon'?"

"Yes." The hairs on my neck stood up.

"That was the name of the guy who kidnapped you when you were a kid. The one we burned to death."

Truth Will Out

My eyes flicked open. Pim had left. I hadn't woken her when I finally got to bed at four thirty. Chai handed me the phone, mouthed "Sankit" at me. I took the phone.

"Still sleeping, eh? It's Monday, you know, weekend's over. Anyway, I've got some information for you. Came from a friend of mine in Crime Suppression. I'd prefer to meet in person, and it is important you come alone. Meet me at the VIP breakfast lounge at the Dusit in an hour. Alone. Don't bring your shadow."

"All right. I'll see you there."

As the crow flies, it's eighteen and a half kilometers to the Dusit. But crows don't have to deal with Bangkok's roads and traffic. I was half an hour late. Leaving Chai with the Maserati, I went up to the VIP breakfast lounge. Sankit was sitting with a cop. There were a couple of other tables occupied but those around Sankit and the cop were empty. I went over, gave Sankit a wai, for form's sake. The cop raised himself out of his seat a little and waied me. I waied him back and sat down. Now that we'd sorted out the pecking order, we could order breakfast. Sankit looked at his watch and raised his bushy eyebrows at me. I wasn't in the mood. I just ignored him. He waved a hand at the cop, wiping his mouth with the other.

"Khun Oh, this is Sarawak Khumthong." Inspector Khumthong to you Farang. "He's with Crime Suppression, based at Hua Mark. Sarawak, you can talk freely with Khun Oh. He is my future son-in-law."

The inspector swallowed nervously, all smiles, nodding his head.

"Sor Sor Sankit had requested some colleagues to assist in finding out about the bombing that took place on Ratchada, concerning Mr. Samuel Harper and your father." I noticed he was careful not to mention it was a massage joint. Polite.

"My superior asked me to investigate. We didn't learn anything new about the bombing other than what forensics told us. However, one of my detectives saw the video of you – sorry, Mr. Harper – and his body-guard after the explosion. It is from the tape of the CCTV. He recognized your bodyguard from another investigation. I asked him to bring me anything he had. He brought me these." Khumthong passed me an A4 brown paper envelope. Just then, the waitress arrived to take my order. Just coffee, thanks.

"What was your detective investigating?" I asked him, opening the envelope. Inside, a thick sheaf of large photographs in color.

"A gang of Cambodians were dealing yaa baa in Lad Krabang. They killed a couple of the local dealers and took over the rest. We got onto them from another dealer, who was scared he was next."

I waited while the waitress poured the coffee and left, then I took out the photos. My blood ran cold. It was Chai talking to the three gunmen from the hospital. The date/time stamp in the bottom corner of the photos said the tenth of May. They were sitting at a table next to a food stall on a sidewalk. In the middle of the stack, a photo of Chai's hand reaching into an inside pocket, a glimpse of paper and passing it to the fat guy, the amulet easy to recognize. I went through all of them. Right to where Chai gets into the Lexus he was driving that day. I remember it. Two days before the explosion and the attack at the hospital. Chai had said he was going to a temple. He'd just finished a long chat with Por on the cell phone. I wanted to puke, but I held it together.

"Thanks for this, Sarawak Khumthong. If there is any way that I may be able to assist you in future, do not hesitate to call on me." He waied me, I waied him back, I waied Sankit. "Father, thank you for breakfast. I have to go. I have business to attend to." I got up and walked out of the restaurant. I managed not to bump into anything, even though my legs were wobbly. "Weak at the knees", I believe is the expression you Farangs use.

I used the washroom on the ground floor, near the lifts. Went into one of the stalls, I wiped the seat and sat down. I was shaking. I breathed out, had to get a grip. I took the photos out of the envelope. There was no mistaking it for anyone other than Chai. I tried to think of reasons why and came up dry. I breathed out hard, the ache in my chest swelling. I squeezed my eyes shut, and something broke inside me.

I washed my face and left the washroom. Walking past the sparsely filled cafeteria on the ground floor, the doors to the car park were opened by a smiling bell boy. Chai waiting outside, moving for the car the second he saw me. He looked the same, moved the same, but everything was different.

Fortunately, we don't talk much, so silence was normal. I couldn't trust myself to talk, the envelope on my lap. It took an hour to get to the Dusit from home. It took a lifetime to get back. I glanced at the cell phone. It was only nine-thirty in the morning. I got out and went straight into the house. Mother wasn't around in the main room.

Beckham was sitting cross-legged on the deck by the door to the guesthouse. He got up and opened the door for me. Mother was perched next to Por. She turned to me, a big smile on her face.

"He woke up just a short while ago. Said your name and went back to sleep. I spoke to Thomas. He said it is a sure sign that Por is recovering fast now."

"I need to talk to you." I flicked my eyes at the nurse on the other side of Por's bed. Mother asked her to take care of some things upstairs. I pulled a chair over from the dining table and sat down next to Mother, her face serious as she read mine.

"This morning, Sankit invited me for breakfast. Said he had some information to give me. Asked me to come alone. He was with a cop from Crime Suppression. He handed me these." I put the photos on the bed and spread them out, propping them up on Por's leg. Mother picked one up, the one with Chai slipping the money to the fat guy. A hand went to her mouth.

"Oh no. Oh, Chance. I'm so sorry." I've never seen Mother cry, but tears welled up in her eyes, the photo in her lap the cause. Tears landing on the image, one on Chai's face, distorting it. She sniffed back the tears and wiped her eyes with the back of her hand.

"Where's Pim?"

"She went to visit some friends. I spent some time with her this morning on the range. Chance, we have to deal with this now, today. We have no choice."

"I have to ask him why."

"It doesn't matter. All that matters is to remove the threat. That is the truth. If you try to understand why everything happens, you can go crazy trying. It can be as stupid but as basic as jealousy. Money, blackmail, position, bad mood, all of them – are why things happen. But when you cut off the source, it all stops."

"I need to know why Chai has done this to me."

"Ggh." The sound made us both jump. We'd been talking in whispers. It was Por. His eyes open. He was trying to talk, but the respirator in his throat made that impossible. His eyes were barely open, but I could tell he was forcing himself to stay awake. He lifted a hand and made a sign for a pen. On the coffee table, a pad and a pen. I got up and grabbed them. I put the pen in his hand. It still felt frail and fragile, but he gripped the pen. I held the pad steady for him.

"not Chai" – he wrote. The pen fell out of his hand. His eyes closed but flickered open. He signaled for the pen again. I put it back in his fingers.

"chai talk ok – Por". The pen slipped off the bed covers and fell on the floor. His eyes didn't open. The heart rate monitor looked normal. He had fallen asleep again.

"You go get ready and meet me at the sala in five minutes." Mother picked up the photos and put them back in the envelope. She pressed the bell for the nurse.

I went to the main garage off the forecourt of the main house. On the rear wall, a bench stood, and above the bench, shelves holding toolboxes. I took one of the toolboxes down and pushed on the panel behind it. The panel pushed in, sliding sideways to reveal a secret shelf. I took out a Beretta M9 and a Gemtech silencer, putting them on the bench. I loaded a magazine. It's like folding a parachute, something you have to do yourself, to be sure. The garage and house were quiet. Each click of a bullet seated like the click on a slide projector flicking through images of our life together. Some images of photos when we were apart. Photos he had of me and I of him. I thought of him as a brother. We were a team. I pushed the full magazine home and put one in the chamber.

I picked up a jacket from my room and went down to the sala. Joom was sitting at the far end. Next to her stood a small table, and on the table, the family Buddha, ancient and worn. I knelt and waied. Mother patted the floor beside her. She was sitting with her knees tucked under her next to the table. I sat down, covering the gun with my jacket. Mother called Chai.

"Chai, come down to the sala now. I want to talk to

you." Mother hung up the phone. It was her style. She turned to me.

"I've told everyone to leave us alone. No one will disturb us. Whatever needs to be done must be, for the sake of the family. Do you understand me?"

"Yes, Mother." I checked that the safety was off, sitting cross-legged, with my hand under the jacket, finger on the trigger guard.

Chai came up the steps to the sala. Shoes off, he paused slightly, a frown crossing his face as he saw the Buddha. He prostrated himself and waied three times as is our custom. Keeping his head low, he crossed to us and knelt on his knees in front of Mother.

His glance took in my stance and hand. His eyes flicked to me, understanding. The corners of his mouth twitched up in a little smile.

"Chai, you will swear to Buddha that you will tell the truth."

"Yes, Mother." Chai looked calmer than he had ever done. His hands folded one on top of the other as if he were at meditation – a calm face and eyes that were smiling.

"Chai, did you pay the Cambodians to kill Chance."

"Yes, Mother. I did." My heart raced. I was truly shocked. He was so blasé about it, like it was nothing. Mother put her hand on mine, the one under the jacket.

"Can you tell us why?"

"No, Mother. I'm sorry, I cannot. I cannot tell a lie, and I cannot tell you the truth. I swore I would not."

"Who did you swear this to?"

"I swore that I wouldn't say."

"You understand that Chance has no choice but to kill you?"

"Yes, Mother, I understand, and I accept it. I am content." He smiled at me. "My brother is ready to be-come Godfather, so my work is done. May Buddha protect him and guide him."

Mother leaned forward, placing the pad with Por's words on it in front of Chai. "Por wrote that today. I think he wrote it to you. Does that change what you can tell us?"

Chai visibly slumped and smiled.

"Por is awake?"

"Yes, for very short periods. He is recovering. Now can you tell us what this is all about?"

Chai waied the ground in front of Mother, holding his hands together in front of his chest.

"I swear, in front of the Lord Buddha, that what I shall say is the truth as I know the truth."

Chai's Tale

"In early May, I went to the showroom to get a car. If you remember, it was the car you took to Hua Hin, when you stayed at the Dusit."

"The seven series BMW?"

"Yes. What I didn't know is that Por had just used the car for a job. He had loaned the car to some Indian financier, and he had it bugged. The bugs weren't taken out until after you came back from Hua Hin. I took the car back to the showroom and picked up another one. Two days later, Por called me to come see him. We talked here. He asked me what I knew about you and Pim. I told him what I knew. He told me that Pim was forcing you to leave the family and asked how I felt about that. I told him the truth, which is that would upset me very much, that you belonged to us." Chai smiled at me. "And you do. You are ready to be Godfather now. You belong here, with us."

I knew what was coming. Could virtually replay every word of the discussion between Pim and I on the drive back to Bangkok. We'd got caught in traffic. I don't know how long Por's tapes lasted, but we talked solidly for three hours. Most of it was about leaving the business.

"Por was upset with the idea of you leaving the family. Said it was the wrong move for everyone, especially you. He left it at that. Told me he was going to think about it, and then he'd decide what to do. A few days later, he called me again. Asked me to come see him. He told me he had a plan, but he needed my help.

"Por said it was time for Samuel Harper to go. His plan was to kidnap Pim, take her upcountry and give her a good talking-to about family values, and have someone try to kill you. I would kill whoever tried to kill you, but it would be leaked to the media so you as Samuel Harper would be exposed. Por said he could take care of all the legal stuff. Once we'd 'rescued' Pim, and you were back in the family, Por planned to retire."

"I asked around, found out about some Cambodians who'd moved into the slum in Lad Krabang. I followed them a bit, got to know their habits, and approached them with a deal. I'd tell them where and when they should hit. If they broke that rule, they wouldn't get paid, and they'd all be killed. They agreed. I went back and told Por what was organized. He said to wait until he was ready. The next thing, the bomb went off in…"

"Chai, I'm perfectly aware that Por was with a girl in Heaven. Please, it is normal," Mother said.

"You sent the photoshopped photos to the Thai Rath?" I asked him.

"It was Por's wish. He was in hospital in a coma, but he came to me while I was meditating. All this time, he was giving me instructions. When he wakes up, you can ask him."

I've known Chai a long time. Up until this morning, I'd have said I could tell when he was lying. If he was lying, I still couldn't tell. His eyes were open, honest, and unblinking, looking from me to Mother with a small smile on his lips.

"Did Por order you to carry out the plan, or did you see that in a dream as well?"

"As I was carrying Por out of Heaven, he asked me about Bank and Red. I told him they were dead, and he told me to follow the plan, to do it, said we needed it now. It was his last order to me, and with Bank and Red dead, he was relying on me. Then he passed out. I went back and got Chance, then I drove you both to the hospital.

"The hospital was a good, controlled environment and public. I called the Cambodians, told them to send three, and it worked out exactly as I planned." He looked at me with a grimace. "From then on, things got a bit out of hand. When the first group of three was killed and you were announced dead, I thought it was good enough. I paid them and told them to stop. That's when they got the bright idea that they'd still kidnap the girl. It wasn't you they were after. It was Pim. That wasn't supposed to happen. That's why I was so angry, I wasn't there. But you did a good job. To make sure it didn't happen again, while you were in Singapore, I killed most of the rest of the gang. They were scum, dealing yaa baa to the kids in the slum. They needed to move on to their next life."

"What about the guy on the pier?"

Chai smiled. "Por showed me in a dream. A crocodile being attacked by a tiger at a watering hole, but the crocodile rolled and bit the tiger in the neck. So, two birds, one stone. I implicate Big Tiger and get rid of the last of the Cambodians."

"He had a double-barreled shotgun pointed at me."

The smile grew into a grin. "I know. I gave him the shotgun and told him you were coming, while you had a smoke. Then I walked up the pier and called you. Waited till you appeared, and he made his move, then I shot him." Chai leaned forward and put his hands out in front. He turned them over to show he had nothing in them. He reached up by my ear and held two 9mm cartridges in his fingers. He smiled again.

"You ordered Pichit and Somboon to put the guy in cold storage and turn the temperature down."

"I did, and he was the last of them. That evening, I sent Thai Rath news desk the photoshopped photos of you, and the next day Samuel Harper was dead and Chance alive. That is everything that happened." He dropped his hands, which had been in a wai all this time, and put them on his thighs, facing Mother. He bowed his head, his chin on his chest.

Mother shuffled forward, her hand reaching to Chai's chin. She lifted his head and leaned forwards, kissing him on the forehead. She turned, looking at me.

"Maybe we can talk later, after dinner. I'm going to take the Buddha back to his room. I'll leave you two to talk things over." She waied the Buddha and picked it up. Holding it in her hands, she rose from her knees. She smiled at Chai. If he had a tail, he'd be wagging it.

Chai looked at me. "I'm sorry."

"It's okay, I understand. It was Por's orders."

"No, I'm not sorry about that. I'm sorry I had to tell Joom your private conversation with Pim."

"You killed five people to keep me in the family."

He grinned, his dark brown eyes wide open, innocent as a newborn babe. "It was nine if you include the one's you didn't see. I killed nine scum who deserved to die. I'd have killed ninety saints to keep you with us." He didn't blink.

There was nothing more to say.

I knew now, how the bomb had gone off in Heaven. I still didn't know if it was an accident or deliberate. The trail ended at the 11th Infantry Regiment Barracks. Sankit had genuinely helped in the Cambodian assassin thing, even though he looked pleased that my own bodyguard had betrayed me. I'd leave him in the dark on that one. I hadn't told Pim any of this. Saw no value in that. Without concrete evidence of some kind, it was all conjecture. I decided to put the matter on a back burner.

I wasn't any closer to figuring out who had grabbed Uncle Mike. Immigration had turned up nothing on Leon, and all the other paperwork was a false trail that led nowhere. It was possible the name was just one of those coincidences, you know, chance. It was possible, but somehow I doubted it. There was something that niggled away in the background, but I couldn't put my finger on it. Just a feeling that there was something I'd missed.

We retrieved Um's body and sent it to his parents with enough money to give a decent funeral. We are not heartless. We did this on behalf of the red shirts and added his name to the list of those killed in the fighting. In a way, it was the truth. I sent the same amount to Ice's father, promising I'd come and see him personally when I had a bit more time. I told him in my note that Ice was a victim of the political violence and that the person who got her involved was dead. I hoped it would give him some closure. I lied about the money too; said it was found in Ice's room and belonged to him. I knew he'd be too proud to take it otherwise.

Loose ends, yes, but I'll take any end to trouble. I still had to decide what to say to Pim, but the choice had narrowed. I couldn't leave the family. Not now. Not ever. The only choices that remained: let her go or be selfish and ask her to stay with me.

I had been thinking about Joom. About the day I first met her. I was picked up at the apartment building by Uncle Mike and Por. I don't really remember much about what happened before, and my memories of what happened after are like anybody's. I remember the first day I met Joom like it had happened this morning.

I got out of the car and saw her for the first time. She was sitting under the house, where the garage is now. Back then it was hard-packed earth with a wooden Thai house on stilts standing on it, grass and trees all around. The river flooded here regularly. There were boats turned over under the house and Joom was sitting on one. She was twenty-two then, but to me as a kid, she was just another adult. We don't figure out age until we've got some.

I stayed where I was. I wasn't scared. My parents had often left me with strangers or alone. Mostly, I preferred being left with strangers. Joom got up off the boat and walked over to us. She squatted down in front of me. She was then and still is beautiful. She smiled.

"Can you speak Thai, Dek Farang." I nodded. I spoke Thai better than I spoke English, as a kid I'd spent more time with Thai people than Farangs.

"You know it isn't polite to nod when an adult asks you a question?"

I remember looking at her and thinking that over. Her eyes were smiling, so I gave her an honest answer. "No. I didn't know that."

Her smile got bigger. "Do you know why you're here?"

I had started to shake my head, but replied, "No."

"Do you know who Buddha is?"

"Yes." I did. My parents were "really into Buddha, you know, man…"

"Buddha has sent you to me. You can call me Mere Joom."

Tum pulled into the parking lot of the Golden Fortune Chinese Restaurant. Chai and I got out. The car park was dark, hot and crowded. I was standing in for Por at the monthly Godfathers' meeting. Held at a different location each month, this month's place had been chosen by Loong Virote. Literally translated, his name means "Tower of Strength". He was being helped out of his old black Benz, the kind with the long vertical headlamps. His bodyguard reached in behind him to collect the aluminum cane he used.

Big Tiger pulled up, Daeng and his boys following in their white van. Tiger got out, yelling at the girl in the car with him. It was Uni girl. Obviously she'd made it back from Samui. Tiger and his boys saw us and started walking over. Uni girl got out of the car, yelling at Big Tiger, calling him a fat old lizard. He just waved a hand and kept walking, his boys chuckling.

I stopped still. The thing that had been nagging at me – the woman's voice – "Leon". It was Uni girl.

MAKING A KILLING

I walked quickly past Big Tiger, heading for the fire exit door that Uni girl had used. I heard Big Tiger call out.

"Hey, Chance, the elevator's this fucking way," but I was moving, as fast as I could without running, Chai a few steps behind. I was thinking: Uni girl on Lilly's phone, how the hell did that happen? I banged through the fire exit door. Yellow-painted walls and a staircase leading up. I took the steps three at a time, running, now that I was out of sight of the guys in the garage. The staircase ended with a door I slammed open. It led into the open-air lobby of the restaurant. Uni girl nowhere to be seen. Then I spotted her. She was getting into a cab about fifty meters away. I ran, Chai hard on my heels. The taxi pulled away before we'd got halfway there. I turned and shouted at Chai, "Get the car. I'll follow them."

Chai sprinted back the way we'd come. I angled off, chasing after the pink taxi on foot. More than a hundred meters ahead of me, the taxi turned left onto Soi Ngam Duphli. I couldn't see the street sign yet, but I knew the street. It was usually blocked with traffic. I kept running. No sign of Chai and the car yet. I ran, dodging food vendors, their carts, and their annoyed customers at the street side tables. Our sidewalks are considered retail space. I nearly collided with a hawker selling balloons and switched to running on the road. I glanced back and saw Chai bouncing the Maserati out of the restaurant's car park.

I turned the corner onto Soi Ngam Duphli and spotted the taxi stuck in traffic. About another two hundred meters further up the soi. It wasn't going anywhere. Hands on knees, getting my breath, I waited for Chai. He cut off a tuk-tuk, barely missing it, and then pulled up in front of me. I got in, and Chai gave the car a little burst, and we were behind the taxi.

"What do you want to do?" Chai asked. "Follow her, or take her now?"

It was tricky here. There were a lot of people around. If she kicked up a fuss … then I had an idea. "Take her now. You stay with the car."

Chai nodded. I got out and walked around to her side of the taxi. She was in the back seat. I tapped on the window and smiled. I couldn't remember her name. She looked shocked, and then she smiled. The window came down.

"I saw you back in the car park having an argument with Tiger. Are you okay?"

"Yes, I'm fine. No problem. I was kind of bored with him anyway. You followed me here?"

"No, no, I was heading out to get some lunch. The idea of having lunch with Tiger and the crowd just didn't appeal. Hey, do you want to join me for lunch? My car and driver are right here. I know a nice hotel nearby." The last sentence was the clincher. I saw the calculator go off behind her eyes. The taxi door opened.

I opened the rear door of the Maserati for her. She got in and shuffled over. I got in behind her and shut the door.

"Chai, can you get us back out to Rama Four?"

Chai looked over his shoulder, a couple of taxis behind us. A bumpy three-point turn later, we were headed in the right direction. I took her hand in mine.

"What do you say to a change in plan? We can head straight to my place. Better than a hotel, more private. We can have a drink, relax, and talk?"

"Talk?" she said with a sly smile. Her tongue poked out and gave her upper lip a wipe.

"Yeah, talk."

She slipped her hand out of mine and ran it up my arm, her fingers softly stroking. Sliding closer to me on the seat, she brought her mouth close to my ear and whispered, "What do you want to talk about?"

I turned to face her, my nose touching hers.

"Leon."

Confusion clouded her eyes.

"Who? What?"

"Leon. Five days ago, in the morning. You walked into a room and called someone Leon. Where were you, and who is Leon?"

She jerked back and tried to open the door. I sat and watched. She turned to me and snarled, "You better fucking let me out of here, or I'll scream and call the cops."

I sat and watched.

"Did you fucking hear me? I said let me out of here now."

Enough. "Listen carefully. This can go one of two ways. One: you tell me everything you know, right now. Be honest and leave nothing out. Then I'll drop you where you want to go. Two: I kill you right now."

Chai handed me a Glock with a suppressor attached. I didn't point it at her, just held it in my lap.

Her eyes got big. "Okay, okay, I'll tell you everything. It wasn't my idea anyway, it was Big Tiger's."

For opening lines, she wasn't doing too badly. She had my attention. I eased myself around in the seat, lifted the barrel of the gun slightly, and nodded my head at her to keep talking.

"I was in Samui with Leon and Ursula, but it was Big Tiger that forced me to go."

"Who are Leon and Ursula?"

"You met them, at Big Tiger's restaurant. Wow, that bomb really did affect you."

Brett and Sheena, Ken and Barbie – shit.

"How do you know I was bombed?"

"Big Tiger was talking about it with Daeng. Daeng is my brother. After you came to the restaurant, the first time I met you, I heard them talking about it."

"What did they say?"

"Tiger said he was fifty per cent happy that you lived because now he could collect. And fifty percent sad because you, and he thought also, Por, had survived."

Chai's visions and Por's warnings. Not to be ignored. "What else?"

"About that?"

I nodded.

"Nothing else."

"Tell me about Leon. When did you know that his name was Leon?"

"Only after we were in Samui. Ursula called him Leon by mistake. He got angry with her, and later, they both told me their real names."

"Were you in Samui the whole time?"

"Yes, at Big Tiger's resort. Mostly we just took drugs, had sex, slept and ate. Sometimes we went for a swim. We didn't do anything wrong."

"Was Leon with you the whole time?"

"Sometimes he went off alone. One time, one of Big Tiger's boys came to get him, and they went off for a while. But most of the time he was with us."

Chai left the expressway and headed west up Sukhumvit. She'd figure out pretty soon where we were taking her, and then she'd freak out.

"I need you to understand that we need to keep you under our protection for a couple of days. You'll be looked after, don't worry."

"You promised I could leave." Tears in her eyes, an accusing look on her face.

"I lied. It really is for your own protection. If Big Tiger learns you've talked to me. He'll have you killed. Probably ask your brother to do it. And your brother will do it. He'll have no choice. So be cool, jai yen, and stay in a room for a couple of days. Okay?"

She sniffed and nodded her head. Chai turned off Sukhumvit, headed for Prakhon Chai. Another ten minutes, and we'd be on home turf.

"Give me your cell phone, please." I held my hand out. She pouted and pulled her handbag closer to her.

"Please. Otherwise I'll stop the car. Put you out there and call Big Tiger myself."

She took out an iPhone, with a flurry of thumbs switched it off, and passed it to me. I took out the SIM and handed it back to her.

"We can leave her at Tum's house." Chai had been doing a little SMSing of his own. "He's on his way."

"Okay, sounds like a plan." I called Mother.

"Yes, Chance?"

"Chai's vision came true, the one with the crocodile. We're on our way to Tum's house. We have someone with us who we need to look after for a couple of days, until we've cleared the problem."

"I'll send someone."

"Thanks, Mother."

"Chance?"

"That other thing that we were going to talk about…"

"Yes."

"Don't think about that. We can talk whenever. I know your heart is in the right place. Just focus on what we have to do."

"Yes, Mother."

"And Chance?"

"Yes, Mother?"

"Don't forget what I told you in the hospital."

"Yes, Mother." She hung up.

"Will you kill my brother?" The reality of what she'd done writ in her scared eyes. She looked younger.

"That depends on your brother, not me. Now please sit quietly, I want to think."

We dropped her off at Tum's place, swapped cars and headed out. Big Tiger was still at the Golden Fortune. I was hot, raring to go, and that's when we need to slow down. Have a good think with a cool head. Both Por and Uncle Mike had taught me this since I was a kid. Of course, Uncle Mike also advocated dropping acid or smoking weed, but that was for a different kind of thinking.

This was thinking about killing.

It was a delicate time. The other families knew now that Por was alive but injured. You can't keep that kind of secret too long. Word gets around. The troubles with the red-shirts and the recent riots had pushed established boundaries into a state of flux. By their standards, I was a "young Turk", perhaps not fit to take Por's place. For the "old men" of the district, the one who has the right to rule is the one who takes it.

If Big Tiger had made a move, it was possible others knew and were waiting to see which way the wind would blow. He'd played me for a sucker, led me by the nose. Even such an act as that is enough to cause doubt that I was fit to be "boss of bosses". The surprise on his face when he saw me that time at the restaurant wasn't that I was alive. It was because he thought I'd come to get him.

I had a big advantage. He didn't know I was coming this time. That would only hold true for a little while. I still wondered why he hadn't just killed me when he had the chance. I wasn't going to give him another one. The disadvantage I had was that I needed to take him alive. We had the boys stick GPS trackers on the white van and Tiger's blue Benz. We didn't call all our boys in, either. We needed to keep everything looking normal, play out our advantage to its fullest. People would notice if we suddenly pulled everyone off the street. It could come to that, but I hoped we could do this quietly.

Without knowing if he had allies or who they were, I had to take Big Tiger quietly. Snatch him, interrogate him and kill him. There are two ways to catch a tiger. One, put a bunch of beaters in the jungle and advance slowly without any gaps. Two, tether a wounded monkey in the tiger's home turf. A plan was forming.

To Catch A Tiger

24 May 2010, Pak Nam, 11:45 pm

Uni girl's name was Pheung, Bee in English. Puffy-eyed, sniffling, she wiped the snot from her nose with the back of her hand. Her other hand held her iPhone with the speaker on, the ringing of the unanswered call loud in the back of the van.

We were parked across the street from the exit of Big Tiger's house. Tiger lived down a small soi about fifty meters from the Ancient Village tourist attraction in Samut Prakarn. Chai had borrowed a standard BMTA (Bangkok Mass Transit Authority) commuter van. Parked in the queue with ten others, it was inconspicuous.

The first two houses in Tiger's soi were occupied by his boys. Lights still shone in the house we could see from where we were. Tiger had been at home for an hour.

"What the fuck do you want?" Tiger's voice sounded

sleepy and pissed off.

Pheung sniffed loudly, the phone in front of her mouth trembling.

"Tiger, I'm scared, please come get me."

"What the fuck are you on…"

"No, no, I'm not on anything, I'm really scared. Today after I left you. This big guy tried to grab me, said he wanted to talk to me about Leon. Where have you been, I've been trying to call you?"

"This guy, what did he look like?" Big Tiger's tone had changed. All sounds of sleep disappeared. I held my breath, this was it.

"Dark-skinned, a scar on his cheek near his eye. Very big shoulders." It was a good enough description of Chai.

"Where the fuck are you now?"

"My apartment, but I'm scared to stay here. What if he knows where I live?"

"All right. Stay there. I'll send that fucking useless brother of yours."

"I've called Daeng. He's not answering his phone. He's probably lying drunk in a bar somewhere."

"Fuck. All right, I'll send some of the boys…"

"No…" she screamed, loud enough that I quickly scanned through the tinted windows of the van to check if any passersby had heard. All okay. My heart thumping, I was worried my breathing could be heard on the phone's microphone.

"…Please come yourself. I promise I'll be nice to you later."

"Oh, fuck. All right. Stay there. Don't fucking move. I'll call your brother first, but either he or I will come to get you. Don't fucking move. All right?"

Pheung sniffed again. "All right."

I indicated with my thumb to shut the call. She did. Chai shifted the barrel of the silenced Uzi, pointing it at Daeng's head. It was cool in the van, engine running, air-conditioning on, but beads of sweat lined up on his receding hairline. We waited.

The phone in Daeng's hand rung. Chai shifted the Uzi a little closer. He answered the call on speakerphone.

"Yes, boss?"

"That fucking sister of yours is causing us grief. It sounded like that goat-fucking Farang's bodyguard tried to grab her today. She's at her apartment. You pick the stupid bitch up and bring her here. Take some of the boys with you. She said she tried to call you. Where the fuck have you been?"

"Sorry, boss. I was getting laid. It's been a stressful week. No need for the boys. I'm driving past her place right now."

"Just get the stupid bitch and bring her here."

I heard Big Tiger sigh and the connection cut. I looked at the time on the cell phone, 11:50 pm. Act one complete. I thought they both deserved Oscars. Daeng had been easy to pick up. Pichit, one of our boys, followed him into the men's room at the restaurant. While he was peeing, Pichit showed him a photo of his sister with a gun to her head and two plane tickets to Los Angeles, California. Cooperate and get a new life, or die. An easy choice for an unappreciated underpaid henchman. Daeng's car, a low slung, five-year-old, five series BMW with tinted windows was parked down a soi a hundred meters away.

We left the van and walked down the street, taking a right down the soi to where we'd parked Daeng's car. Daeng got in the driver's seat, Pheung in the passenger seat. Chai and I got in the back. No one said anything. It was warm in the car. Daeng turned the engine on and turned the air-conditioning up. I checked the cell phone, another eight minutes to go.

Across the street, a pack of soi dogs stood looking at the car. Noses in the air, they could smell, but not see us. One of the pack got too close to the leader. The leader turned, snapping at the encroacher's neck. The bitten stray took off up the soi, yelping, tail between its legs. The rest of the pack chased it. The leader turned back to us with his nose in the air. A group of teenagers crossed the front of the soi, laughing and pushing each other. The dog's head turned towards the sound, and then he trotted over to our car. He stopped by the front wheel passenger side and cocked his leg. This was his soi. Point made, he trotted off into the shadows.

Five minutes left. Chai touched a button on his comms pack.

"Get ready. Five minutes. Five minutes," he repeated. We had Beckham and Tum parked further down the road. If our plan went wrong, back up was a hundred meters away.

"Go. Take the route I showed you and no faster than twenty," Chai said.

He pressed the button on his arm rest, winding down his window. The black eighty-percent film he had taped in place looked like a window. Once we reached the main road, we ducked down. Mini cameras taped in the rear window gave us a view of either side of the car.

Daeng turned right on the main road and drove at a steady pace. The car slowed as we approached the entrance to Big Tiger's soi. Deang opened the window on his side and his sister's. We approached the barrier, a red-striped metal pole across the soi, and a guard's hut with a window, the guard rubbing his eyes, yawning.

"Open the fucking gate. Tiger's expecting me." I heard Daeng say. The car moved forward, tires crunching on soft gravel. I checked my weapon again. I'd chosen an HK UMP 5 .45 ACP with a Gemtech suppressor. Twenty-five rounds per magazine. I had it set on full auto, stock folded. I didn't want a war, but if one started, I wanted to be dressed properly.

The front gate of Tiger's house appeared, a huge Tiger face emblem set in the middle of its bars. Daeng drove close to the wall and pressed a button on the intercom, arm out of the window.

"Who is it?" Tiger's voice.

"Daeng, I'm with Pheung."

The gates started to open, rolling back. Big Tiger's house was set back from the soi by about fifty meters. I could see in the right side monitor a circular driveway enclosing a garden with a large fountain and pond in the middle. We went left. I watched the left monitor as the front door to Tiger's house slid into view. We drove past a little more and stopped. Safe from being seen, I sat up and clicked my weapon off safety. Daeng had parked at a good angle to the front door. Chai brought his milspec M26 Tazer to bear, aiming through the film.

The door opened. Big Tiger looked out and peered

around cautiously. Then he stepped out, wearing nothing but a pakama and a gun. He moved quickly for a fat guy. Chai lined up, but Tiger had walked too fast, moving behind the car. Daeng opened his door and started to get out. Tiger's gun started to come up. Shit! He was going for it right here. Chai moved. Flinging the car door open, he got out and turned. I opened my door, gun ready to fire. Tiger's face was shocked as he recognized me. His gun swung towards me, and then the twin electrode darts of Chai's Tazer hit him in the chest. Tiger's legs fell out from underneath him, the gun bouncing on the red bricks of the driveway. Tiger's body twitched, and a pool of piss spread out from underneath him.

"Pop the trunk," Chai ordered Daeng. I took up a position near the fountain, watching the gate and the front windows of the house. Nothing moved. I could hear dogs barking out on the road. Probably the same pack we'd seen in the soi. A frog croaked in the pond. Daeng and Chai lifted Tiger and rolled him into the trunk of Daeng's car.

"Chai, find Tiger's phone," I whispered into my microphone.

Chai nodded and went into Tiger's house. I dialed Tiger's phone to make Chai's job easier. While Chai was looking for the phone, I collected Tiger's gun from where it had fallen beneath the car. Chai reappeared, nodded at me, and we got back in the car. With Pheung lying on the floor at our feet, Chai and I crouched low on the back seat. I checked the time. Less than three minutes. We went back up the soi, Daeng flicking his beam lamps at the guard. I watched as the guard, shielding his eyes from the bright lights, lifted the barrier up. Nice touch, Daeng. We turned right onto Sukhumvit Road. I sat up and gave Chai a grin. I like it when a plan comes together.

The white BMTA van we'd been using was parked on our side of the road, two kilometers further up. Chai told Daeng to pull over in front of it. We got out. Daeng and Pheung got out. They looked scared and nervous. Chai handed them each an envelope. I walked over to them and indicated towards the van.

"Beckham and Tum will take you to a hotel, then to the airport in the morning. You've got a new life in those envelopes, new names, new place, money to spend. Don't come back."

They nodded and waied me. I watched them get in the van. Tum pulled out. They'd spend the night at a short-time motel near the airport. In the morning, Tum would take them to the airport. Chai had argued for death. It was the right thing to do, but I wanted to give them a chance. Whatever their faults, they'd played their parts well. It was a risk, but one I was willing to accept.

We got back in the BMW and turned left into Bang Pu Industrial Estate. We had a warehouse here, one we seldom used. Deep in the heart of the estate, the corrugated iron building behind a chain link fence looked run down. Weeds grew in the cracks of the cement driveway and unloading area. Chai dragged the wide door open. I drove in and popped the trunk. Chai closed the door behind us.

Together we heaved his body out of the trunk and dragged him over to the gantry hoists. Chai tied Big Tiger's hands over his head and his feet together at the ankles. He made a loop each end and connected the loops to the hoist's hooks. Green button up, red button down. Tiger moaned, he was coming around. Chai pressed the green buttons on both control boxes. Tiger rose from the floor, the ropes around his wrists and ankles biting hard into his flesh. Chai stopped before Tiger was fully stretched out, face up, his body horizontal about waist height.

Tiger puked. Messy. Then he wet himself. Messier. I hoped we were done with the bodily functions. Lucky we hadn't duct taped his mouth. He didn't look too comfortable hanging there. I stared down at him. Eyes rolling and blinking rapidly, puke and drool hanging from the corner of his mouth.

"Tiger, do you know who this is?"

"Oh, fuck." His voice had lost its power. He sounded like he looked, naked.

"I want to know about the kidnapping and Leon. I want you to tell me everything. If I believe you, I will let you live. Now talk or…"

"Fu-fuck off."

I nodded at Chai. He pressed both green buttons. The gantry motors whirred, and the cables tightened. Tiger straightened out a bit more. His eyes darted from side to side as he thrashed himself about. Reminded me of when we capture a crocodile by the mouth and tail. He had risen to chest height. I walked behind Tiger's sagging head and nodded for Chai to stop.

The echo of the motors died, the only sound was Tiger's panting. Tiger looked up into my eyes.

"This is a bad way to die, Tiger. Just tell me what happened. We're not far from your home. You could be back there in five minutes. But this is it. This is your last chance to talk. I'm tired, and I want to get some sleep. So if you don't talk now, I'm going have Chai duct tape your mouth shut, and then he's going to tighten the cables until either your arms or your legs pull off. At which stage, you'll either get a nasty bump on the head or you'll be legless. You might die of shock at that point or you'll bleed to death. Either way, it shouldn't take more than five minutes. Your call." I looked him in the eyes, letting him know I had no problem doing exactly what I'd just said I'd do.

"I'll talk."

I thought he might. I thought of Lilly, and a part of me wished he'd been "old school".

Bungalow # Thirteen

25 May 2010, Seat 14A PG103, 6:55am

A flight attendant's voice woke me up. "…and gentlemen, the captain has turned the seatbelt sign on. We will be landing in Koh Samui shortly. Please make sure your window shade is up, the tray locked securely to the seat in front of you and your seat is in the upright position. Thank you for flying Bangkok Airways, and we wish you a pleasant trip." I eased my seat into the upright position and pushed the window shade up. We'd just made the six am flight. I'd fallen asleep before we took off.

Tiger had been recycled. By now, he'd be in several of the twenty baht bags of "Croc O' Licious" that we sold to the tourists. So far there'd been no unusual activity reported from his turf. He'd talked. Told us everything we needed to know and a bit more besides. Then I shot him in the head.

Leon was the son of the man who had killed my parents. Only he never knew that part. He was born after his father died. He only knew that his father had come to Phuket on a yacht from Singapore and had never returned. Forty years later, by accident, he learned about Uncle Mike, Por and Joom. It was Big Tiger who had told him about me.

Big Tiger wanted a Farang to be the one on the call. In exchange for twenty percent, Tiger offered me up. Part of the deal, and the reason I hadn't been killed, was Leon wanted me alive so he could burn me to death. Brett and Sheena were Leon and Ursula. Ursula's sister, Natasha, actually in Moscow not Odessa, was the honey to sucker Uncle Mike. Leon and Ursula had been at Big Tiger's resort since the time I had dinner with them. Big Tiger complained about the bill they were running up, waiting for a second chance at me.

The plane came in over Chaweng Beach and touched down, taxiing back to the terminal. In business class, we got off first and walked through the open-air terminal. It was hot and humid, but the air had that sea smell that lets you know you're near a beach. Backpackers, families with kids, the usual mix of tourists, everyone looking happy and relaxed. We didn't even try to blend in.

At the exit from the airport, a stocky guy wearing camouflage trousers and a black T-shirt handed Chai the keys to a black Range Rover parked curbside. Chai clipped the GPS unit to the dashboard and started the engine. The route to Big Tiger's resort at Thong Krut beach already entered, we waited for the GPS to lock on and sync. Bright blue sky, not a cloud in it – hell of a day to die.

It was twenty-three kilometers to Big Tiger's resort, and we wanted to be there before eight. Seven am now, we had to motor. Chai put his foot down. I reached around and took the bag off the back seat. I unrolled the beach towel. A Walther PPK/S .38 caliber, a suppressor and a magazine. I checked and loaded the weapon. The other beach towel had a Sig Sauer .38 and the same accessories. I checked and loaded it as well. I handed the Sig, safety on, to Chai. A glance over the other materials on the backseat confirmed that Chai's contact had been reliable.

We stayed on the 4169, running down the east coast of Samui. People were out on the beach already, the ocean flat calm, aquamarine blue ready for a holiday snap. The going was slower than we liked. We got caught behind a truck carrying sugar-cane crawling up a hill. Once over the hill, Chai got past him, and we made better progress. Past Lamai beach, we came through Maret and turned off onto the 4170. The road had less traffic on it, and we made better time.

We turned off the main road, driving down a small dirt track, jungle either side of the road. Chai turned off the track and went into the resort car park. The Tiger resort was on the eastern side of Thong Krut beach. The resorts villas ran back from the beach in two parallel lines, a restaurant, swimming pool and bar in the middle between the bungalows. Chai parked nearest the entrance, under the shade of coconut trees. He looked up to check that the coconuts were young. They make a hell of a dent if they fall off and land on your car.

Chai collected the supplies off the back seat. I hung the beach towel around my neck to hide the butt of the gun. Leon and Ursula were in room thirteen. We walked into the resort. The path threaded through thick bamboo and jungle. We passed an old couple with smiles and good mornings, Germans, by the sound of their accents. Outside room thirteen as requested, a large laundry basket. The path was quiet. I looked in the basket for the spare key to room thirteen. We'd had Tiger call the resort manager and order him to put the key in laundry basket outside the door to thirteen. I found the key under a sheet. Chai put the supplies in the basket, and we went up on the porch.

A nod at Chai and we pulled masks over our faces. I slipped the key into the lock. Holding the door handle, I slowly turned the key, until I heard the latch snick. I pushed the door slowly inwards. A small, short hallway, a double bed and a door to the bathroom. The bathroom door was shut. I could hear water running. Leon was sleeping on the bed. Ursula must be in the shower. Good, if we could do this without having to sedate her, so much the better. Leon was lying on his side. Legs curled up, hand on the pillow beside him.

I shot him in the temple. It was kinder. Let him go in paradise. I lifted his head to check the exit. There wasn't one. The bullet was in his head. I kept a watch on the bathroom. Chai dodged out to the laundry trolley and unrolled the plastic bag onto the empty space on the double bed. We rolled Leon onto it. Chai put a plastic bag over Leon's head, securing it in place with a couple of tight cable ties around his neck. I worked the zip of the bag quietly closed, keeping an eye and ear on the bathroom door. Bag closed, I searched the bedside drawer. Leon's passport, wallet, watch. I took a hundred thousand baht out of my packet and left it in the bedside drawer: Leon's guilt money for Ursula.

Chai nodded at me from the door. I heard the water in the shower stop. We picked Leon up and carried him out the door, putting him quietly in the basket. Chai threw his beach towel in after covering up the folded body bag. I pushed the lock back in on the door and closed it behind me. A last glance showed the bathroom door opening. I was glad Ursula was taking a shower, we didn't need the baggage. Chai was already turning the corner up the path to the car park, the laundry basket's wheels rattling on the brick path.

Chai opened the rear door of the Range Rover. I got one side of the laundry basket, and we lifted it into the rear cargo area. Back on the main road, we turned left and headed up the west coast of the island to the main pier and car ferry to Don Sak.

We drove west up to Taling Ngam. Outside a gas station on the intersection to the pier, we pulled over. I had a bowl of red pork Kuai Teow with wontons for breakfast.

After eating, I called Mother.

"Our friend has already left for Singapore. I'll send his arrival time by email." I took out Leon's Australian passport and took a photo of the identification details page. I sent the photo to Mother. Leon would be entered in Thailand's immigration computer as having traveled from Samui to Bangkok and then Singapore. He was already on his way.

We drove down to the roll-on roll-off pier, Chai at the wheel. Traffic was heavy, pedestrian and vehicles. I got out and walked to the ferry. I climbed the stairs to the upper deck and stood leaning against the railing. The sun sparkled on the sea, glints that made you squint your eyes as their brilliance hit you. A couple of kids shrieked, startling me as they chased each other up the stairs laughing. Their mother called to them to be careful. I sighed. The day wasn't done. We had more chores to do, starting with getting rid of Leon's body.

I called Cheep.

"Hey, Cheep, how you doing?"

"Chance. I'm good, really good. What's up?"

"I need your help. Want to go fishing, about five miles offshore, deep water. Can you organize?"

"Sure. Can. When you need?"

"This afternoon. We should be there just before 5:00 pm."

"No problem. Consider it done."

"And, Cheep, just us. I have a special kind of bait."

"Understood. I'll drive."

"Thanks, Cheep. See you later."

The ferry to Don Sak would take between two and a half to three hours depending on the captain's mood. I looked around. There was a wooden bench seat up against a bulkhead. I sat down. The morning sun felt hot on my face, warming the material of my shirt and my jeans. Chai came up the steps and stood by the railing, looking out to sea. I put my arm across my eyes and stretched out. The warmth felt good. I pushed an image of Leon, curled up in the body bag, out of my mind. Time enough for that later.

After the ferry ride, it was a two hundred and eighty-seven kilometers drive to Phuket, most of it on twisty mountain road. More time to sleep.

Sunset Cruise

25 May 2010, Phuket, 4:45pm

Between the sleep I had on the ferry and the first couple of hours driving to Phuket, I was refreshed. I had taken over driving a couple of hours ago, to give Chai a chance to get some sleep. I nudged his shoulder as I rolled down the sandy track next to Cheep's, actually Uncle Mike's, resort.

I turned left on the track just before the beach and drove down to the fishing pier that Uncle Mike had built. It was illegal, but the navy, whose ground it was on, turned a blind eye in return for a monthly envelope. I parked the Range Rover at the end of the pier and got out. The sun hung low on the horizon now, the sky a faultless blue, the sea undulated calmly, not a wave to be seen.

At the end of the pier, Cheep was standing next to an open speedboat. From where I stood, it looked like a fast smuggling boat. Chai and I got the laundry basket out of the Range Rover and down onto the wooden pier. We collected everything from the Range Rover, tossing it into the laundry basket. Chai pushed the basket, rattling its way down the pier.

Cheep looked nervous. Hands clasped in front of him, but he came forward to give a hand.

"Sawasdee, Khun Chance, Chai." He waied. Unusual, he'd never done that before, always treated me as a Farang, as Uncle Mike's nephew. I waied him back.

Getting a square basket, loaded with a man, from a pier onto a smaller boat is not easy. As we lifted the basket down, Cheep stumbled, and the body bag tumbled out onto the floor of the boat. After that, it was a piece of cake.

The boat was basic. A center console with twin 300HP mercury engines on the back, seats arranged fore and aft. Cheep cast off from the pier and spun the boat around. He eased the throttles forward, the boat lifted its bow, and we headed out to sea, cruising at about ten knots, not up on plane. I went and sat in the right corner of the boat.

The air was cool with the speed of the boat. The sea lay flat, like a mirror. Just us and a couple of fishing boats heading out for a night's work. I took off my shirt and my jeans, putting the Walther and my phone into a small locker next to me. The air felt good against my skin. I stretched my arms out either side of the boat. Chai was sitting up front, with Cheep steering, sitting sideways on the captain's seat, one hand on the wheel. I squinted and put a thumb between the sun and the horizon. Clouds formed up ahead, orange rays putting down lanes in the ocean.

Once we got a decent distance offshore, Cheep pushed the throttles forward. The boat's bow rose and then fell as we came up on plane, the beach steadily fading to a smudge of white against a background of dark blue and green behind us. I started to feel cool and reached into the bag we'd brought with us. New jeans and a new T-shirt. I put them on. Face feeling gritty with the salt air.

The sky in front was a riot of orange and purple, behind dark blue fading into a black green smudge on the horizon. Here and there I could see the lights of fishing boats ducking in and out of view, twinkling as we rose and fell on the slow swell. I got up and reached across, tapping Cheep on the shoulder. He cut the speed, the rear of the boat rising as the last wave of our thrust passed beneath us. It caused me to stumble, and I held onto Cheep's arm. He grinned at me, steady on his sea legs.

Cheep turned the engines off. The sound of the sea slapping against the hull the only sound in the silence that followed. We prepared to put Leon to rest. Cheep and Chai pulled a long length of chain and the spare anchor out of the fore locker in the bow. They dragged it to the middle of the boat. I collected the gun from the locker I'd stowed it in and checked that there was one in the chamber.

I picked up my cell phone and selected media. I turned the speaker on and pressed "play".

Dire Straits "Money for nothing" sounded tinny from the tiny speakers of the phone. In the evening on the ocean, the sound carried out across the waves. Cheep's shoulders slumped where he was crouching with Chai, sorting the chain. He turned and looked at me. Chai carried on sorting the chain, but eased himself back on his haunches, moving well out of the line of fire.

"When did you find out?" Cheep asked me.

"Last night, from Big Tiger."

"Who's in the bag?"

"The Farang, 'Leon'."

"What did he say?"

"I didn't give him a chance to say anything. In his way, he was innocent. It was you who caused this. Out of all the places he could have chosen to come for a holiday, he chose your resort. I suppose there's some kind of karmic fatality in that, but the real twist is that it must have been you to put two and two together and come up with a hundred million. Why?"

"I didn't want to hurt anyone. Just thought we could pull it off."

"Lilly?"

"She wasn't supposed to be there. She normally went shopping, but that day she changed her mind and came back. I didn't have a choice. She saw me, and I panicked. I knew that ringtone was a problem. I forgot to change it."

"Yeah, I asked Uncle Mike last night. He said it was your favorite. You played it every trip after a successful delivery."

"Does he know?"

"No. Not yet."

"Will you tell him?"

"I haven't thought about it yet. Probably not. I'd have to tell him I executed one of his best friends."

Cheep looked at me and nodded.

"Why?" I asked him.

He sighed and looked out to sea. "The tsunami wiped me out. My bars, and I had a small restaurant. Gone. Nothing left. Mike let me run the resort but, man, we did the same trips, and he owns half of Phuket, and I'm wondering how to make my next car payment."

"He put you in charge of the resort. He paid you to look after it. You weren't hurting."

"Nothing, Chance. Nothing. That's what I had. Mike and I, we did more than half of those trips together. We got busted on any of them and I was looking at five to ten. I'm fucking sixty and not a baht to my name. I never intended for Mike or you to get hurt."

Chai banged the chain against the hull of the boat. A look at his face confirmed his anger. Cheep looked at the floor of the boat, shame written across his face.

I blew out hard. I'd shared a lot of drinks with Cheep, a lot of years. The snapshots rolled in my head. In most of them, we were laughing.

"How do you want it? Front or back?"

Behind Cheep, the sun plinked below the horizon, the sky ablaze with orange and scarlet, blood red.

Cheep slowly stood and sat in the left rear corner of the boat, looking out back at the beach we'd come from.

"My family…"

"We'll take care of them. Make sure they have enough to live and for Nong Wan to go to school. We always would take care of that, Cheep. You know that."

"Yeah, I do, Chance. I'm sorry. Sorry for everything. Sorry for Lilly."

"Me too, Cheep." I pulled the trigger. The silenced pistol spat, the sound lost in the slap of water against the hull. Cheep slumped forward, hanging over the bulwark of the boat. I tossed the gun in over the stern, the cool sea breeze drying the tracks of my tears.

We put Cheep and Leon in the laundry basket and weighted it with the chain and both anchors. I helped Chai lift and tip it over the edge of the boat. I watched as the white canvas laundry basket disappeared from view, sinking fast, bubbles rising and then just the sea.

Chai started the engines and turned us around. He drove boats like he drove cars. I sat in the stern as we powered our way back to the pier and the Range Rover. We had seats booked on the 10:10 pm Bangkok Air-ways flight out of Phuket back to Bangkok. If we hurried, we could still make it.

I tried and failed to push the image of Cheep's daughter's eyes out of my mind. She stood at the front of a growing queue, all demanding the attention she was getting. The rhythmic thumping of the hull beat in tune to the glare of her eyes burning in my mind.

Beckham was waiting for us in the arrivals area of the domestic terminal at Suvarnabhumi, Suwanna-poom to you Farang, Airport in Bangkok. I was tired. My feet felt like lead as we walked to the car park. Beckham handed a packet to Chai. Chai took a look the contents and passed them to me. We were walking across the footbridge on Level three, to the car park. It was just past midnight.

Inside the A4 manila envelope, the money, passports and tickets I'd given to Uni girl and Daeng. Chai paused, fell in step with me. Leaning close.

"We couldn't take the risk. Sorry to disobey you, but we decided to act this way in your interest. Sooner or later, they'd have told someone or got busted and spilled their guts. It was painless. They went in their sleep." His voice, matter of fact.

Furious at my orders being disobeyed, I kept walking. There was nothing to say. Maybe I knew, deep down, it was what they'd do. We used the stairs to go up to level four where the car was parked, following Beckham. At the car, Chai put his hand on my arm, looking at me. I flicked a tired glance at him. I understand. His eyes held mine, narrowed a fraction. I nodded. He squeezed my arm, gave me a curt nod and opened the car door for me.

In Joom's Benz, the perfume-scented leather gave me a strange sense of comfort. Beckham provided a rundown of the day's activities in the district. The district was quiet but talking about Big Tiger's disappearance. There was speculation and not a little gambling going on as to why he'd disappeared. So far none of the other families had made a move. I had some work to do in that area. Big Tiger's confession had revealed a couple of threats, but it wasn't urgent. More of a hint, of a rumor on the edge of a breeze, heard on the balcony of a house at the edge of town. Bosses waiting to see which way the wind will blow. The wind had blown. Come and gone. Reap the whirlwind.

Walking through the airport, in the car park, and on the drive back home, I had the strange feeling I was moving between worlds: the real everyday world and an alternate world, my world. The people in the real world can't see in, can't see me, even though I'm moving among them. I am invisible.

We pulled out of the car park and took the first exit out of the airport onto the old road. Containers, gas stations and warehouses flanked the road, Chai and Beckham talking softly in the front of the car. I was sitting in the back, thinking about the five people I'd killed in the last twenty-four hours. I included Daeng and Uni girl, they were as much on my head as anyone who had pulled the trigger. I guessed it would have been Tum, under orders from either Chai or Beckham, perhaps even Mother. There wasn't any point knowing who had done it. It was done.

It was Por who taught me long ago. You can't change the past. Maybe you can't change the future. All you can do is change the present moment.

LOOSE ENDS

I woke up. Pim was staring at me, her head lying horizontal on the pillow, her big eyes centimeters from mine. It was a great way to wake up.

"Morning," she whispered and smiled. She shifted in closer, my hands touched skin. I ran them up her body, a lot of skin. She was naked under the sheet. Her smile grew broader as her eyes turned naughty. She sank below the sheets.

A while later, I was taking a shower, feeling a whole lot better about life. Pim had already showered and gone downstairs for breakfast. I was taking my time, enjoying the feeling of the hot water on my body. The last couple of weeks had been one crisis after another, and I wasn't out of the woods yet. I still had Yakuza Steve and the issue with the hundred million to resolve. But the snakes in the backyard had been cleared. I felt bad for Daeng and his sister. I felt bad for Nong Wan who had to grow up without a father. That was a choice her father made when he recognized a tourist's tale.

Who knows what karmic strings were pulled to cause Leon to book a holiday at Uncle Mike's resort and to cause Cheep to be there when the drunken Leon had told a tale of his father going missing in Phuket many years before. If you believe in spirits, as we do, Farang, you would say it was his father calling him. It's as good an explanation as any. Or perhaps it was just pure chance. It was Cheep who contacted Big Tiger and got him to finance the operation.

Leon was an out-of-work actor living in Sydney's eastern suburbs. His new girlfriend, Ursula, recently divorced, had enough money to buy them a holiday. Leon chose Phuket. Leon chose Uncle Mike's resort. It was Cheep who put two and two together and came up with a hundred million. It was Cheep who flew to Sydney and talked Leon into coming to Bangkok. He hadn't planned on Leon going crazy. That was an accident. Or perhaps it was just another twist in the great karmic balancing of all things. They would have killed Leon, but needed him to keep making the phone calls to deflect attention away from them. At least, that's how Big Tiger had told it.

Big Tiger went out thinking he'd survived. Well, maybe he did. Hard to know what another man's thinking before a bullet goes through his brain. He looked relieved, though, when I told him we were taking him home and released him from the rack. It gave his spirit a happier start on the next life. A small thing, but we think about the small things.

The post-adrenalin rollercoaster had bottomed out, and I was on a gentle decline.

I got dressed and went downstairs. There was no one around. I went out to the guest house. Beckham and Chai were sitting on the deck outside the house. I waved them down as they started to get up. Looking through the window, they were all there. I slipped my shoes off and went in. Pim was sitting next to Por. Por was sitting up in bed. All the tubes were gone. He smiled at me. I crossed the room and knelt by the bed. He put his hand on my head and stroked my hair. Pim moved out of her chair and, with a touch on my shoulder and a flick of her eyes, told me to sit in it.

Mother was on the sofa, talking to Uncle Mike.

Por inclined his head slightly towards Mother. He looked tired, his eyes half closed.

"I've heard you've had an interesting time while I've been sleeping."

"Yes, Por."

"Mother told me you've decided to get married?"

"Yes, Por."

"She's a good girl. I talked with her already. Reminds me of Joom when I first met her. Same kind of iron in her backbone…" He'd drifted off to sleep again. I got up and arranged the pillows around him. The nurse came and edged me out of the way in the way that nurses do. I looked across the room.

Pim and Mother were listening to Uncle Mike tell one of his stories. Now was as good a time as any. If you thought I was going to do the honorable thing and tell or ask Pim to leave me, you're insane. There was no way I was letting that much beauty out of my life. She was born for me and I for her. I had a whole speech prepared. I'd put the finishing touches to it in the shower.

"…And Dennis, man, Dennis, he was so stoned, he'd put his leathers, you know, leather trousers for riding a motorbike … yeah, he put them on backwards and when he went to take a piss, he looked down, and he screamed, 'Oh God, my dick has disappeared!' Oh, man, what a character." Mike, standing with his hands around his groin, bent double, laughing his head off with Pim and Mother – a Kodak moment.

"What did you say to Por?" I asked Pim.

"I told him we were fucking like rabbits, making the first of many grandsons."

Out of the corner of my eye, I saw Mike's jaw drop, and then he rolled on the floor holding his stomach. To say that I have an unconventional family would be an understatement. Well, we all have our quirks. The trick is to love them. I sat back in the sofa looking at Pim. She smiled innocently at me. I mentally ripped up the speech; didn't need it.

"Don't worry. I spoke in Thai."

"I'm not worried. Really. Not about anything. How's your shooting going?"

"You know about that? How did you find out? I wanted to surprise you. But it's going good. What do you think, Mother? Have I improved?"

"You're doing very well, Pim. You have a natural talent."

"What weapon have you been training on?" I loved it when she poked the tip of her tongue out like that. Sent shivers up my spine.

"Mother's teaching me the AA-12 first. Based on the," she paused and glanced at Mother, "minimal time to mass destruction potential concept." She looked at Mother, making sure she'd got it right. Mother beamed at her student.

My phone rang. Yakuza Steve.

"Is now a good time to talk."

"Sure. Go ahead, how was your trip?"

"Yeah, good, interesting. Why don't we meet, and I'll tell you about it."

"When, where?" I thought I'd give him the option of being cool about a smart place for us to meet.

"Rossano's off Sukumvit, off Asoke. Do you know it?"

"Sure. What time?"

"Lunch okay, about noon?"

"See you there."

Steve didn't sound too worried, sounded casual even, but that's when you have to be at your most careful. Rossano's was an okay place to meet, reasonably safe. If Steve had invited me to Thaniya, I would have known that the Yakuza Board wanted my head.

"Yakuza?" Mother asked me.

"Yes. Sounded okay, but I'll take some of the boys with me just in case."

"Can I come?" Pim asked.

"Not this time. It's a bit tense, and you haven't learned how to shoot a handgun yet. Walking into Rossano's with an AA-12 shotgun might cause a bit of a stir."

"Come with me to the farm, Pim. I want to show you how it all works."

Uncle Mike was sitting cross-legged on the floor, leaning against Mother's leg.

"I'm heading back to Phuket tonight," he said, turning to glance up at Mother.

"We need to talk before you leave," I said and got up. "I have to get going, I shouldn't be too long. What time are you leaving for Phuket?"

"Not sure yet, I was hoping to have Cheep pick me up at the airport, but he's probably out fishing or something. Not answering his phone."

"I'll be back by four at the latest. I'll take you to the airport, and we can talk on the way."

"Yeah, cool, man. Thanks."

After kissing Pim on the cheek, I went to get dressed. I put on a jacket to hide the Glock 17 in the shoulder holster. I didn't expect today to turn into Baghdad, but if it did, I wanted to be appropriately dressed.

Rossano's is in a converted house, just off Asoke – upscale Italian in a relaxed atmosphere. There's a car park, fancy name for an abandoned lot, next to it. We pulled into the lot, Tum driving, Beckham in the front, Chai and me in the back. I had kept the Maserati, I liked it, and if we needed speed to get us out of trouble, it had plenty of it. I recognized Steve's van by a decal for JAL in the back window.

If there was going to be a hit, that's where it would come from. Nothing moved, including the traffic in the soi. Bangkok was back to business, snarled in a tangled web of stalemated opportunities waiting for a green light. If the Yakuza Board hadn't accepted Steve's explanation for the loss of the money, they'd want it back. I wasn't prepared to give it back. We'd gone through a lot, and I had some plans for that money. It would mean war with the Yakuza, and that would be a problem. Last count, the Yamaguchi-Gumi clan had about forty-five thousand members. We had about a hundred at full stretch. Bad odds, and I don't gamble. Wars are bad for business. This whole area could attest to that. Last week, a gas tanker had been parked less than two hundred meters away from here, with red shirt protestors rolling burning tires at it, trying to get it to explode. It's on YouTube. Check it out.

The air-conditioned lobby was a welcome respite from the brutal heat outside. I left the guys in the car park, keeping an eye on the van.

"Good afternoon, sir. Do you have a reservation?" she spoke English to me, a natural enough assumption on her part, and I replied using English.

"No, I don't. I'm meeting someone. A Japanese guy."

"Oh yes, he's sitting outside." She turned, hand extended to show me the way.

"Is he alone?" I asked her as we entered the empty restaurant.

"Yes, he's alone," she said, and opened the door for me.

Terracotta tiles, low sofas, glass tables on black iron, and big comfy easy chairs decorated the outside area. Overhead latticework hung with fake, but very real-looking vines, grapes hanging down. Low-hanging fruit.

Steve was sitting at the sofa facing the door, a bamboo wall separating him and the car park. Behind him, a concrete pillar. Good choice for a seat, decent cover and a good field of fire.

"Chance." He rose, extending his hand. I shook it. A glass of red wine stood on the table in front of him, and a Mild Seven burned in the ashtray. Cosmopolitan was our Yakuza Steve.

"Hey, Steve, if your guys are waiting for you in the van, can I suggest they join my guys in the bar and have a drink while we talk?"

"Sure. Good idea."

He took out his cell phone. I did the same. Called Chai told him to join the Yaks in the bar with Tum and Beckham. Over the top of the bamboo, I saw the Sumo brothers get out of the van. It was warm outside. A big black box of a fan sprayed a fine water mist into the air, keeping the worst of the heat at bay. I still felt hot with the jacket on. Steve was also wearing a suit.

The waitress brought me a cool towel and a second glass for the bottle of red that Steve had opened. She poured me a glass with a twist of her wrist before putting the red back into the ice bucket. Room temperature here was at least thirty-one degrees Celsius. She went back into the interior of the restaurant. I glanced backwards to check where she was and took off my jacket. I slipped off the shoulder holster and put it under the jacket on the sofa and sat down next to it.

"Good idea," he said and smiled, copying my actions. I raised my glass to him.

"Cheers."

"Cheers," he said, and we touched glasses, making eye contact. Trying to read what was there and failing.

It was his meeting. I'd let him do the talking. I took another sip of the wine. Tum, followed by the Sumo,

Beckham and Chai, filed past the opposite side of the seating area, heading for the bar in the lobby. I relaxed a little bit. It didn't look like anything heavy was going down. Steve took a long drag on his cigarette, the smoke whisked away by the breeze from the fans. Elbows on his knees, he brought his hands together clasped in front of him.

"I met with the Board yesterday, updating them with the results of my investigation." He broke off as the waitress came out with menus, handing one to each of us. She started to leave, but Steve stopped her.

"It's okay. I just want a pizza Margherita, thanks."

"I'll go with the spinach ravioli, thank you."

The waitress left us alone. Steve lit another cigarette. I took a sip of wine. He looked me in the eye. Didn't blink.

"I was convincing enough, even though I don't believe your story." He smiled. You kind of have to smile when you call someone a liar in our business. I didn't react, poker face, looking him in the eye.

"Anyway, no matter how convincing I was, the Board has a proposal that they want me to discuss with you."

"I'm listening."

"They want you to expand your business. Japan, the States, Europe, maybe even Eastern Europe, Russia. We will be your partner, fifty-fifty, and we will also be a customer."

So we were off the hook for the hundred million, but with conditions attached. I shook my head. "Not going to fly. We don't do fifty-fifty partnerships. However, we have been thinking of going inter with the business, and in certain markets, we would of course partner with local partners to manage the local business. We could do fifty-fifty in Japan, and a minority share in other markets as funding requires. We would also offer you a discount on services if you give us the global franchise on your body disposal business."

Ken nodded. "I think it's possible to work out something, but perhaps you could make it a sweeter deal, like say in the States. Next year, we're expanding our operations retail and wholesale. Disposal logistics have become somewhat problematic and unreliable lately."

"You still outsource your disposal to the Italians, right?"

"Yes, and their grip has been slipping. They got too big and greedy. The Ndrangheta, they're coming up, but they don't have the facilities, and we're competing in too many channels. The mafia, you know they're on the decline. Their leadership issues aren't going to be resolved any time soon."

"What are the Italians charging? Ten?"

"Ten."

"That's cheap, but are you getting the quality you need?"

"Honestly, no. That's why we want to invest in a downstream operation likes yours."

"Okay, well, let's work it out. It sounds like we have enough in common with our goals to talk in more detail. Are you the point-man on this?"

"Yeah. I'm reporting back to my boss, who's a VP and sits on the Board. He's been given the task of getting this issue fixed. He would like to meet you."

"Why don't you invite him here? We'll give him a tour

of the farm, demonstrate the facilities, and we can talk more then?"

"Sounds like a plan." Steve reached across the table with his hand. I took it, and we shook on it.

Lunch was pleasant enough. When we left the restaurant, we were greeted with a sight that would have terrified any casual walk-in customer off the street: Chai, Tum, and the Sumo brothers all lined up at the bar in the lobby. Beckham and one of the Sumos were about to arm wrestle. Money was on the bar. I smiled. You can take the boys out of the district, but you can't take the district out of the boys. Luckily, the restaurant was empty. Wars are bad for business.

"Hai," Sumo number two shouted, releasing his massive paws from the clenched hands of Beckham and Sumo One.

"What are their names?" I asked Steve, pointing with my chin at the Sumo brothers.

Sumo Two bounced around the bar. Yeah, I remembered, very light on his feet. Held his hand out to me. "Hi, I'm Ailana," he said with a huge grin and in perfect American-accented English. "That's my brother, Ailani. He's about to whip your guy's ass."

I had to grin. I counted five thousand baht out.

"I got five thousand says Beckham cleans the bar with your brother's shirt sleeve."

"Hah, cool. You're on."

Ailani had weight and not all of it was fat. Beckham had technique.

The rope-like sinews in both men's necks were the only sign of the intense battle. Beckham's wrist was only centimeters from the bar, but he was holding. Ailani's jowls were beginning to shake, beads of sweat popped on his forehead. He was straining now, full thrust down, grunting. Beckham's face turned a bit redder, but otherwise he was holding, letting Ailani wear himself out. Ailani breathed out with a rush, and Beckham struck hard.

His brother turned to me. "Dude, that guy can arm wrestle. We got to get him over to the States. We'd clean up."

I glanced at Steve. He gave me a little shake of the head. Sumo didn't know what we'd discussed. Just a coincidence.

"I'll ask him for you," I said, smiling.

He handed me five thousand baht. Like I said, I don't gamble. I gave it to the lone waitress. It didn't look like she'd be getting any tips for a while.

A Sting in the Tale

Uncle Mike had cried when I told him I'd killed Cheep. It wasn't something that I could let lie between us. He had to know. I told him why. I didn't tell him how. He didn't need to dwell on that. Revenge for the sake of revenge is a pointless exercise. The Japanese knew that. It's why we reached a pragmatic Asian-style compromise. They knew I'd stolen their money, but going to war would cost even more. Going into business would recover the loss.

I had hugged Mike at the departure gate and told him I'd see him next week. He planned to move out of the villa and into the resort. He told me he didn't want to even visit the villa. Thinking of Lilly, I understood. Uncle Mike was part Thai. When you've lived here long enough, it happens through osmosis.

I'd driven Uncle Mike myself. I didn't want him to be

embarrassed in front of others, knowing how he'd react. The airport was a ghost town. Not quite as bad as when the yellow shirts shut it down, but emptied of all tourists just the same. My car was parked on the same level as the walkway from the main building.

When I returned, I opened the door and froze. On the driver's seat, an envelope. Written on the front, "Boom" and a smiley face. I reached down and carefully turned it over. On the back, written in large black felt tip, "From the guy who gave you a Benz". I squeezed the packet gently, rang my finger against it. Didn't feel any wires – felt like a DVD.

I upended the envelope, ignoring the taped end and gently tore open the bottom of the envelope. A plain, blank, white DVD was inside. I looked around the car park, not expecting to see him. I could feel him watching me, a tingle at the base of my neck. I saw nothing suspicious, just a cleaning lady pushing a bunch of trolleys, and a guard staring down at the empty road below. I sat in the car and turned the engine on.

After paying the parking fee, I headed out onto the main expressway back into town. Traffic still hadn't returned to normal, and it was pretty light. I kept my speed low and popped the DVD into the player.

Ronin's voice came loud and clear through the car's speakers.

"Hey, Mr. Lucky Nine, I told you I never forget a favor. Consider this a gesture. Maybe I'll need your help again one day. Stay safe. Oh, and don't share this with anyone else. It would identify the source and compromise a friend of mine. Strictly for you only." Silence.

The player showed Track Two in its display.

Man #1's voice: "We need you deliver a birthday gift to our friends downtown. Urgent request, it must be before four pm today."

Man #2's voice: "Understood. Consider it done." I knew that voice. It was Um. I'd listened to some of the voice messages he'd left Ice. They were still on his computer. These were the tapes the DSI or secret military forces had of Um.

Man #1's voice: "What's the number you have?"

Um's voice: "Zero eight one, eight six zero, eight seven zero nine."

Man #1's voice: "Zero eight one, eight six zero, eight seven zero nine?"

Um's voice: "Correct."

Man #1's voice: "Don't be late. Use the girl to send it."

The player showed Track Three.

Man #1's voice: "You've got to get out of Bangkok. Leave now. Today. Your faulty bomb killed a mafia boss and his son. Your life is in great danger."

Um's voice (sounding stressed, tearful): "Who's following me? Who's onto me? Can you tell me who you are? Can you protect me?"

Man #1's voice: "You know I can't, but I'm your friend. You have to run, now."

The DVD player automatically flipped over to the iTunes mp3 play list. Bob Dylan's "Like a Rolling Stone". And that happens sometimes, when a piece of music matches the moment we're in exactly, like the music's in harmony with our life. Bob's stuff always makes me think, and I had some thinking to do.

Bob was singing about diplomats and Siamese cats. I could have told Um who he was talking to. The guy talking to Um was Sankit, Pim's father.

Made in the USA
Lexington, KY
27 August 2018